THE SCAR

ARTHUR CALDER-MARSHALL was bo
includes novels, books for children, biographies, memoirs, and travel books.
He once remarked, "I have never written two books on the same subject or
with the same object," and this is reflected in the wide variety of his work.
His thriller *The Way to Santiago* (1940) was adapted for film by Orson Welles,
but the film never came to fruition. His memoir *The Magic of My Youth* (1951),
reprinted in 2022, recalls his youth in 1920s England and his search for the
occultist Aleister Crowley, an influence on the author's formative years. He
is perhaps best remembered today for his fantasy for children, *The Fair to
Middling* (1959). He married in 1934 and had two daughters. He died in 1992.

ARTHUR CALDER-MARSHALL

The Scarlet Boy

VALANCOURT BOOKS

The Scarlet Boy by Arthur Calder-Marshall
First published in the United Kingdom by Rupert Hart-Davis in 1961
First U.S. edition published by Harper in 1962
First Valancourt Books edition 2023

Published by Valancourt Books, Richmond, Virginia
http://www.valancourtbooks.com

ISBN 978-1-954321-91-5 (paperback)
ISBN 978-1-954321-92-2 (hardcover)
Also available as an electronic book.

Set in Dante MT

CONTENTS

AN UNREPEATABLE BARGAIN

The story undoubtedly began, as far as I was concerned, on Monday, April 3, 1959, when I received the following letter from my old schoolfriend, Kit Everness. I give it in full because its flavor is distinct for that of the average Q.C.'s (if such exists), and certainly from that of one of such established reputation.

It was written on printed paper in Kit's own carelessly academic holograph. The letterhead informed me that it was from Sir Christopher Everness, Q.C., P.C., K.C.B., of 1 Staircase W, Outer Temple, London W.C.2. The handwritten date was April Fool's Day.

How've you been, my dear George, since we met in El Vino's in, unless memory cheats me, Sept. '48 and split that excellent Volnay?

Busy I know, from those biennial biographies reverently pinpricked by the Times Literary Supplement *and cleverly denigrated by the* New Statesman and Nation.

I did enjoy that reprint of your Third Programme talk on Gissing in the Listener, *which I read in Delhi when suffering from dysentery. Poor fellow! I find him as binding as sulfa-guanidine. Quite a tonic in my fluid then.*

This is to ask what you will instantly refuse, if you have at last managed to control your milk of human kindness. After years of wanderlustiness, the Evernesses (Nieves especially but me a furtive bit too) want to Strike Roots. At least for the next six years. An eternity I would have imagined it 30 yrs. ago. But now with the flashing past of months, just a Long Moment.

We want A HOUSE.

My daughter, Rosa, aged 11, is a boarder at St. Clare's School for (Church of England) Young Ladies and HATES it. Perhaps my fault. I had not realized that too many hotels in too many capitals in too many continents confuse the young. So Nieves maintains and I must make amends.

Nieves wants a house in Wilchester from which Rosa can attend St. Clare's daily and where she, Nieves, can pursue her art without being dragged around by me. She is right. She has considerably more talent than the critics credit her with. At least, I think. If she can settle.

We have, thanks to Comrade Kadar, a most charming Hungarian, Magda Kovacs, who for some insane reason prefers to cook for us rather than work in the Hungarian section of the BBC—where she was offered a job. She would run the house and keep Nieves company. I'd give up the flat in Wessex Place and sleep at my chambers, when I couldn't get down—that is, if we can find a house.

But here I implore your discretion, dear George. People think Q.C.s wallow in wealth. I have some; needn't go through Building Society hoops. But I do not, Repeat NOT, want a period piece which some brigadier's widow has bought for a song, spanked up contemporary and wants to sell at 100% profit. Find me for preference the run-down shell of a place that we can make over to our own idea of home; in the center of Wilchester if possible, but with a garden and plenty of room. We like as a family to spread—to have room to sulk in. And of course if Nieves is to start sculpting, as she wants, she needs room for all those bits of stone.

I wouldn't presume on your good nature, my dear George, if I did not know that the Wilchester estate agents would only inundate me with sheafs of duplicated and mendacious hand-outs. And this presumption is a sign of trust. Though we meet so comparatively seldom, you are, I realize with something of a shock, my oldest living friend—the only person whom I have known for over forty years.

Perhaps that means little to you with your sense of continuity. You probably have dozens of old toddling pals whom you have known since you played together in your rubber rompers throwing sand into one another's eyes. But to discontinuous me, you are the symbol of a tradition which I like to know is there, while disapproving intellectually of your persistence. If you can understand that.

Ever Johannically yours,

KIT

To George Grantley, Esq.
The Chantry
Wilchester

By subscribing himself "Johannically," Kit was almost presenting a long unpaid account. At St. John's School he had been my "parfit knight" and I his devoted squire. Though in the same house, he was two years my senior. In my first term, he found me being bullied by my contemporaries and with that passion which has characterized his later career, he came to my rescue. From that time onward he remained my mentor and protector until he left St. John's (where he had been Captain of School) to take up the First Classical Scholarship at Balliol. When two years later I followed, a humble exhibitioner at St. Edmund's Hall, he helped me with advice, invitations to parties and even commendation of my feeble undergraduate verse. Without him, Oxford would have been a place far more terrifying to a person of my reclusive nature. In a sense, he blew me up into somebody I could become.

We had met infrequently since then, perhaps a dozen times in thirty years. But at every meeting the friendship had been renewed as spontaneously as if we had seen each other a couple of weeks before. This was the more curious, because my life has been passed in Wilchester apart from the excursions necessary to collect research material, whereas Kit's had ranged far and wide, farther and wider even than one might expect in a left-wing barrister of international repute.

My Conservative friends considered him warped, irresponsible and even downright traitorous. But I find they regard me with almost equal suspicion, because I belong to no political party and am unsinged by the burning issues of the day.

I realize that it would be a disaster if everyone were as perversely partisan as Kit or as indifferent as myself. But it is fallacious to consider that the Universal Will should be held by every individual. The Universal Will should spring from the impetus of conflicting forces; and I felt that Kit and I shared the belief that a society threatened by conformity needed the tonic of dissent. In a world governed by Yes-men it matters little whether you say "No!" or "A plague on both your blouses!" We were both against the same side.

But fond though I was of Kit Everness as a distant friend or lifelong acquaintance, I was not certain whether I would welcome him as an inhabitant of my native town. I did not know him as a family man. His wife, Nieves, was a refugee from Spain, whose brother had been killed on the Ebro fighting against the Falange and whose father, a POUM leader, had been tortured to death in Barcelona by the Communists. I had never met her. But Frank Cusek, who claimed that he had and may even have done so, described her variously as the "Improbable Lady Everness," "a fierce Iberian bitch" and "that peninsular painter to which Kit has hitched his jolly boat." How she and her child Rosa, to say nothing of his Balkan domestic, would fare in Wilchester gave me some faint disquiet. But in loyalty to Kit, I felt that I must try my best.

I took Frisk with me. She demands exercise as much as I need it. I have had an unbroken line of spaniel bitches from that first puppy which Helen Scarlet gave me on my tenth birthday. Frisk is ninth in the line of succession, which makes me feel old, though her antics keep me young.

I eliminated the estate agents one by one. They had a collection of the "3 bed 2 recep" monstrosities with which the old town is being encircled. But there was nothing that suited Kit's requirements. "You know as well as I do," said Bardsley of Bardsley & Beard, the best agents in a bad bunch, "everybody is clamoring to find 'something really individual' within thirty miles of London. We haven't even a broken-down piggery."

"Why doesn't somebody hit on the idea of building disused granaries, bakehouses and pubs 'Suitable for Conversion'?"

He looked puzzled for a moment. Then he said, "You might have something there at that," and made a note on his pad.

In Wilchester, as in all country towns, the most interesting properties change hands without the intervention of estate agents. It gets around that the X's are emigrating to New Zealand, Miss Y has had another coronary or Mr. Z has been offered promotion to Aberdeen, and immediately the future occupation of their *Lebensraum* becomes a matter of public business.

My best-informed spy is Norman Newman-Turner at the Book Shop. In his search for stock, Norman has built up an elaborate intelligence system. He knows the interiors of all houses worth knowing, what books they contain, the owner's expectation of life (or removal) and other circumstances which might induce a selling mood. Attics are his favorite stamping ground and while looking for copies of the Gutenberg Bible and Shakespearean First Folios, he has time to examine the state of the rafters as well as the bric-à-brac which may interest colleagues in the secondhand furniture, china and curio trades. Though he has been in Wilchester only eight years, he knows more of what is going on here than I, who have lived here all my life.

He was engaged with Mrs. Corbett, the Hon. Sec. Conservative Women's Association (Wilchester & District), who wanted a book on lilies, the name, author and publisher of which escaped her, but Norman must know it because it was *the* Book on Lilies and it was bound in half calf and was always in the middle shelf of the bookcase by the boot cupboard where her father kept all the gardening books.

As he stood there as patient as a great Dane listening to the yapping of a Pomeranian, he gently lowered one eyelid in a slow-motion wink at me. "If you had a snapshot of your father's boot cupboard," he suggested mellifluously, "perhaps you could enlarge it and read the title with a magnifying glass."

"But I haven't," Mrs. Corbett complained, "and anyway it wasn't *in* the boot cupboard."

"That *is* a pity." Then as he moved in my direction, he added consolingly, "Anyway, it would probably have been illegible."

He had a book for me and we went together into his office to fetch it from the reserve shelf. "At least Job did not have to serve Mrs. Corbett," he muttered. "Were Bardsley & Beard able to fix you up?"

"How on earth . . . ?" The efficiency of the Wilcastrian bush telegraph never fails to astonish me, or at least its speed.

"Rushmore," Norman said. "Saw you going in. What are you looking for?"

I explained in general terms, but suppressing everything about Kit except that he was an old friend. "You'd like him. Might be a good customer too. But there's nothing here."

"You might drop along to Scarlet's," Norman said. "John Scarlet asked Yerbury if he would be interested in some furniture from Anglesey House. And the sister is due back from the West

Indies this week. Just straws in the wind. I've never been in the place myself."

I had been there many a time, but not since that hard winter of 1947 in the January of which John Scarlet's step-grandmother Helen had died. "It's an idea," I said. "It must be dilapidated enough."

I called to Frisk and took her, puzzled, in the direction of Market Street. A dog has a way of emphasizing the setness of our habits. In all her lifetime, I had never taken Frisk into Market Street, which leads from the High Street out onto the main road to Sodbury; whereas The Chantry is on the opposite side of town, just off the Chipstow Road.

But Market Street looked much the same as it did when I was a boy and used so often to run down to Anglesey House and play. During the expansionary years between the two wars, none of the invading stores coveted its sites, because it was so narrow. They set their garish shop fronts in the broad High Street: and now that Market Street has been scheduled as a bottleneck of historic interest, it will gradually change from a run-down country side street into a fashionable residential quarter.

There were already signs of this domestic revolution. A number of the houses had been bought and refurbished by daily commuters who worked in London and slept in Wilchester. A critic as fastidious as Osbert Lancaster would probably have found their good taste ghastly, because there was little individuality, just variations on a few simple themes. But I thought they compared well with the uniform shabbiness of the unreclaimed, in which a variety of past fashions were overlaid with a common neglect. Jealous as I am to preserve what is good, I have no regret at the passing of what was declining even in my boyhood.

Anglesey House stood out from the other houses in the street, whether languishing or refurbished, because its double Regency bay windows encroached conspicuously on the narrow pavement. Though it was now the shabbiest, it had been the most gracious in its heyday, even a trifle grand. Now it stuck out as an obtrusive eyesore, like a gigantic tramp in a line-up of spivs and runts in an identity parade.

The sight brought a pang to my heart. There had been a time

when walking down Market Street I quickened my steps because it was the second emotional center of my Wilchester world.

Beside the house was a blind alleyway which in the old days had led up to Blagrove's slaughterhouse. I remember well the Highland cattle being driven up there, heads down, eyes rolling with the unknown fear of what lay at the end, Tom Blaze the drover and Squirrel his son, hollering and belting their flanks with ash sticks to bolt them up the cut; and the packed woolly scuffle of the young sheep, like a flood of dirty soapsuds after market on a Wednesday.

Blagrove's shop front was on the next street south, the Woolpack. The animals scampered in from Market Street on Wednesday and went out again the other side in small pieces wrapped in newspaper. It fascinated and appalled me as a child.

When I heard the phrase, "In the midst of life we are in death," it evoked—and still evokes—the stampede up the cut to Blagrove's shambles, the lowing, the bleating and the squeals; the cans of blood which Mr. Allfrey, Helen's gnomelike gardener, carried bumping against his knee and sprinkled at the bases of the rose trees.

The sheep and cattle were killed without sound by "a humane killer," who I imagined was a gentle assassin who lived at Blagrove's and never ventured abroad. I was disappointed when I was shown the little stub-pointed pistol.

Helen's son, Charles, and I used to stand beside the back gate and shout "Oy! Gerr on! Atcha!" in imitation of Tom Blaze and Squirrel, feeling very brave but ready to dodge back and slam the gate if there was any sign of retaliation from the scared beasts.

The pigs were different. They were strung up from a hook by the hind legs, Mr. Allfrey said. They squealed with fear, which changed to agony as their throats were slit. I imagined the squealing getting all mixed up with the blood from their necks and bubbling out of the wound as the dark blood pulsed and spurted into the pans ready for Mr. Allfrey to fill his watering can.

I found out later that this was a picturesque invention of Mr. Allfrey's. Perhaps being so small, he hoped to make himself more impressive. But I have never been able to bring myself to eat pork.

When the town slaughterhouse was erected in the early

twenties, all meat was butchered there. Blagrove's shambles was converted into a workshop by a war veteran named Bill Wagstaff, a carpenter who had a silver plate in his head as the result of the Battle of Mons. When he was drunk, he cried and asked people to feel it. He died in the black-out during the Second World War, but his son Perce carried on the business, a sick man who looked as if he had swallowed a mouthful of tin tacks. He used the same small notice board as his father, painting out the W and inserting a P. This was the only thing still legible.

Beside it on the wall was a smart board which was new to me.

WILCHESTER SCHOOL OF EQUITATION
Prop. Miss P. Spreckles

Up in the yard a stable girl was grooming a pony and in the cut lay little piles of organic fertilizer.

The windows of Anglesey House had not been cleaned for months, or perhaps years. But through the dust could be seen, bister with age and spotted with fly dirts, a piece of cardboard on which was written in indelible pencil:

TO BE LET FURNISHED
Inquiries ask at Scarlet's, No. 63

The paint had flaked from the windowsills, and where it adhered it provided a damp trap rather than protection against the weather.

The notice and general condition of the house were typical of John Scarlet. He would not employ an estate agent, I imagined, because he did not see why he should pay another man for letting a house when he could do it as well himself. If he failed to let the house, he wouldn't throw good money after bad by paying a woman to clean a place in which no one was living.

John Scarlet had always been an enigma to me. He was the same age as myself and Charles Scarlet, who had been my real friend. But there was a confusion of the generations. Charles was the son of Albert Scarlet by his second wife Helen Kent. John and Miriam were the grandchildren of Albert Scarlet by his first wife Miriam Anglesey, through Albert's son, Ernest.

Charles and John and Miriam and I should have been natural playmates as children. But Albert Scarlet, an industrious apprentice who after his employer's death had married his employer's daughter, had held strict views on education in his first wife's day. What had been good enough for him, a remarkable man, was good enough for his son and grandson. "The shop's a lad's grammar school," he said, "and his university beside."

The shop had been Albert's university. For the son Ernest it was a grammar school, in which Ernest learned the laws of commerce as if they were the Ten Commandments, never to be challenged or revised. And for John, it was a kindergarten. He never fully mastered the four R's; while from outside came an invasion of new men and new chain stores with different methods of business. In that branch of the family, there was a progressive stunting of each male generation.

Helen Kent on the other hand, better educated than Albert or his first wife, demanded that Charles should be given a decent schooling, at least as good as Albert had conceded that a girl should have. A girl's schooling, in Albert's view, was her dowry. He had sent Celia, his daughter by his first wife, to St. Clare's; and his granddaughter Miriam went there also as a matter of course. Of our age group only John Scarlet remained underprivileged.

It seemed to me that through lack of cultivation even the qualities which John had inherited from his grandfather had degenerated. Albert's shrewdness, his flair for seizing the main chance, became in his grandson a sort of instinctual cunning. I've known some men in which this is a more than adequate substitute for intelligence, enabling them to cope with situations without realizing how or why they were doing so. But John Scarlet was not one of these. He had the illusion that everybody was an enemy, seeking to swindle, outwit or deride him. Without any of the armory of reason, he skulked in his warren of suspicion, defending himself from attack—and he interpreted as an attack any approach however well intentioned—by immediately taking the opposite attitude.

Helen, who after her stepson's death had to treat with his son John as one of her trustees, turned him into a comic character. "John is so easy to deal with," she said. "If I don't ask him to tea, he imagines that I am cold-shouldering him. But if I do, he immediately asks himself what I want to get out of him. So if I have to see him, I ask him for any day except the one I want and then I give way when he insists that this is the only day he can manage."

It was twelve years since I had seen John Scarlet—at Helen's funeral, when he had invited me back to eat corned-beef sandwiches. As I went to No. 63, I wondered how I should find him and the family emporium.

I could recognize the shop from a distance by the paraphernalia on the pavement. It looked as if John was expecting a visit from the refuse collector and had turned out the sheds at the back. There were some dust bins and a defective incinerator on which was stuck a placard "SIMPLY CANNOT BE REPEATED." Under it someone had penciled the comment, "Obviously!" Since this was the spring season there was a display of pea and bean sticks, rolls of galvanized iron wire and a secondhand lawnmower without box, to the handle of which a drawing pin was affixed from which dangled a card saying "£2 Bargian!" John's spelling was always weird.

I went into the shop, which was a sort of Hieronymus Bosch vision of The Hardware Hell. Ironmongeries are susceptible to chaos. There are so many things to be stored and such little space in which to store them. From the ceiling dangled an array of coils of wire, rope, kettles, bast, frying pans and so on which must have cost far more to purchase than they could ever recoup on retail in their dilapidated condition. Stock stood about me like the guards outside the Kremlin.

In the gloom I detected a customer, like the solitary denizen of a pond which was being drained for brackishness. And behind the counter between a rusty pyramid of Snowcem and a pyramid of Ceilingite as rusty, I perceived the faithful Lucy Worplesdon looking even more harassed than when I had last seen her in 1945, when she could deny the presence of anything in the shop because there was "a war on." She was now huddled over a catalogue about a foot thick, trying to find the price of a small object, which might be listed as "KNOB plastic for the repair of kettle-lids tin" or "KETTLES, tin, knobs plastic for the repair of lids of." The hairs of her mole, I noticed, were turning gray.

I find something endearing in anyone as reliably inefficient as Lucy. "Why is it she always looks so *worried*?" I once asked Helen Scarlet. "Wouldn't you," she answered, "if your bottom was slipping down to the back of your knees?" I could have watched her for hours, but Frisk was sniffing some pressed paper flowerpots in an ominous fashion.

"I know it's either sevenpence ha'penny or fivepence ha'penny," Lucy said as she began to flick wildly through the catalogue at T for "TIN," P for "PLASTIC" and L for "LIDS." Then, nervously aware of my presence, she turned and called, "Mr. John, please."

From a cupboard about the size of a telephone box, but with the word OFFICE frosted on its glass door, John Scarlet emerged, bent with care.

"Excuse me, Mr. John," Mrs. Worplesdon said, "are these sevenpence ha'penny or fivepence ha'penny?"

John Scarlet took the knob between finger and thumb and scrutinized it as if it were a crystal bowl on the far side of which could be seen its price. But behind that mantic gaze lurked the terror that his assistant knew the price already and had only invented this test to expose his incompetence. "*Six*pence ha'penny," he pronounced, and then realizing that he had laid himself open to contradiction if Lucy ever found the place in the catalogue, "to you, Mrs. Squelch."

He smiled on Mrs. Squelch as briefly as a light on a pin table and then he turned to me, washing his hands in invisible soap. "Good morning, Mr. Grantley," he said. "And it really is, isn't it, for once. Ha! Ha!"

I found it absurd that John with whom I had played and squabbled as a boy should call me Mr. Grantley; yet it would have been even more ridiculous that this frightened creature who took refuge behind titles should have called me George. Mr. John Scarlet ironmonger was even further from common humanity than the little boy who tried to avoid any games, because he was always the last to be picked and the first to fail.

"By God! Helen," I remember hearing old Albert exclaim to Helen in little John's hearing, "Miriam's the man in Ernest's family."

"One might think it was a day in May," Mr. Scarlet said, "if one did not know that it was April. A real May day, eh?" His conversation was like a labored progress across ice floes during the break-up. He leaped hazardously onto a phrase and tried it again and again to make sure that it would not sink. "A May day! Yes. Mrs. Worplesdon, wouldn't you say it was like a day in May, um?"

Mrs. Worplesdon did not hear. She was still worried about where the price for the tin kettle lid knob was to be found and was ruffling through the pages of the price list like a dog looking for a field mouse under a pile of beech leaves.

"I made a *special* price for Mrs. Squelch, Mrs. Worplesdon." Mr. Scarlet turned back to me. "She's an old friend of the house, Mrs. Squelch is, an old friend of the house." I by implication was no friend of the house, buying my mousetraps and Sluggit elsewhere; but John clearly felt it too pointed. "It is nice to see you after all these years," he said, leaping onto another conversational floe. "Very nice after so many years." He drew in his breath sharply, a gesture the significance of which was interior. "Very nice after so many years." His eyes wandered across the shop, not in search of anything but to avoid my own. "They pass, don't they? 'Like silent footsteps on the grass,' as the poet says. How right! How true!"

He had scored a bull. I have no literary memory. When anyone quotes a gobbet, I am thrown into a fluster. "The years that pass, like silent footsteps on the grass." Surely not Marvell, too flaccid. Ninetyish? Not Dowson. O'Shaughnessy? Dora Sigerson Shorter? A felicity from Ella Wheeler Wilcox?

It gave John Scarlet the respite he needed. "A visit from Mr. Grantley does not happen every day, does it, Mrs. Worplesdon? To what do you think we owe the pleasure? Indeed, no," he added, turning to me. "This is quite an occasion, an event, a red-letter day."

I thought I detected a thread of hatred in his hardware humor. But perhaps he was just using Roget's *Thesaurus* to keep his conversational end up. "I will make a note of this in my diary," he said, drawing his breath in sharply. "I must make a notch on my recording stick, ha! ha! This is a Date!"

"I came about Anglesey House," I said. "Someone I know is looking for a furnished house in Wilchester. For a few months."

His eyes went darting round the shop as if they were following the crazy progress of a may bug. "But it isn't . . . really you know . . . not to let, I mean. You see, my sister, Mrs. Schroeder . . . she's coming today. The whole thing is . . . well, fluid. It's in the melting pot, to coin a phrase, the melting pot."

"In that case it doesn't matter," I said. "My friend actually is rather interested in a place near Chipstow. It was selfishness on my part. And of course loving Anglesey House. As it was in the old days."

"The old days!" Mr. Scarlet said, drawing in his breath. "The good old days! We'll never see the like of them again." He shook his head sadly.

I wondered whether the alchemistry of memory had really transmuted his miserable childhood into a golden age. I chose a ball of sisal cord and handed Lucy Worplesdon a ten-shilling note. The cord was only sixpence more expensive than in my usual shop. "You and Miriam and me!" I echoed, shaking my head in imitation of his. "There aren't so many in Wilchester remember those times . . . and I'll wager that Miriam's become so grand now that she wouldn't come round to see me in that shabby old home of mine."

"Of course she would." It was a reflex action. "At least I think so. And if you'd like to look over Anglesey House, why don't you take the key? You can slip it through the letter box if we are closed for dinner. It might be just the thing for your friend."

"I'm sure Miriam and her husband would want to live there, if they're back for good," I answered. "But I'd love to look it over all the same."

He went into the office and took an enormous rusty key off a rusty nail. "We shall see what we shall see," he told me delphically. "Meanwhile it's in the melting pot."

2

IN THE BEGINNING IS MY END

In saying that the *story* began on Monday, April 3, 1959, I realize that I have been doubly misleading. In the first place, I am not telling a story, as the professional storytellers in the Eastern market places or the Western fiction lists tell stories. This is something which happened to me, and only recently. It is a fragment of autobiography, as factual and serious as any of my biographical, historical or antiquarian studies, but more difficult to write because I was, and still am, intensely engaged in it. I cannot pretend to be objective and if I did, I would falsify what happened. I am now a very different person from the George Grantley who took the rusty key from John Scarlet that Monday morning and calling Frisk to heel walked back toward Anglesey House. In retrospect I appreciate that I, and all the rest of us, had to change before what happened was able to.

This may sound paradoxical. We tend to think of ourselves changing or developing as a result of experience. But in this case, it seems to me, the process was reversed. We only experienced as a result of our own change or development. I would go even further and say that the logic of this narrative is inexplicable in terms of human thought and will and act. (That of course is true of real life far more often than novelists would admit or puzzled historians and biographers would like to acknowledge.) Perhaps we are always actors in a Mystery drama, most happy in our predestined roles when we act them with the conviction of free will.

In the second place, though the *story* began on that Monday, all the components had existed for a long time before that. Imagine, for example, a performance of Shakespeare's *Antony and Cleo-*

patra in a modern theater on that day. It could begin punctually as the curtain went up. But not unless Antony and Cleopatra had lived and loved and died and Plutarch had written his *Lives* and North had translated them and Shakespeare had written the play and the theater had been built and all the company assembled; in fact, only after an enormously complex series of events.

That Monday was the start of a drama, but no more definite. The world had been going on for billions of years, all of which in some way or other, though I could not sense it, were remotely connected with that moment. We have these daily connections with the past. The gallon of gasoline in the tank refined from prehistory may drive us from here in a car smash to eternity.

But that Monday I had no sense of this. What I did have was an acute sense of the role which the Angleseys and the Scarlets had played in the life of Wilchester and especially of what Anglesey House had meant to me and to my lifelong friend Helen Scarlet, who had lived there for the forty years following her marriage to Albert Scarlet, John Scarlet's grandfather. It was a sad history of decline.

The hardware business, now known as Scarlet's, was until the beginning of this century known as Anglesey's Stores, the business of that branch of the Anglesey family resident at Anglesey House. The Angleseys are as old a Wilcastrian family as the Squelches and rather higher in the social scale. The earliest one I discovered in my book on Wilchester was a miller in the reign of Queen Elizabeth the First. Under one spelling or another they crop up in and around Wilchester, Chipstow and Sodbury with their intervening parishes as farmers, merchants, yeomen, bailiffs and so on. A few rose into the landed gentry, a few fell into the ranks of plowmen, herds and drovers. But the majority remained burgher stock.

Anglesey House had been built originally by a William Anglesey in 1603, so far as the deeds show. But as in so many of these cases, it was not quite clear whether there had been another building already standing on the site, to which additions were made. William Anglesey was a tanner and the south wing of the house, running back from the street, was built as a tannery.

It was not converted into dwelling accommodation until 1670, when another William Anglesey, "overblessed with progeny by the bounty of God and the fecundity of his wife, Chastity," found it necessary to make over the tannery into dormitories, "it being said that Mistress Chastity, distressed with the stench of hides, had sworn to breed her master into new quarters."

The proliferation of Angleseys dates from the mid-eighteenth century. They became farmers, surgeon-barbers, millers, general merchants, such of them as did not join the Church or the armed services or emigrate abroad.

Anglesey's Stores had been a general shop, in fact *the* general shop, in the middle of the nineteenth century, a sort of premature Universal Provider selling anything from cheese to ribbons, saucepans to sausages.

As a family the Angleseys had shown a tenacious *savoir survivre*. But Ernest Anglesey, John Scarlet's great-grandfather and architect of the Universal Provider, was unfortunate in producing only one child, a daughter Miriam, who was cursed with an extraordinary ugliness and a curvature of the spine which no backboard would straighten. None of her cousins could bring themselves to propose despite the business. And when her father died in 1882 at the age of fifty-nine, Miriam was left a modest but ill-favored heiress in her late and desperate twenties.

Albert Scarlet, who in the course of twenty-five years had risen from errand boy through the ironmongery section to chief assistant, proposed to Miriam that he should marry her and manage her business. He was accepted on both counts.

How can one sum up in a few lines the life and character of a man who lived his three score years and ten? Brevity must be unjust. And memory is false, if one knew the man as I did only at the end of his life.

Albert as I remember him in his old age was a Person. When he came into a room, you could no more ignore him than you could ignore a conger eel just landed in the bottom of a boat. Life persisted in him just as tenaciously. Cut a conger eel in steaks and five hours later each steak is nervously alive. Albert was like that. If anybody had sliced off his feet at the ankles when he was walking, they would have got home on their own.

The family was furious at Miriam's marriage, blaming her for taking the business outside the family, even though none of them was prepared to take over her with the business.

It was not a marriage of convenience, at least as far as Miriam was concerned. She adored this large vigorous red-faced man, saddened only by her failure to give him the enormous family he wanted. She produced two sons, Ernest in the first year of marriage, Percy under two years later, and then there was a succession of miscarriages, broken only by the production of a daughter, whose constitution was so delicate that her survival was pronounced by the doctor as little short of a miracle.

Miriam was a martyr to maternity, like so many women of her time. Exhausted by too many pregnancies, she failed in health and died of a consumption in 1902, leaving Albert a vigorous widower of fifty-eight with two sons of an age to work in the shop but still living at home and a daughter of twelve with a nervous disposition that made her difficult, even before the onset of pubescence.

The one person to whom this child, Celia, showed devotion was a schoolmistress at St. Clare's called Helen Kent, a woman of about thirty at that time, who by the photographs which I have seen (curious period pieces with straw boaters on piled hair, elaborate leg-of-mutton sleeves, minute waists and long full skirts hiding the mystery of the feminine leg and foot) must have been extremely handsome, and by reason of her delicacy very attractive to a man of Albert's coarse vigor: his unattainable opposite.

She certainly attracted me as a boy. I was filled with guilt because I envied Charles for having a mother so much more beautiful and gracious than mine. Mine, with her freckled homely face and the old hat of my father's she wore shoved on the back of her head as she scrabbled in the herbaceous borders weeding and trying to lug a trug too heavy for her to the rubbish heap, was a six-days-of-the-week mother. But Helen Scarlet was a Sunday-go-to-meeting mother, cool and fresh and deeply tranquil.

In my treacherous way I could understand why old Albert Scarlet loved her so. I, as much younger than she as he was older, knew exactly how much he loved her. And what made her so exciting, compared to dear old freckly Mum who'd let herself go, was this intense awareness she always had of being a *woman,* not just a wife, or a mother or the mother of a friend.

Reading through this last paragraph I am afraid that I may have given a wrong impression, as if there was something sexual about Helen. There wasn't. She was the least physical of women. There was something about her which was, though it may sound ridiculous, "ethereally feminine."

When I used to trot down, ostensibly to play with Charles, her son, my excitement was due to the fact that I would see her. Charles was physically very like her. He had very soft fine black hair, as she had in a glorious abundance, and those strange blue eyes set in the olive-complexioned face with the very small underneath-the-skin freckles.

As far as I was concerned, Charles was an extension of Helen, a more approachable, playable part of her. If I had thought of him as himself, I would not have liked him. Even as a boy I realized that he was obscurely vicious. There was a house built in a tulip tree toward the end of the garden. It was "The Crow's-Nest" and we used to take our meals up there in the summer and eat them. It had a rope ladder, which we drew up, "weighing anchor" we called it, and then we were alone above the adult world.

We could hear the adult sounds below, but they did not belong to us. We were withdrawn in a leafy universe. I remember one Wednesday afternoon. This was a year after Albert died, which he did quickly one Sunday after a *full* lunch—at least my father said so. They were killing a pig in Blagrove's shambles. It escaped and there were shouts from Tom and Squirrel as they dodged to corner the beast. There was fear in their voices; but when the pig was caught and roped, the fear left the men and entered the animal.

"Oh, I wish we could stay here," I said, "forever and ever."

Down on the ground was fear and agony and suffering, not just for the animals who passed through the cut, which I thought of as "the valley of the shadow of death," but all over the earth and especially in Flanders where my father was among those fighting.

"Oh, come on," Charles said fiercely. "Get on with the game."

The game was Tortures and I never really understood what it

24

was all about. It followed fierce rules which Charles understood and involved tying him up in different ways. I did not like playing it, especially when we were in the tree house, because it "spoilt things."

But I obeyed all the same. Charles was normally an equal sort of companion, but when he was playing Tortures, he became quite a different person, almost as if he were possessed, and I was too frightened by this strange creature within Charles not to do what I was told.

On this particular afternoon, I had to truss Charles up like a chicken and I had just about finished when I heard Helen calling us from the house.

My instinct was to answer immediately—it was such sweet pleasure to obey her—when Charles gripped my wrist and shook his head.

I peeped through the sides of the tree house and between the leaves I could see the white of her summer dress and then someone in that bright hospital blue which they gave to convalescent fighting men.

"She's coming," I whispered, "with Cousin Andrew."

Cousin Andrew was a distant Anglesey relative who had landed in England with the Australian Expeditionary Force, a tall, sunburnt, handsome soldier, who had looked immensely dashing in his uniform and khaki bush hat. Albert had been taken with him, admiring manliness in all its forms, and had told him to make Anglesey House his home whenever he was on leave.

Since that first visit, Albert was dead and Andrew himself had nearly died of a deep shrapnel wound that they feared would turn gangrenous. But now he was mending and had secured a transfer to Wilchester Manor, which had been turned into a convalescent hospital. He spent much of his time at Anglesey House, and when Charles jealously asked why, his mother answered, "Your father would have wished it so."

It was plain to me, even then, that it was through no mere deference to her departed husband that Helen made her cousin welcome. The marks of tenderness, as now when she took his arm to help him up the terrace steps of the garden, were clear for anyone to see. Yet when I had asked my mother whether she thought that

"Aunt" Helen would marry Cousin Andrew, she laughed and said tartly, "And forfeit everything to Ernest! When Andrew hasn't a penny!" But when I tried to fathom the meaning of this cryptic remark, she shut me up; and it wasn't until years later I understood her. By his will, Albert had made over Anglesey House and a sum of money in trust to Helen and Charles, for Helen during her lifetime and then to Charles if he survived her. But, by a codicil, he had made this dependent on Helen not marrying again. If she did so, half the trust money was to go directly to Charles and the other half and Anglesey House to Ernest, the residuary legatee. Ernest was the only surviving child of his first marriage, Celia having succumbed to tuberculosis at the age of eighteen and Percy to a German bullet a few weeks after his father died.

Despite this barrier to marriage, I think that Helen and Andrew were desperately in love, Helen with the passion of a beautiful woman conscious of the near approach of middle age and Andrew with perhaps a more complicated feeling compounded of loneliness and longing for love and gratitude for having escaped death and the fear that when he recovered he would be sent back to the trenches again for the Germans to finish the job they had botched the first time.

I saw them coming closer and I looked down at Charles lying on the floor of the tree house, thinking that I must at all costs untie him. I had been aware, vaguely, that grownups would disapprove of this game; but there was a lot of things which grownups disapproved of which were quite harmless. Now for the first time I realized that Tortures was not one of them. It was evil. It was what I prayed every morning and evening to be delivered from without ever being quite certain what it was. I started to untie one of the knots, but with a power I had not suspected him to possess, Charles seized both my wrists and dug his nails into my flesh so hard that I had to bite my lip to prevent myself from crying out.

Helen and Cousin Andrew came to the foot of the tree. Helen called up, "Charles! George! Cousin Andrew's here."

"You must answer!" I mouthed at Charles.

But he shook his head. He was tense, not like himself at all, but not frightened nor awed. I had the feeling that his lying up there, bound like a prisoner, with his mother below unable to see him, had brought the game to its supreme climax.

"Perhaps they aren't there," Cousin Andrew suggested in the faintly Australian voice, which I found rather attractive.

"Don't be absurd, Andrew," Helen said. "They've pulled the ladder up after them. They must be." Her voice was quite audible, but she raised it to call to us again, telling us not to be foolish. She did not sound angry, however, and when Cousin Andrew said, "Why don't we leave them be, Helen?" in a voice intended only for her, she took his arm and they walked back toward the house, Andrew telling her of a hide-out he used to have as a boy "down by the creek, a beaut of a place."

That was the last time I played Tortures with Charles. He tried several times to persuade me, but I refused. I was frightened of something to which I could not put a name, except that it was evil.

After that Charles played more and more with Miriam and John. My invitations to Anglesey House became fewer and fewer that summer of 1916. I did not like what Charles was becoming and Aunt Helen was taken up with Cousin Andrew. I was insanely jealous and I noticed that each of them took every opportunity to call the other by Christian name. "Helen" and "Andrew" were like caresses exchanged in public.

That summer mother and I spent August staying with Aunt Peggy at Deal. I did not enjoy myself. For one thing my cousin Harry Waybridge was only five—half my age—a soppy kid who couldn't swim or do any of the things I liked to do and who cried at the slightest provocation. For another, we could hear the guns across the Channel where my father was fighting. Every time we heard one of those distant booms, we both thought, "Maybe that killed him." With that limitation of sympathy common to the young, I did not worry about any of the combatants except my own father; but for him I was in constant apprehension. We momently expected that dread telegram from the War Office, announcing his death.

But what came instead was a letter in a black-edged envelope with a Wilchester postmark. My mother read it at breakfast. Or rather she began to read it, turned very pale and then placed it folded beneath her side plate.

"Something wrong, Kay?" Aunt Peggy asked.

Mother shook her head, meaning "Not now!" And for the rest of the meal, we tried without success to pretend that there was no black-edged letter waiting to be read.

Later in the morning, when I was digging a sand castle with a defensive fosse, she called me to give me a bun. The tide was coming in fast and I was trying to reinforce the fosse with seaweed.

"Darling," she said, "I've got some bad news for you."

I took the bun and dug my teeth into it, looking for fresh supplies of weed.

"That letter that came," she said. "When you go back, you won't be seeing little Charlie."

Charlie wasn't little. He was my height. "It said he was dead?" The black-edged paper could mean only that.

"It was an accident," mother said, bursting into tears. "Poor, poor Helen!"

I looked toward the sand castle. A wave sprinted up the strand, carrying with it a ribbon of foam. It bit into the base of the fosse and surged around it. I wanted to run back and prevent its being overwhelmed. But in the distance came the thunder of gunfire and the earth shook and all around was evil and death.

I went over and stroked her freckly everyday face with the back of my hand.

She caught hold of my hand and half-pulled me down to sit beside her. "A terrible, terrible thing!" she said. "At her age! To have no one!"

"How did it happen?" I asked.

"He fell and broke his neck. It was all over in a moment, Helen said. I can't believe it."

I let her fondle me, watching the castle vanish beneath the waves. "In the midst of life, we are in death" with the cattle scampering wild-eyed up the cut and the guns thundering across the sea. "Deliver us from evil, for thine is the kingdom." One learned words but how much longer it took to learn their meaning.

Not only did I never see the Scarlet boy again, but I never saw Cousin Andrew. They patched his young flesh up and sent him back to Vimy Ridge, to be killed after two days.

I didn't see Helen Scarlet either, until the Christmas holidays. I was shocked by her appearance. She was no less beautiful, but in a sense transfigured as people sometimes are by a severe illness. She said she had some things for me and asked my mother if she would let me come to tea alone on Saturday to collect them. "As a treat for me," she said, "I'll bring him back myself."

My mother agreed with some reluctance, torn between pity for Helen Scarlet and fear that now she had no child of her own Helen would try to win me over. My love for them both made me aware of their tension, even at that age; though there was no reason for it that I could see. I loved them each in such different ways.

When I went to tea, I found that Helen had gathered together all Charles' books and toys and games. "You were his friend," she said, "I want you to have them all."

I shook my head. Up to that moment I had felt nothing about Charles dying. But the thought of being given all his things so excited me that it made me actually glad he was dead and that was an evil from which to be delivered. Besides, my mother would never let me keep them. "Why can't they stay here for when children come to play?"

"If you'll come," she answered. "But you wouldn't want to. Not now."

I could see her poised in apprehension. To me it was inconceivable that she should want me in her house. I fumbled in vain for words. "You know, you know . . ." I said, tears spurting into my eyes. And then she was on her knees, hugging me and rocking me from side to side.

We had muffins and Australian flapjacks for tea and afterward we did a jigsaw puzzle and before I left we packed all the games away in the bottom drawer of her great big German corner desk. She locked it and she showed me a little secret drawer in which the key was kept. "Only you and I shall know about it," she said, "but you can open it whenever you want."

"What about Miriam and John?" I asked. "Can't they?"

"It's time to get your things on," she answered, "or your mother would never let you come again."

And that was the beginning of a relationship with my "second mother" as Helen called herself, lasting more than thirty years. It was not a very accurate description of my feeling for her, which was both less and more than that. But that it truly described her feelings for me I saw from the frequency with which, especially later in life, she called me "Charles" by mistake.

3

RAT'S FEET OVER BROKEN GLASS

The key which John Scarlet had lent me was to the back door of Anglesey House. It was typical of the man. I do not mean that being a tradesman he naturally chose the tradesmen's entrance; though it is true, I am told, that he always enters his own house through the scullery door. To John Scarlet a front door was something to be barred against the outside world, proof that an Englishman's home was his castle. He was the sort of man who screws a cage over the letter box to prevent bills and income tax demands from invading his privacy.

In Helen's day the enclosed back yard leading to the trades-men's door had been scrubbed twice a week and one of the gardener's duties was to prevent grass and plantains growing between the stone flags. But now a green moss covered the stones and between them were the dead weeds of previous years. The door of the coal shed hung by one buckled hinge, leaves clogged the trap of the soak-away and the back door itself had been gnawed through by rats.

I closed the gate from the cut behind me, let Frisk off her leash and opened the door by the coal shed to give her exercise in the garden while I reviewed the house.

Though I had had the run of the house as a child (apart from the grownups' bedrooms and the somber room on the ground floor called The Office, where Albert Scarlet had wrestled with his business problems and drunk whisky with his cronies) I had never examined the place with an adult would-be purchaser's eye.

It could scarcely have been better from Kit's point of view.

Between what it had been allowed to become and what it could be made yawned a chasm, inviting the bargain hunter with capital. The site would have been very valuable, if only the bottleneck outside had not been scheduled as an historic monument. As it was, the house was a shell filled with what any surveyor could prove to be an encyclopedia of the ills to which man's building is prone. There was wet rot beneath the stairs, dry rot by the door, rising damp in a dozen places, condensation in the hall. There was woodworm in the staircase and, no doubt, in the rafters. The kitchen, over the modernization of which I remember Helen spending in the late twenties a legacy (much to my mother's envy), was the most modern and most obsolete part of the house. The rusty refrigerator, the no longer Ideal boiler, the superseded sink and the out-of-date electric stove were the saddest things in that sad house. (Really old things, like wooden kitchen spoons or earthenware mixing bowls, seem to have far longer survival value than modern gadgets.)

From my, though not from Kit's, point of view it was terribly depressing. All the doors were covered with chocolate paint, which as Randall Rushmore says is not a color but a state of mind. That light blue Morris-papered drawing room, which my mother had regarded as Helen's shockingly daring innovation as the second Mrs. Scarlet, had become reconciled in dust with the furniture which she had never persuaded Albert to abandon.

When I was a child, what seemed a small army of helpers was employed on the daily polishing of furniture and brasses, so that they gave off reflected light. Everything shone and sparkled, dark though it might be. But now it was dull with dust and verdigris. Whatever life was in that heavy oppressive furniture, the tables with dropsical legs and the sideboard carved with clusters of grapes and hanging pheasants, had retreated into itself, like a snail in a dry season. The rooms had become resolved into that somber browny-mauvy purple which makes the backgrounds so difficult of jigsaw puzzles called by such titles as "A Toast to the Pretender" or "The Play within a Play"; Vandyke dirt, Rushmore calls it.

Yet the front rooms, facing the street, despite their northern aspect, were full of decorative possibilities. They were only of medium size, but well proportioned. With mirrors, bright paint and wallpapers, they could be made cheerful and satisfying. And if, as I should have done, Kit threw the dining room, the hall and the drawing room into a single room, it would be gracious and even exciting.

Helen herself had gradually abandoned this part of the house, as the wages of servants rose and the yield of her trustee stock declined in purchasing power. It was opened up again during the Second World War for the reception of evacuees, but for some reason the evacuees did not stay. The place, I imagined, was too old-fashioned, inconvenient and run-down even for them. So Helen was left to herself again.

By that time Helen had withdrawn to the two most southerly rooms in the garden wing, the downstairs living room having a staircase of its own leading to her bedroom immediately above, and these were the only two rooms in the whole house which gave any impression of having been lived in, in recent times. They were the most attractive, by reason of their views of the garden and the sunshine which on a good day flooded them from dawn to near dusk. John Scarlet's tenants since Helen's death had clearly gravitated there away from the gloom of the rest of the house.

But separating Helen's living quarters from the main part of the house were four other rooms, two up and two down, which were even drearier than those facing the street. The original conversion of the garden wing from tannery to living quarters had never succeeded in welding the house into a single domestic complex. The William Anglesey who had made the original conversion in the seventeenth century must have thought that all this sleeping and living accommodation would be needed only for a single generation. The original work had been done on the cheap, without regard for quality or beauty since it was only to accommodate children or servants, both in their different ways lower castes who should be kept aware of their condition by the inferiority of their surroundings.

I glanced in at the first of these bedrooms, a sort of maids' dormitory, with an ugly varnished pitch-pine closet for linen in one corner and a low ceiling in the center, from the huge oak beams of which the plastered roof sloped down on either side, with a small dormer window on the eastern side.

The next room had been the Scarlet boy's; and I had slept there with him on one or two occasions, when my mother had been called away to visit her parents. Even with the companionship of Charles, I remember that it scared me, perhaps because of its coldness, perhaps because of the noises in the night which Charles told me were the scamperings of rats beneath the roof and the chirping of birds nesting under the eaves.

I tried the door into Charles' bedroom, curious to see what it had become over the years. It had always been bleak, a pair of truckle beds, a deal chest with white china knobs which came out when you tried to open the drawers, brown-patterned linoleum cold to the feet and tiny worn rugs beside each bed and before the washstand, with its flowered bowl and ewer in which the water froze in winter. But the connecting door was locked and looking through the large keyhole I could see that it had been left as a lumber room, just as it had been at the end of Helen's time. There were the old tin trunks, the abandoned towel horses, cardboard boxes filled with forgotten rubbish, a commode with a floral carpet top, a picture of Bubbles advertising Pear's soap.

I went back and down the main stairs and through the connecting rooms on the ground floor. At the end I could see Helen's sitting room dazzling in the sunlight, making the desuetude into which the intermediate rooms had fallen all the more depressing. One had been, I remembered, a sort of workshop for Albert Scarlet, to which he retired when wanting privacy. He specialized in carving wooden boxes with elaborate but unlovely designs and in making objects in poker work, letter racks, holders for pipes and toilet paper or mottoes to which calendars could be glued. Helen encouraged him to give them away as Christmas presents; and though she never said a word except in their praise, she made a clean sweep of these objects after Albert's death, presenting them to his friends and relatives as "something special to remember dear Albert by."

The other room had been Charles' playroom but was later converted into a sewing room. Helen's antiquated treadle sewing machine stood against one wall with dust thick on the oak veneer of its barrel cover. There was the chair she sat in desperately sewing curtains while Mrs. Allfrey and I knelt on the floor measuring and cutting the yards and yards of thick black cloth that were to hang like mourning for the long years of the Second World War. So many windows and so little money! She had implored Ernest to find some way in which the trust could be broken, so that in return for Anglesey House she could have a little cottage or a flat to live in. But Ernest, who never forgave Helen for marrying his father, insisted that there was no way of varying the trust without damaging the residuary legatees. It gave him, I think, a savage pleasure to think of her crippled by the maintenance of a house too big for her, yet too proud or set in her ways to let part of it off or convert it to a guest house.

Up to this point I had viewed the old house with little personal emotion; the sadness which I always feel at something allowed to fall into decay through neglect was counterbalanced by specula-tion about what might be done with the injection of new capital and ideas. I was Kit Everness' go-between.

But in the sewing room I felt that I was on the threshold of an experience which had nothing to do with Kit Everness or Angle-sey House. Helen Scarlet was in an odd way the most important person in my life. My dear father and mother, he with his schol-arship and his scrupulous practice of the law, she with her love of house and garden, her placid acceptance of tradition, which was not just convention but a very real sense of the continuity of human history, despite its imperfections—she followed the Hebraic tradition, without any curiosity in the ancient Chinese or regard for Asoka—gave me my workaday philosophy. But Helen inspired me in all sorts of ways; with the mystery of the feminine personality, for example. She also made me challenge my parents' standards, taught me that no one is the same all through, that unpredictability is not a vice of personality but a sign of richness. I loved her in quite a different way from the way in which I reverenced my parents; and yet she had passed through the same terrible stations to the grave, the fears about money—in her case justified—the assaults of senility, in which I was Charles first, then Andrew and later even Albert.

I went upstairs to her bedroom, in which I had visited her so regularly during those last weeks of her life, when she lay bed-ridden after the fall which broke her hip. It had seemed a night-mare room, with its little one-bar electric fire scarcely taking the edge off that terrible cold of 1947. I had brought round a larger fire and promised to pay her electric light bill, had scrounged a few hundredweight of coal and some sacks of wood, but Helen, haunted by the fear of penury, refused to let Mrs. Allfrey light a fire in the hearth or use my larger fire. The bedroom was like the grave.

And yet she always rallied for these visits of mine. Mrs. Allfrey told me that when she was working in the living room below, she used to hear the noise of weeping. But when I rang the front doorbell, Helen's handbell would sound immediately and she would have to hurry to the bedroom before opening the door to me. "Keep him," Helen would say, "wait till I ring for you." And Mrs. Allfrey would bring her mirror, brush, comb and toilet things so that Helen could make herself ready to receive me.

I was touched by her brave but haphazard toilets. It seemed to me a life-preserving vanity which could so rally her to put a good face on to meet a man. And when I came in, there was no doubt about the pleasure which it gave her to be held and hugged. She knew it was a man, though she was never quite certain of my name. And despite her age, I was very conscious of her as a woman, rather than as an old lady on the verge of death. She was as tremulous and grateful of caresses as a young girl.

There is something refreshing about the approach of death. Even my mother, who looked a very old, old lady in the last year of her life, began to look younger as her hold on life relaxed and on her deathbed was like a bride. And Helen was transfigured. The wasting of her face in those last weeks stretched the skin across the skull into a Red Indian fineness which smoothed away the wrinkles gathered in the years of compromise with widowed life; and the fever which never left her lit the cheeks with a flush almost of health.

But I was uneasy. Her spirit was restless. The mind, unhinged, swung creaking through the arc of her long life. Time seemed to have been ironed out, but not the cares and guilts that creased it. She clutched my hand between hers and said, "Oh, Charles, I failed you. My poor, poor Charles."

I tried to comfort her, but nothing I said would help. She had passed beyond the realm of reason. I did not ask her if she wanted to see the rector, Martin Turner. She was a strict evangelical and she disapproved of Martin as a "Puseyite." The idea that she might need to make a confession or receive the absolution of a priest would have appalled her.

But I told Martin and he went round to see her and something happened which seemed to give her peace. What exactly it was I don't know. Martin said to me later, "A sacrament can be a sacrament, even if someone doesn't realize it." So I suppose she must have confessed whatever it was that troubled her and been given absolution without realizing it. At any rate, she died in peace; and she knew who I was the last time I saw her. She called me George. "Pray for me, George," she said, "and pray for Charles. And Albert. Out of your innocence." It was the last thing that she said to me and I was deeply moved to think that she with her great purity of spirit should consider me innocent.

I remembered this, as I went up to Helen's bedroom, expecting to feel myself very close to her. But I was wrong. John Scarlet had modernized this room. In the place of her four-poster bed (which I suspected he had sold without consulting Miriam), there were twin divans with interior-spring mattresses. On the floor was a large, cheap, gay, Indian carpet the pile of which was molting like a yak in summer. A shoddy contemporary style of furniture had superseded the late Georgian and early Victorian pieces which Helen had chosen out of the clutter of Albert Scarlet's furniture.

Looking round the room, I realized, for the first time, despite having attended her funeral, that Helen was dead. Her spirit, wherever it might be, was certainly not here.

I looked out of the window at the terraced garden, which had been her pride, even to her last summer. With her sadly knotted arthritic fingers she had plucked at weeds and with her failing eyesight sought for garden pests. The order had declined, but in her day it was still a garden, the triumph of the human cultivation of God's finest flowers. Now it had fallen into utter neglect and I felt for John Scarlet, whose civilized duty it was to uphold it, a contempt which bordered upon hatred. Like children and animals, gardens are defenseless and when someone starts a society for the prevention of cruelty to them, perhaps people like John Scarlet will be prosecuted. A dozen years of negligence had obliterated half a century or more of love.

I had been rather uneasy about Kit's determination to get a place on the cheap, feeling that he was rich enough not to haggle, but when I saw that garden, I hardened my heart. The cheaper Kit bought the place, the more he could afford to spend on putting it back into condition; John Scarlet had forfeited my sympathy.

Suddenly I heard a furious barking and saw hopping through the tangled grass and weeds a rat, so slow and clumsy that I thought it must be pregnant, as Frisk herself was. I hate rats, obscene vermin with their wiry tails and fleas and mangy coats. Frisk caught it in her jaws and tossed it in the air with a movement that should have broken its neck. But the rat spun in the air and fell in nettles and I could see their stems waving as the filthy creature scuttled toward the wreck of the old hen house, which stood on stone toadstools.

I flung open the window and shouted, "At her, Frisk! At her!" But my voice distracted the dog for a moment and in that moment the rat gained the lead it needed to escape. Then recovering, Frisk darted after it under the chicken shed and I was left facing the fact that the sash cord had broken and the window in its rotten runners was liable to fall out unless I was careful.

I locked the window and went down to Helen's living room. It was the one room in the house where life still flickered. Though it had been changed out of recognition in the meantime, there still survived in its old corner the great Danziger desk, and even in its lower drawer, though sadly battered, the games which Helen had tried to give me, the compendium of Ludo, Chess, Halma and Snakes and Ladders, the box of letters for Word Making and Word Taking, the bone Spilikins, the checkers and the jigsaw puzzles. I found the key in our little secret drawer.

After the Second World War, we had discovered that the back of this desk was riddled with woodworm. Helen was too poor to have it renewed and I insisted on paying for the work myself.

Helen was proud and we had quite a row before she gave way.

"It's yours anyway, after I die, George," she said. "I want you to have it to remember me by. It's the only lovely thing in this place which belongs to me."

But she omitted to make any mention of it in her will; and when I told John Scarlet that it had been promised to me, he turned guiltily red, scarlet one might almost say. "Really!" he said. "You really surprise me! You surprise me very much indeed!"

I couldn't think why.

"Her very last words to me," John Scarlet said, "her Dying Words to coin a phrase ... she said, 'I want that desk to stay in the family. That desk belongs in the family,' she said. 'It's a family desk.'"

I was going to say that John Scarlet was a very bad liar. But in a way he was a very good one. There are two ways of telling a lie effectively; one is to appear to be telling the truth and the other, in which John excelled, is brazenly to persist in untruth. There had been nothing I could do. But I was determined, if the desk was offered to Yerbury, that I should have the first offer of it. It was no use trying to buy it from John himself, because his reflex action was to become an unwilling seller if he knew he had a willing buyer.

It was a very large piece and the only reason why he hadn't sold it earlier must have been that he knew he would find it difficult to dispose of. He had sold all the smaller things—and I wondered how much of the money he had received had been paid over to Miriam. He was quite capable of getting Yerbury to make out two different bills and splitting half the smaller amount with his sister.

That was a mean thought of mine and it made me anxious to leave the place which had provoked it. I looked at my watch. It was five to one and my housekeeper, Mrs. Ambrose, was as much a creature of habit as I was. I had not been late for a meal in ten years. But today I would be late however much I hurried. I opened the French windows and called Frisk.

She is a most obedient bitch. I have a way with dogs. But she did not come, even when I called again and again.

I went out into the garden, over the tangle of matted grass and dead weeds through which the spring growth was thrusting with the blind urge of the living to rise above the dead. I felt as I imagine a diver must feel exploring a submerged wreck. There were the shapes of the man-made garden but overgrown with weeds as a ship with barnacles, anemones and seaweeds.

All this time I was calling Frisk, but she did not come to heel. I thought that perhaps she was so excited in digging out those rats beneath the chicken house that she could not hear, or at least obey, me.

There was a great tangle of dock and nettle around the chicken house, but I could hear Frisk whimpering, even though I could not see her. I bent down and looked under the shed. There was a dark shape, like a bundle of rags, and the waggling white of Frisk's tail. She was caught in something and trying to back out to come to me she was strangling herself.

I called, "Down, Frisk, down!" But she was frightened, as I had never seen her frightened before. She struggled, shaking her head and tightening whatever it was she was caught in tighter around her throat.

I ran round to the other side so that if she came to my call, she would at least be straining in the opposite direction. On that side there was a tremendous overgrowth of ivy. It hung down in bitter evil-scented trails over the entrance to the chicken house. I tore it away but it fell about me, engulfing me so that I could not see what I was doing. Frisk's whining was almost like the whimpering of a child.

I heard another noise—a sort of scrabbling, squealing, which it occurred to me was the noise of rats, turning to attack Frisk now she was entangled beneath the hen house. I shouted and tore myself loose from the festoons of tendrils.

The interior of the hen house was dark, but I could see that one of the floor boards had broken in two and the others were rotten, eaten within to powder by woodworm. I caught hold of the plank above Frisk and wrenched it up. There was the scurry of a rat in retreat and then I bent down and patted Frisk on the head, saying "There, there, it's all right, my darling."

How she had managed to get herself so entangled I could not imagine. Beneath the hen house was an extraordinary litter, broken glass from the wine bottles in which old Mr. Allfrey had brought his lunchtime draught cider perhaps, rusty strands of wire, crumpled wire meshing mixed with lengths of fiber rope. Frisk was caught in a noose of this rope around her neck and her struggles to escape had only involved her legs and fur more firmly with the rest.

It took me about ten minutes to free her and I could not have done it so quickly if she had not stayed so obediently still.

As I worked, I thought that I would have to warn Kit Everness of the dangers of the garden for his daughter. The wreck of the house in the tulip tree would have to come down and preferably before the child saw it, or she would be demanding a new tree house in its place with all the attendant dangers. And there ought to be a visit from Collie Tickner, who used to be known as The Ratter, but is now entitled the Rodent Disinfestation Officer.

Yet as I walked rapidly home to face Mrs. Ambrose's silent disapproval, I thought how all the disadvantages of the place were conspiring to secure the property at the bargain price which Kit was keen on. He could build up a case which made it appear a favor for him to take it off the owner's hands. But he would have to be very careful not to overplay his hand with John Scarlet.

4

THE WEREMAN AND THE WHITE EMU

I am not a hasty man. I did not sit down and write a letter to Kit. Anglesey House was a possible. But until I had engineered a meeting with Miriam Schroeder, I could not advise Kit how best to set about negotiations.

As it happened, I did not have to engineer the meeting. I had forgotten to return the key of Anglesey House to John Scarlet and next morning Miriam rang up to ask whether she and her husband could come that evening for a drink and pick up the key. "It would have to be earlyish, if you don't mind, because we've got to put Andrea to bed. The granddaughter, you know. Molly's eldest. We've taken her for a week." She had a nervous pipping-comma voice, without any of her brother's pomposity but a defensive little laugh which I thought was her particular shield against the unfriendly world.

I asked them both for a quarter to six and for the sake of politeness added that I would be pleased to see John also, if he could come round after the shop was closed.

"Oh, no, I think not," she said, laughing. "Anyway he wouldn't come."

It was thirty years since I had seen Miriam; but it gave me a shock to think of her as a grandmother. My recollection of her was of a healthy, self-contained girl with a face like a speckled brown hen's egg, and certainly not cracked. I had never speculated what she was really like, because in those days I was incurious about those to whom I was not attracted. But I envied her the experience of parenthood and the pleasures of grandchildren. I regretted that I had left it until too late to marry.

I am a bachelor not by conviction, but by ambition in the first place and duty later. At Oxford I fell passionately in love with a girl, but I never proposed marriage because I knew that despite the attraction which drew us each together I should have to devote the rest of my life to earning enough money to maintain her in the condition to which she was accustomed. I knew that I could not do this by the books I proposed to write, at least for many years.

When my father died in 1930, I made my home at The Chantry partly because it was my duty to keep my mother company but also because it was a good place in which to work. I had what I considered then my necessary biological accommodations, which I now recognize as sinful relationships. I think my mother knew about them, but her silence was the price she paid for my companionship. I never broke a home. In fact, I seemed to find by instinct those who wanted the sort of love I could give not as a substitute for their marriages but as a cement. Since some of them are still alive, it would be a cruel thing to be more specific. It is enough to say that where there was passion it was measured. If it fell short of the high sublimity of love, it seldom sank into the abyss of lust. Though there was much of which I was ashamed, there was more of which the repentance was formal.

41

There was only once that I was caught terribly in the snares of love and that was in the first year of the war, in June, 1940. It was a mad time, when it seemed obvious that Britain was going to be invaded and conquered within a matter of months. I was aged thirty-six, too old for the call-up as of that time—and rather gratefully so, because though I loathed Hitler and was shocked by the bombing and machine-gunning of Guernica, by the "Rotterdammerung" and "Coventration," I foresaw that we would only win by atrocities as degrading; the heroism of the dambusters who drowned women and children in their sleep, the fires of Hamburg carrying people into the air like flaming bits of paper, the blasting of posterity at Hiroshima.

I volunteered for agricultural work and was sent to a farm—the location of which I shall not specify. In charge was Elizabeth X, the wife of a stockbroker-farmer who had been a major in the Territorial Army and was promoted to the rank of lieutenant colonel, before he was reported missing and presumed dead at Dunkirk.

I was with her the night this news came through and it was the first night I slept with her. It seemed the least I could do. My body clasped to hers was like a first-aid dressing bound to a battle wound and I was just a service orderly. It was a staunching embrace.

But there followed others, which were good in themselves. And a child was born, who, I was convinced, was my child but might just have been Weeny's (that was the hideous nickname of Elizabeth's enormous hero-husband). The boy, Adrian, was mine. I could see it by a dozen of my characteristics, the set of his eyes, the double-jointed elbows and so on. I pleaded with Elizabeth to have Weeny's death confirmed so that we could marry. But nothing could be proved, she said, until the war was over.

In the meantime we lived together as man and wife, but with a discretion which at times infuriated me. In bed Elizabeth was so full of love, so yielding and so demanding, but during the day she was Weeny's exacting bailiff. "We must wait until the war is over, George," she said.

And of course she had known all along that Weeny was alive. When she told me he was coming back next day, we had a flaming row. "How could you do that, when I wanted to marry you?" I asked.

She kissed me. "You're a lovely lover," she said, "almost as good as Weeny. I shall miss you."

I was outraged. I loved the little Adrian as my child.

Elizabeth laughed. "Shall I show you the birth certificate?" However beautifully physical love may flower, it is rooted in an earthy soil. Since the beginning of war, wives have defended their chastity by taking husband substitutes to ward off importunate lovers. Perhaps in the absence of Odysseus Penelope favored secretly one of her suitors to give her the strength to resist the others.

There was nothing I could do but retire, when the husband returned almost as small in body as he was in nickname. The poor chap had contracted tuberculosis as a P.O.W. and for some years I waited in the wings ready to appear upon the stage again if the tubercle finished the work captivity had begun. But the healthy life of the farm, the tender care of Elizabeth and the company of Adrian cured him completely. And by the time that I recognized this, I discovered also that I had let life slip by me. I seemed to take a dive from youth to age without an appreciable interval of maturity. I had missed the chance of marriage and paternity, between devotion to my mother and Helen on the one hand and my biological accommodations on the other. When looking in the mirror, as I have to in order to shave or brush my hair, I am filled with distaste at the body which is my habitation. It is the penalty of my earthly love of physical beauty that the years should fill me with repulsion at the sight of myself.

I frankly envied Miriam Schroeder now that, plain though she had started, she had enjoyed the experience of marriage, children and even grandchildren. Her life had been richer than mine. I was resigned to bachelordom. It had its compensations. My life was admirably organized for work—far better thanks to Mrs. Ambrose than ever seemed likely through a marriage of convenience to some middle-aged widow seeking security at no matter what sacrifice of standards. My only worry was The Chantry, toward which I felt the sort of responsibility lack of which for Anglesey House I deplored in John Scarlet. The Chantry needed love and care, without which it would soon fall into a decline as alarming as that of the Scarlet house.

There were no Grantley relatives to succeed me. Ours was a dying strain. But on my mother's side was Harry Waybridge, the young cousin with whom I had tried so unsuccessfully to play at Deal. I had been in correspondence with him during the last three years. He had married for a second time and was farming in Tanganyika. Though he was by his accounts doing well, I detected in his letters a nostalgia for England. He and his family were coming to stay with me that June. Though I had made no mention in my letters, I hoped that Harry's wife and children might fall in love with the place. If they did, I proposed to make them its custodians after my death. Otherwise it would be better to present it to the National Trust and let them appoint tenants of their choice. Deprived of my own blood, Adrian—for which I had only my own sinfulness to blame—I had to regard as members of my family anybody who would love and cherish this house as I did.

During the day, I wondered whether Miriam Schroeder felt toward Anglesey House as I did toward The Chantry, or if this deep feeling which I have for places was merely a transposition of parental and grandparental love toward the only thing I had to love, a house and garden.

Punctually at five forty-five a new Ford Anglia stopped in front of the door and a couple of minutes later Mrs. Ambrose showed in the Schroeders, Miriam advancing quickly first, her husband lagging sensitively behind.

All resemblance to a brown hen's egg had disappeared. With her small head and beaky nose, the crest of white hair and thin legs supported on stiletto heels, she was like a bird, a white emu wearing a black suit and a white silk shirt blouse. "George Grantley," she said, grasping my hand, "I'd have known you anywhere—after all these years—despite the heightened forehead." It was a lie prepared in advance and I could not return it.

"Even to my barber," I answered, "I am bald."

But she had not finished her rehearsal. She turned to her lagging husband. "You haven't met Karl," she said.

He was a tall broad-shouldered man, who clicked his heels and bowed slightly, as he shook my hand. "Karl Schroeder," he said and as he did so, his face was contorted in a nervous spasm which bared his teeth. What was the cause of this affliction, which recurred, like his wife's laugh, at any moment of social stress, I haven't the least idea. Kit Everness, when he met him later in the negotiations, nicknamed him *l'homme garou* maintaining that here was a reversal of the werewolf practice. "He's a wereman, my dear George; a wolf that becomes a man during the day." Kit was physically so secure that he could find the physical infirmity of others funny. A baldpate like myself is schooled in pity; or rather knows that within the oddest bodies live some of the loveliest spirits.

It was an unexpectedly cold afternoon and Mrs. Ambrose had lit a fire. I placed them either side of it and gave them sherry and cigarettes, drawing Miriam out on her impression of Wilchester after the lapse of so many years. While she talked, revealing that her observation was sharper than her intelligence, I watched the husband out of the corner of my eye. He held his hands toward the fire, long-fingered clever hands, impatient either with being here at all or with time wasted on trivialities. The flames, or pictures he could imagine in the fire, interested him more than those on the wall, my Cotman, my Puvis de Chavannes. His face stopped twitching and it was so handsome, or rather strong, that I could not remember he had this spasmic weakness.

When I turned the conversation toward their plans, Karl looked away from the fire toward his wife. We were coming closer to the point. They were not going back to the West Indies. Karl had been transferred to head office in London, for which they were glad because they could see more of their children and grandchildren. Miriam assumed that I knew all about her family affairs, I suppose because John Scarlet had kept her posted about mine. There seemed to be a daughter called Eileen who was married to a bank manager in Nottingham, a son who was a research chemist in ICI and a less satisfactory daughter whose husband had failed in his own business and was now a trade representative, working largely on commission. "But they're happy," Miriam said. "Aren't they happy, Karl?"

"Oh, yes!" The wolf within shook Karl by the throat. "Much in love."

"Which is the most important thing, after all," Miriam said doubtfully. "Isn't it, George?"

"I don't think so," I answered. "But what are you going to do? The two of you?" An interchange of glances showed me I was getting warm. But despite the granddaughter waiting to be put to bed it took a long while for me to piece together what worried them.

Karl was open in his contempt for John Scarlet. But Miriam was torn between pity for her brother, fear for the impending bankruptcy of the family business in which she held a quarter share and despair at the possibility of helping him.

As far as I could gather, John was in debt. How heavily it was of course impossible to say. I could imagine John's vague clichés—"temporary embarrassment," "struck a bad patch," "certain liabilities"—to cloak the results of years of muddle and mismanagement. For years there had been no distribution of profits and Miriam, abroad, had been content with vague statements about "building up stocks" and "necessary renovations."

Karl interrupted here to say that he had told Miriam over and over again that she ought to demand an annual statement of accounts. "Business is business," he said, "and within the family you can't be too businesslike."

But it was impossible for the unfortunate Miriam in San Fernando, Trinidad, to be businesslike with a brother in Wilchester who never answered letters. I could sympathize with her not provoking a quarrel which would have achieved nothing. John was a man who ignored unpleasant facts and refused to admit that he had ever been wrong.

Karl was sure that John had almost reached the end of his credit and the patience of his creditors. But John put his desperate call for help as if it were a proposal for mutual aid. It consisted in two parts which he tried to link together. The first was that he should take in as a junior partner Leslie, the Schroeder son-in-law who had failed in his own business. He wasn't getting any younger, John said, and who else was there to step into his shoes, when the time came to retire? The second was that the Schroeders should buy John's half of Anglesey House (for a sum which after sounding I judged to be about £3,500), which would enable

Karl and Miriam to make a home for themselves and for Leslie and his family.

Moronic though John might appear, he had his complement of cunning.

"How much would you say Anglesey House was worth?" Miriam asked me.

"What would you?" I asked turning to Karl.

"If it were in the High Street," he said, "it would be a very valuable site."

"What was the probate valuation?" I did not want to make a guess, which might be taken as an unofficial bid on Kit's behalf.

"It was £3,500," Miriam said, "but John says that prices have gone up since then; and of course probate valuation is always very low."

I pointed out that though house property might have gone up in the last twelve years, the condition of Anglesey House had gone down, as nothing had been spent on it.

I could see that they agreed. "If only Market Street hadn't been scheduled!" Miriam sighed. "And you remember how pleased John was, when he told us about it?"

"It depends what you want to do, doesn't it?" I suggested. "If you pretend you're interested, on Leslie's behalf, you can have your accountant examine John's books without offending his pride or doubting his honesty. That would give you an idea as to whether it would be worth your while to pull the business round. If it is, paying John twice as much as the house is worth would be a diplomatic way of refinancing the business."

"And leave that cretin as senior partner?" Karl asked, "when he isn't fit to be the office boy!"

"Insist that Miriam and Leslie should both be partners, each with equal voting powers. If he's as desperate as it sounds, John will agree."

"What about your friend?" Miriam asked. "Is he really interested?"

I said I had done nothing about it, because John had said nothing of the house being in the market. "Surely you must make up your minds what you want to do first?"

Miriam rose and picked up her bag. "There is one thing I am

determined about, whatever happens," she said grimly. "Nothing would induce me to live in Anglesey House, nothing."

"Why ever not?"

"Stepgranny Helen," she said. "I could never feel the house was mine." She spoke with a rancor which surprised me, coming from her in the first place and being directed against the gentle Helen in the second. "Of course, I'm sorry, George," she said. "I'd forgotten . . ."

"What?"

The white emu face grew pink. "You were one of her *followers*, weren't you?" Into the word "followers" she injected a load of poison, which infuriated me.

"If you mean that I loved her and admired her, yes," I said stiffly. "In that sense, I was her loyalest follower. And still am."

Karl, unaware of anything except that in some way his wife had caused an offense which she was trying to cover up with muttered excuses about relatives seeing a different side of people's characters, came between us with thanks for the time I had devoted to the discussion of their problems.

Up to that time I had felt the ambiguity of my position, having to advise two conflicting parties, Kit and the Schroeders, on an issue where their interests might conflict. But now I saw my way clear. If Miriam felt like this about Helen, Anglesey House was not the place for her. She would fill it with "contemporary" furniture, multipurpose units, sofas which turned into beds, dining-room tables concealing sewing machines, cocktail bars which were television sets, bookcases or china cabinets. There would be horrible occasional tables like boomerangs on three legs and deep armchairs with drawers underneath for storing blankets. "I take it then you would like me to tell my friend that the house is for sale?"

"Please," Karl said. "Please."

I looked at Miriam, who nodded agreement. "Who *is* your friend, by the way? I suppose someone very famous."

"If you've been abroad, I don't suppose you'll have heard of her," I answered. "She's a Spanish painter. Nieves Mariposa. Not very well known outside her own circle."

"It doesn't sound as if she was rolling in money," Miriam said.

"Not many people rolling in money are interested in houses backing on a shambles converted into a riding stable and a carpenter's workshop," I answered. "Her little daughter's a boarder at St. Clare's. She wants the child to be a day girl; and a studio to work in."

"Isn't she married?"

"Oh, yes," I said. "But he's abroad a lot of the time. It'll really be her house, not his."

That evening, I wrote a full report to Kit, explaining the half-lie I had told.

I think you had better send your wife down to make the preliminary reconnaissance; or if you come yourself, be the husband of the artist. It is just the sort of place which you were wanting. There are snags, of course. Apart from the fact that the structure is suffering from most of the defects to which house property can be an heir, the neighborhood is patchy; but it will improve steadily and in five years' time may be one of the most select residential neighborhoods in Wilchester, when the new by-pass has siphoned off the traffic.

However you must appreciate from what I have told you of the interplay between John Scarlet and the Schroeders, the psychology of house purchase must be most carefully studied before you make even an initial approach. Perhaps it would be a good idea if we all met before we did anything and concerted a plan of campaign.

5

BUYERMANSHIP

I received no answer to my letter, but on Saturday morning Kit telephoned me from the Wilchester Arms. "I've got to deliver some bloody Founder's Day Speech and present the prizes at St. Clare's," he said, *"Black Beauty* and the *Puce Book of Fairy Stories,* you know. No, Nieves couldn't come. She's painting a vegetable still life and the onions have begun to sprout. The point is I shall want a drink beforehand to get into the mood for the bland lies I've got to tell the poor girls. And equally I shall want one afterward, to forget the hideous deception. And which, if either, can you give me, Georgie pie?"

I hate drinking during the daytime—it makes me so sleepy. But I had finished a chapter and I wanted time for my thoughts to muster the material for the next, so I asked him to come straightaway.

He arrived in a gray Jaguar, before I had finished tidying my desk and arranging the reference books I had been using in orderly piles. But I had time to warn Mrs. Ambrose that I was expecting an old friend. "There's no need to ask his name," I said, knowing that if she did, it would be round the town before lunchtime next day. "Just show him up. And put that bottle of Steinwein Boxbeutel in the refrigerator—the pretty bottle, you know. He might prefer it to whisky. We'll see."

I could sense my housekeeper's resentment. Between us, we had built up such a rigid pattern of mutual habit that any variation of it on my part aroused suspicion on hers. My lateness for luncheon earlier in the week with the lame excuse that I had been unexpectedly detained had already aroused her curiosity. When the Schroeders came, she said, "I suppose it was about Anglesey House," just to show that she knew what the unexpected detention was. Now she was aware that this caller was the person interested in Anglesey House. I had had the good sense to burn Kit's letter, so that she could not know his identity. But when I saw that Jaguar come up the drive, I hurried down to open the door myself.

"I'll go myself, Mrs. Ambrose," I said, "it's quite all right."

From the flash of her rimless spectacles I could see that for her it was not as all right as that. I had posed her with a mystery which she was determined to solve; but if I had taken her into my confidence, the secret would have been passed on even quicker. People who love the anonymity of London say that this is the tragedy of small-town life. I used to think so myself, but I have come to the conclusion that it is the corollary of the virtue of belonging to a small community.

I opened the door just as Kit was raising his arm to press the bell. I caught him for a moment facially unprepared and in that instant found him rather sad—like a large house in Mayfair deserted for the opening of grouse shooting—the same impressive façade, and lack of life within.

But when he saw me, the lights flicked on. "George!" he said. "To be opened unto by the master, this is a surprise. An honor." He had a latter-day Wildean manner, floridly handsome, expensive bags beneath the eyes, a fine-cut mouth, if petulant. His tailor had tried to discipline the paunch and his barber had succeeded in making his partial baldness into a distinctive coiffure. He was balder in the center than I was, a sort of shiny pink ostrich egg of a skull, fringed with a curly black tonsure. But it gave him distinction. He looked, as Mrs. Ambrose hovering in the hall undoubtedly noticed, Someone; though whether it was a bishop, a politician, a TV personality, a Harley Street specialist or a black magician was not so certain.

I took him quickly to the staircase. Mrs. Ambrose was still hovering, hoping that she could find his name. "I would like you to meet Mrs. Ambrose," I said, "without whom life would be unendurable. She wants to know whether you would prefer whisky or Steinwein Boxbeutel."

Kit held out his hand and clasped Mrs. Ambrose's. He still had his own teeth and though they did not flash as brightly as when he first won West Carshalton for Labour, his smile won Mrs. Ambrose. "I should prefer whisky," he said, "but Miss Binks who is the Principal of St. Clare's would, I am sure, prefer me to reek of wine."

Mrs. Ambrose looked puzzled.

"The Steinwein Boxbeutel," I explained.

But Mrs. Ambrose had understood what Kit meant. Her puzzlement had sprung from her recognition of Kit's face as familiar and her inability to give it a name. As she followed our progress up the stairs, I saw the light dawn in her eyes. Of course, as a Wilcastrian she would know who presented the prizes at St. Clare's. I was glad, because this childish deception had made me uneasy.

Kit was oblivious of Mrs. Ambrose. He marched up the stairs and into my study, looking around him in a way that was at the same time sharp and cursory. "Cotman. Rowlandson. Puvis de Chavannes." He paused before the pictures just long enough to identify their painters. They were not works of art but terms of reference. Similarly he paused at the torso on the bookcase, not because of its beauty but because he could not place it. "Syracuse?"

"Paestum."

He nodded to it as graciously as if he were the Queen Mother in Stepney and then swept the room with his gaze. "Excellent! Typically you. It would have been worth while visiting Wilchester merely to see the Grantley bird in his native habitat." He looked down on me from his six feet two with a teasing smile and then, noticing the pain he had caused me, grasped my hand effusively and said, "It's good to see you, by George! It literally is."

"I suppose you want to see the house."

He clapped me on the shoulder. "I've seen it. I can't imagine anything better, short of a Plantagenet morgue."

"I'm glad you've decided to come out into the open. I thought all this . . ."

There was a light tap on the door and Mrs. Ambrose brought in the wine and glasses. "Would you pour Sir Christopher a glass, Mrs. Ambrose?" Once the cat has been let out of the bag, it is best to pretend that it was never in it. "Sir Christopher and I were at St. John's School together. He stopped me being bullied."

"I thought it was him from the papers," she said. "Well, I never. You never told me, Mr. George. Not that you couldn't stand up for yourself, Mr. George, judging by now."

She fussed around a little and then reluctantly retired.

As the door closed, Kit raised his eyebrows. "Wise, you think?"

"She reads the *Wilchester Gazette*," I answered. "There'll be a photograph of you in the next issue. Going round to Scarlet's is a different matter."

He tasted the wine. "Steinwein Boxbeutel is the second good reason for visiting you, my dear George. Another gap filled in my oenophilic education."

"What did you make of Scarlet?"

"I did not see him myself; but my Mr. Dawkins, whose judgment of the human species is unerring, pronounced him 'a proper cretin.' Mr. Dawkins is my chief clerk, a shrewd and misleading fellow. People think that his brain is as wild as his aitches. He is an unconscious master of mispronunciation and solecism. There is nothing more disarming than a first-class intelligence operating behind a shield of ill-educated pomposity. While you rack your brains trying to decide exactly how he has misused some word, he's in under your guard."

While Kit had driven down in the Jaguar, which he parked in the yard of the Wilchester Arms, Mr. Dawkins had gone ahead in his Morris Minor 1953 and called on John Scarlet, saying that he understood Anglesey House was to let. The notice was still in the window. When told that the house was now for sale, Mr. Dawkins took the key, saying that purchase was possible, if the price was right.

I was shocked by the deviousness of Kit's mind. "John Scarlet smells a rat even when there isn't one. If Dawkins is pretending to buy Anglesey House for himself . . ."

"Dawkins has merely said 'Purchase is possible.' " Kit walked over to the tray and replenished his glass. "No one, not even a proper cretin, could imagine Mr. Dawkins would pay an inflated price; and yet this pea-stick vendor Scarlet lent him the key. He must be prepared for a realistic starting price, from Mr. Dawkins."

"You're just making trouble for yourself, when Scarlet finds out that Dawkins is dealing for you. Even if you succeeded, it would be all over town. It might amuse people to think of John Scarlet being outsmarted . . . but they wouldn't think very highly of you."

"You mean, *you* wouldn't," Kit said, smiling down at me to cover his embarrassment. "You should know better than to think that I would do anything to forfeit your high regard, dear George."

"You're rich enough not to play underhand tricks."

Kit lit a cigarette. "I'm more famous than rich," he said. "Have you ever heard of Clifford Mulgrave? No. Mulgrave is an expert on patent law. He earns, I suppose, five times as much as I do—but nobody outside the profession has ever heard of him. Nobody knows what he looks like. Nobody cares. He could walk into Scarlet's shop and buy a bottle of Flytox and give his name without causing a flutter of interest. Well, next week I'm going out to East Africa to defend N'gozi. It'll be in all the newspapers and the proper cretins will think that I've been given a whacking great fee. In fact, I'm doing it for nothing. The Defense Committee pays my fares and hotel expenses. But the office, my staff, my family, the flat in Wessex Place, Rosa's school fees—those come out of my pocket—or the income tax I don't have to pay because I've earned nothing." He waved my protests on one side. "I know it has its satisfactions, power, fame, ego-bolstering. But I'm bloody fed up with the popular idea that if a man has a public name, you can double your price and get away with it."

He turned away angrily and filled his glass again.

"I'm only telling you about Wilchester people," I said. "If it gets around that you've used Dawkins as a front man, your reputation will stink in this town. I shan't tell people; but in a town like this when they start putting two and two together, they make the most alarming totals."

He turned back to me and walked over to the window, looking out at the cypress. "You're not being very consistent. You tell me that I have to use the psychological approach. But when I initiate one of the elementary ploys of Buyermanship, you attack me without even troubling to ask what I'm up to."

The Steinwein Boxbeutel was stronger than it seemed and Kit was drinking on an empty stomach. I went and gave myself a second glassful. "It had better be more ingenious than it seems."

"You assume that I'm going to use Mr. Dawkins as a 'front man,' whatever that may be. In fact, we have a situation in which a very stupid man has very stupid ideas about the value of his property. I want to buy his house. But I don't want to buy it at an inflated price. If you know a really reliable man here, get him to value it. I don't want to swindle Scarlet—any more than I want him to swindle me."

"Randall Rushmore's the man," I said.

"All right, if you say so." Kit was impatient at the interruption. "But how do we get Mr. Scarlet to see sense? After all, there's no fixed price to a house; it's what the buyer will offer and the seller accept. That is where Buyermanship comes in. Mr. Dawkins is not going to buy Anglesey House. But he is going to soften Scarlet up. He is going to beat Scarlet down to the lowest figure which he is prepared to accept—at the moment. Subject to survey, of course. Then he is going to bring in every weapon in the surveyor's arsenal. You've told me of the woodworm, the dry rot, the rising damp and so on. But there are other things. The electric wiring; it's rotten. The guttering needs renewing. The roof ought to be relaid. The plumbing is appalling; the lead pipes need renewing. The drains don't correspond to the council regulations and so the house could never be converted into two without their being completely overhauled. I'm willing to bet anything you like they're clogged underground with roots."

"This isn't a brief," I said.

"This is not a brief," he repeated as though he was in court. "These are facts; facts which the ostrich-like Mr. Scarlet has chosen to ignore. If, that is, he ever knew them. Somebody has to tell him those facts. But whoever does will fail to buy Anglesey House. He will incur the hatred of Mr. Scarlet for having brought him into such unpleasant contact with reality. Mr. Dawkins on the strength of the surveyor's report will withdraw his initial offer, but he will make another offer seven hundred and fifty or a thousand pounds less than the figure which Mr. Rushmore has decided is a fair price for the place. Then your friend, the painter Nieves Mariposa, who has probably been unavailable during this period, visiting her relatives in Mallorca—or would Ibiza be more convincing? By the way, you must meet her. You have some Spanish, haven't you. You may find her less overpowering than most of my friends. Your friend Nieves, to resume my flow, comes along and makes her bid—for a thousand pounds more than Mr. Dawkins finally offered. And in her unsophisticated way, she makes no mention of surveyors. An artist, she is only concerned with the amount of money she can rustle up for the purchase. (It will be her house, by the way, not mine.) And no building society will offer anything on a property of this age. And John Scarlet, egged on by the Schroeders, will close, we hope, eagerly, thinking what an unworldly ass she is, not to ask for a surveyor's report."

"You've worked it all out, haven't you?" I said, as he poured out the remainder of the bottle, giving himself the lion's share.

"You are quite wrong, my dear George," he answered. "I've

been making this up as I went along. Strategically I think that it may be sound enough, but tactically we must keep it fluid. If the Schroeders stay with John Scarlet much longer, for example, you may find the situation becoming very much more fluid." He glanced at his watch, swallowed the rest of his wine at a gulp and said, "God, I'm late. Maybe I'll be able to skip that glass of South African sherry in the headmistress' den before the corned beef and beet root."

But though he was late, he found time to say good-bye to Mrs. Ambrose and congratulate her on the wonderful job she was doing with me. I felt as if he was the master in the parable, with Mrs. Ambrose as the faithful servant making the most of me, the talent.

From the *Wilchester Gazette,* I learned later that Sir Christopher Everness in his urbane manner had made a most brilliant speech on the tradition of selfless service, as embodied in St. Clare's in contrast to the Modern Supermarket.

Three days later I received a letter from him, from his home address in Wessex Place, which showed the fluidity of the tactical situation.

> *Flat One, 43 Wessex Pl.*
> *London, W.1*
> *April 10*

JORGE MIO,

While we were sinking your pretty Stonewine, the redoubtable Dawkins continued his researches over bread and cheese and a tankard at a hostelry you may know called "The Intrepid Fox," managed he swears by a Mr. and Mrs. Guppy, the former "a lippy lad" and the latter "easy on the eye."

Being a stranger, he was regarded with a certain amount of suspicion, which he tried to allay with casual hospitality on what, to judge from his expense account, was a lavish scale.

He was rewarded in the end by Mr. Guppy's remarking in the words of Mr. Dawkins' confidential report, "Of course it depends if you believe in ghosts. Me, I don't, so it cuts no ice."

Mr. Dawkins goes on. "When I pressed the landlord to explicit him-

self, his wife interrogated, 'Oh, shut up, Charlie. That's nothing but a lot of idle gossip and it doesn't bear repeating.'

" 'Where there's smoke, there's fire, the saying is,' I said.

"The husband conquered with me, but his wife said Wilchester folk was so dull they had to make up things just to make life interesting; but it didn't signify, what they said. And there was quite an alternation between them.

"If it had been just him, I wouldn't believe it, sir, because he's got a wharfed sense of yumor, but she couldn't see a joke if you stuck it underneath her nose; and even if she does not credit it herself, it's as plain as a pikelet, some do, though I couldn't asseverate names.

"I think it might be a useful ace to keep under your hat, in the event the selling party proving difficult, being able to say how could Lady E succor domestic help in a haunted house."

I find it hard to believe that if there were any rumors of this sort, you would not yourself have heard them. But of course if there is any such superstition, it could rightly affect the purchase price. So I wonder if you would make discreet inquiries.

Will you let me know when you are liable to be in London? I fly to Nairobi tonight but will be back in a week's time at latest. Nieves wants to meet you, so perhaps you could manage dinner here one evening. To Comrade Kadar we owe the acquisition of a cook, who, while she is learning the subtleties of the English language, is thank goodness not forgetting those of Hungarian cuisine.

Per Sanctum Johannem in saecula saeculorum,

CHRISTOPHERUS AETERNITAS

I did not know Mr. and Mrs. Guppy personally—not having visited "The Intrepid Fox" since before the Second World War. From the little I had heard, they were Londoners, he a rather rough but good-hearted cockney, she a pretty but neurotic woman who in their eight years of residence had made as many enemies as her husband friends. It seemed to me unlikely that they should know more about Anglesey House than I did; but on the other hand they might be better informed about the gossip which hangs over a place like Wilchester as oppressively as the smoke clouds over an industrial city. I owed it to the Evernesses to find out.

6

THE LOCKED ROOM

But how was I to find out?

My experience in biographical research has proved how fatal it is to ask leading questions. People are very suggestible. I had only to hint to A that someone called X had said that Anglesey House was haunted and within a couple of days, even if A said he had heard no such thing, B, C and D would come to me and volunteer the confirmation of X.

As a doctrinaire rationalist Kit saw the whole thing as a sort of joke. He was so concerned in the battle of what he considered right against what he considered wrong that he had no time for good and evil. But I knew, as much by experience as by faith, that evil exists and spreads its kingdom wherever faith in its dominion prepares the way. The frontiers between belief in evil powers and their actual dominion are shadowy. Charles Guppy, even if he had merely said that Anglesey House was haunted as a joke, might have started something which could end by the place being possessed. I prayed for guidance, that I should not spread what I was trying to verify.

Prayer can be answered with extraordinary rapidity—but on the other hand it may not be. That is a fact that makes the religious life at the same time so much more exciting and hazardous than the rationalist's life of coincidence.

The telephone rang in a couple of minutes. It was Miriam Schroeder. She said, "George. May I come round and see you? This morning?"

"Of course."

"You were upset with me the other night, because of what I

said. And I'm sorry. Karl was angry with me. I didn't mean to hurt you."

"You didn't hurt me." I was sincere in saying that, but the moment I had said it, I realized that she had in fact hurt me more deeply than I had admitted to myself. "Is something wrong?"

"I can't explain over the phone. But I want your advice. Karl sees it all without the personal complications."

I told her to come round right away. I wanted to deal with whatever was troubling her before I settled down to work. Then it occurred to me that Miriam's call might be the answer to my prayer. She was probably the only person in the whole city of Wilchester who could answer my question about the haunting of Anglesey House honestly without spreading the rumor around the town.

I went down to Mrs. Ambrose and discussed the shopping. Mrs. Ambrose is the only person I have met who has been able to cook a good meal without losing her own appetite in the process. If she had been cooking merely for me, I should have felt guilty about the excellence of her food. But she enjoyed the dishes herself as much as I did. I gave her the widest latitude in what she bought and how she cooked it. I might, for example, suggest that some form of veal kidney might be nice for luncheon only to discover that she had prepared *moules marinières,* which she knew that I preferred on the rare occasions when she found fresh mussels in the shops. The post-breakfast discussion of the day's menu was merely a symbol of my interest in her cooking; the real business of the day was the review of the meals served, how far short of perfection a dish fell and whether the fault was in the material or the cooking. She was an artist who insisted on stringent criticism in order to prove that I was worth cooking for. I suppose I wouldn't have been so contented a bachelor, if we hadn't shared these gastronomic adventures together. The only uneasiness I ever felt was that I suspected Mrs. Ambrose would have liked to eat together with me in the kitchen so that we could compare bite-for-bite notes.

Miriam Schroeder's ring at the bell cut short our formal discussion. I took her up to my study, glad to have her alone. Her husband had inhibited Miriam on the previous visit. She felt far more entangled with John Scarlet than she had dared to show in Karl's presence. I suppose however far apart a brother and sister may drift, there remains the original family loyalty which conflicts with the later loyalties of marriage—and of course the guilt of cutting away from that original loyalty.

"I'm so worried," she said. "We called in an accountant on our own. John has been using Arthur Anglesey, who is just as hopeless as he is. It's a desperate situation. They've been waffling on all these years. We haven't any idea what the real position is; except that it would be madness for Leslie to go into the business. Our man says the only thing is to liquidate the whole concern. There hasn't been a realistic stock-taking since father died. John's just been playing at the thing."

I could believe that.

"But if we do that, what is going to happen to John?" she asked. "I can't come back from abroad and ruin my brother."

"But you haven't. You won't. Your brother has ruined himself."

"That's what Karl says. But don't you see, George, he's my little baby brother. I could see this happening right from the start. You remember when old Grandpa Scarlet had those races, who could get up the tulip tree first, and you and I and Charles ran for it and John hid in the raspberry canes. And John was frightened of the dark and I used to laugh at him. I used to pretend there was a witch in the cupboard under the stairs, and he believed it. And I told him that the Scissors Man in *Strüwelpeter* lived in the corner cupboard."

"But, my dear Miriam," I said, "John Scarlet is what he is because your mother didn't feed him properly—at least according to my mother, she didn't—and lots of other things. You mustn't take this guilt on yourself."

"But don't you see, I hated him because he was a boy and I was only a girl? It's ridiculous now, when we're in our fifties. We ought to have grown up. But poor little John never has. And I know it's my fault. Not just mine. But if I'd only understood. He never *was* normal; and I made him worse deliberately."

This—and a great deal more like it—coming from a grandmother about a fifty-year-old ironmonger must appear to the reader as ridiculous unless he or she is of an equal age and has discovered that the patterns established in childhood repeat themselves until the end of life. If John had not been her brother, she could have viewed her present problem objectively; but childhood guilts and jealousies obscured her judgment.

Mrs. Ambrose brought coffee for us both and I sat back, trying as I imagined a psychoanalyst would do to allow this personal material to order itself in my mind, so that when the time came to offer advice I could offer a solution which would satisfy Miriam emotionally as well as tackling the problem of John Scarlet's indebtedness. There was little coherence in her outpourings and it was only gradually that I realized she had passed from discussion of the shop to Anglesey House, for which a bid had been received from Mr. Dawkins that morning. She was reluctant to disclose the amount of the bid, wanting me to elicit a counterbid from my painter friend.

"I don't like auctions," I said, "but if you want to conduct one, you have to give some clue as to what she is up against."

Dawkins had offered £4,500, subject to survey. "Karl and I think it's a reasonable figure, having regard to the condition of the house. But John is sticking out, because he knows that his half won't cover the debts of the shop."

Knowing what I did, I felt I had to warn her. "John's debts have nothing to do with the value of the house," I said. "I'll pass on the information. But I shan't advise her even to come down to see the place. I think Dawkins' offer is too high and I believe he'll have to withdraw it when he gets his surveyor's report."

Her birdlike face crumpled with dismay. "Oh, dear! Oh, dear! What *are* we going to do?"

"It's for you to decide what you do about the house," I answered. "But I think you would be foolish to think of trying to keep John Scarlet in business. He hasn't the capacity to run one. He's one of nature's office boys. Sell him the idea of giving up the shop with one of those face-saving phrases he loves; call it 'realizing the site value of the property.' It's a jolly valuable position, even though it is in Market Street. You'd never get planning permission to start a new shop there. But they can't object to a conversion to a supermarket for example, if the façade is untouched. It runs a terrific way back. There's an unloading yard behind. He could probably pay off his debts with the sale of the stock alone and have enough capital to buy a sleeping partnership in a business where he wouldn't be allowed to do any harm."

She looked at me suspiciously. "You haven't been talking to Karl?"

"No. Why?"

"Because it's just what he said. But I felt so sorry for John. I couldn't bear to think of it."

"If you get him out of this mess, he'll get himself into another in five years' time, if not sooner," I said. "That is, if you allow him to be his own master. He'll be far happier taking orders from somebody else. He's terrified of responsibility."

"Karl said that, too." She seemed relieved at the coincidence of our opinions. "Well, I mustn't waste any more of your time."

As she pulled on her gloves, I said, "There was one thing I wanted to ask you. Is Anglesey House haunted?"

"Haunted?" She gave me a look into which she put all the surprise she could, but my impression was that this wasn't the first time she had heard the suggestion. "Whoever told you that?" She gave her little birdlike laugh.

I could not disclose my sources without danger of betraying my connection with Dawkins. So I lied. "I forget exactly where. I think it was from Mrs. Ambrose."

"Considering how well you knew Stepgranny Helen and the house," Miriam answered, "I should have thought you would be in a better position to speak than Mrs. Ambrose."

I agreed. "I merely asked you, in case you'd heard any rumors."

"Do *you* believe The Chantry is haunted?" she asked.

"Of course not."

"And yet some people do," she answered. "In a place like Wilchester any house more than a hundred and fifty years old is supposed to have its ghosts."

When Miriam had gone, it occurred to me that I should have asked her who had said that The Chantry was haunted and by what sort of ghost. And if I felt that, Miriam would probably feel the same. So I went into the kitchen to make Mrs. Ambrose privy to my deception.

I found her studying a racing form in the interlude between preparing the midday meal and putting it on. She is an inveterate punter, placing each day a sixpence each way accumulator, content if it comes up two or three times a season. "I hope you don't mind," I said, "I told Mrs. Schroeder that you had told me Anglesey House was haunted."

"Of course not, Mr. George," she answered, making it plain that what she did mind was being interrupted in her daily calculations.

I assumed that she had not really taken in what I had said. But while I was working on my notes upstairs in my study, it suddenly occurred to me that she might have been so unperturbed because she took it for granted that the place *was* haunted. I tackled her after luncheon.

"But of course," she said. "Why else couldn't John Scarlet let the place after the old lady died, when you couldn't find a furnished place for love nor money?"

I suggested there were good enough reasons in the extortionate rent John asked for a place so dilapidated and the fact that he wouldn't use an agent.

"Wouldn't use an agent!" she answered. "They wouldn't touch it, not after Bardsley & Beard had all that trouble with the first people who wouldn't pay the rent on account of the ghost and wouldn't get out neither."

"But why didn't you tell me about this?"

"Because you're not interested, Mr. George. You and your reading and writing. I didn't want to bother you with what's really happening."

I looked at her in astonishment. The frankest criticism is that which is made unconsciously. I, with what I regarded as my unselfish devotion to scholarship, was someone who could not be bothered with what was really happening! It was the more damning because Mrs. Ambrose took it for granted.

"But if it were haunted, Mrs. Scarlet would have known," I protested.

"Of course, she knew," Mrs. Ambrose said. "That's why she kept the boy's room locked. She never used to go through that room even if she wanted to go to the toilet, Mrs. Allfrey said; she went down all them stairs and along the corridor and up the other side. Just so she wouldn't have to go through the little boy's room."

I couldn't believe it of Helen, with whom I had had this wonderful intimacy, this in her own words "spiritual kinship." "She would have told me. She was able to tell me things she had never dared to confide in anyone."

"Perhaps she thought you knew," Mrs. Ambrose said darkly, "seeing as everybody else knew. Or maybe she liked you because you were so in the clouds you didn't notice."

"But why in Charlie's bedroom?" I asked. "It isn't Charlie?"

"That was his name," Mrs. Ambrose said. "The little boy what hung himself. Of course I was only a girl, but Mum told me."

"But he didn't. He fell and broke his neck. I remember the letter coming. He fell out of the tulip-tree house."

"Maybe that's what you heard, Mr. George," she said. "Your mother always tried to shield you. But that wasn't the way it happened. There was a proper scandal because of John Scarlet being in the same bedroom; and he never woke up, he said, not till the next morning."

I looked at her in astonishment. Her idea of the family relationships was so utterly wrong. "It isn't possible. John and Miriam sometimes came round to play. But they never stayed with Charles. They didn't get on together, Helen and Ernest Scarlet."

"But this was an emergency, you might say," Mrs. Ambrose said. "Mrs. Ernest was rushed off to hospital with an appendix; and so Mrs. Albert took the children; and then this happened. That was when the real split came. Before that they only didn't like one another, as relations don't."

That definition of a normal family relationship, "They only didn't like one another, as relations don't," impressed me with Mrs. Ambrose's natural wisdom. It was a fantastic thing that though she had been working in The Chantry for fifteen years, I had never had a conversation like this with her. We had talked of food and prices and domestic matters, but we had never discussed people. "Where did you get all this from?" I asked.

"I keep me ears clean," Mrs. Ambrose said. "And Mrs. Allfrey used to live just around the corner."

"I should have thought she was very loyal," I said.

"Oh, she was. Else she wouldn't have stood by the old lady right till the end. Scared stiff she was, many a time. In the blackout too. With air raids on; and this, whatever it was, inside. And poor old Mrs. Albert not allowed to get away, not by the Trust. You can't say Mrs. Allfrey wasn't loyal."

By this time I had finished my coffee and Mrs. Ambrose was waiting to take the things away to wash up. (Not, I may say, in order to place her bets, which she always phoned through before luncheon, but because she was due to leave at half-past two.) I kept her for one last query. "Do *you* think The Chantry's haunted, because Mrs. Schroeder's been told it is?"

"It's what you mean by haunted," she answered. "Not if you mean being unhappy, it isn't. But I always feel your mother's here. Maybe it's fancy. Because she loved it so, and you too. Much more than she ever let on, with that sharp tongue of hers. Of course I can remember; so it isn't a real test. I'll never forget that funny old hat of hers as she knelt on the sorbo mat grubbing out the weeds in her gardening gloves; and arranging the flowers; and picking raspberries. She's still here all right, in my mind. But it wouldn't be haunting—not as I reckon it. Just a sort of lingering love, like. To see you don't get into mischief."

7

A DUSTY FILE

I knew, from writing my *History of Wilchester,* that no files of the local papers were kept before 1921. But Helen had used my father's firm, Grantley, Grantley & Oakes, as her solicitors and Neville Fairchild, the present senior partner, was an old friend of mine. If necessary, the name of Sir Christopher Everness could be brought in; but I suspected that my own would be enough to gain me access to the information I needed. It certainly obtained me an immediate interview.

"I suppose you've come at last to discuss that will of yours," Neville said.

"I'll be discussing that with you later in the summer," I said. "After I've seen Harry Waybridge and his family."

Neville leaned back in his armchair tapping his splayed fingers on one another. He was a great finger-tapper. It was his way of saying, "If you're not busy, I am."

"Do you remember Helen Scarlet's boy, Charles?" I asked.

He nodded. "Vaguely. Never spoke to him, of course. In fact, we only came to know *her* socially when I joined the firm. My parents were howling snobs, bless 'em."

"I want to know how he died."

"Of course I was still a schoolboy. But there was a post mortem, wasn't there? It must have been before July, 1917. I was called up then."

"It was August, 1916. We were at the sea, but if there was an inquest . . ."

Neville pressed down a red key on the interoffice telephone. "I want the file for Mrs. Helen Scarlet deceased, 1916." He released the key. "Would it be rude to ask why you are interested?" he asked. His mouth, which had puckered since his teeth had been superseded by dentures, twitched with amusement at the absurdity of the literary profession. "You are not contemplating a *chronique scandaleuse* of our fair city, I trust."

A girl whose youth cried shame at this dreary office brought in a faded box file and laid it before him. "I've dusted it, sir."

Neville tried to formulate a light rebuke at having been told that the girl had done what was her plain duty, but his time was too valuable to waste in telling her it had been wasted. He opened the box and lifted out the papers, which were kept in folders year by year, tied with pink tape. The largest was that for 1916.

A girl's voice on the internal telephone said, "Mrs. Corbett is here and would like to see you, sir!"

Neville raised his eyes to high heaven. "Can't Mr. Anglesey cope?"

"Mr. Anglesey isn't back from court, sir, and Mr. Stephen is busy."

"Ask her to wait a minute." Neville bundled the papers back into the folder and tied it up. "If only that woman had less money what a lot she would hear to her spiritual advantage!" he said.

"This is strictly unprofessional, George. But you're the son of the firm and it's all dead stuff anyway. Take the file home and let me have it back tomorrow. It ought to have all you want in it." He slipped it in a foolscap envelope and for once I made for home at a faster pace than Frisk demanded. Holograph material always excites me. One can read so much in the handwriting and its variations. But this was the first time in all the years devoted to biography that I had ever been engaged on research affecting my own life.

The letters were from Helen Scarlet to Geoffrey Oakes, the partner who had held the fort while my father was at the war. Oakes had been exempt because his left arm had been atrophied through poliomyelitis. There were also two letters from Dr. Pidgeon, the G.P. who had fascinated me in childhood because he had a clean-shaven upper lip but a mustache running down his nose. He had seemed to me then an indifferent doctor and my impression was confirmed by his letters. There were also depositions taken, I imagine, by Oakes himself in longhand in that very office where I had seen Neville Fairchild, except that in those days it had no devices for the interruption of privacy, except an old-fashioned outside telephone. The main deposition was from Helen Scarlet. But there were others from servants, Bessie Toole cook and Lizzie Allfrey parlormaid, from Miriam and John Scarlet, and Albert Allfrey gardener. There were notes on an interview with Ernest Scarlet and there was a letter from Corporal Andrew Scarlet, A.E.F. Transit Camp, No. 3 Southern Command, written obviously just before a posting oversea, which Andrew would have liked to be postponed so that he could give evidence at the inquest, but without success.

If I were writing a work of biography, I would print all the relevant evidence in an appendix so that the reader could draw for himself conclusions against which he could check my own. But I have decided here to ask the reader to trust me, in the light of the standards which I have shown in such diverse works as my *Richard Middleton, Feudal Sodbury, The Ecstasies of St. Egfrith* and *Joanna Southcott and others*. These may be all works of a specialist interest. But of them all, it would be true to apply the remark of the reviewer of my *Wilcastrian Worthies* in the *Times Literary*

Supplement, "If nothing else, Mr. Grantley is scholarly." So I can vouch for the general accuracy of my account.

Mrs. Ernest Scarlet woke on the morning of August 18, 1916 with a feeling of severe pain. Dr. Pidgeon came at 8:45 A.M., diagnosed an acute appendicitis and dispatched her forthwith to hospital, where an immediate and successful appendectomy was performed.

Ernest before opening his shop slipped across to his stepmother and asked whether Miriam and John could stay with her until other arrangements could be made. Helen immediately agreed and the children moved into Anglesey House that morning.

The children did not get on with one another very well. Miriam played with Charles up in the tree house, but John refused to climb up. Helen said that the reason for this was that he was frightened of climbing the rope ladder. John said he didn't like the games Charles played, such as Prisoners and Tortures. Asked if they had played such games in the tree house, Miriam said Charles had suggested them, but she had refused. Against this, Oakes had penciled, "Lying, because ashamed?" John characteristically had spent the morning digging worms on the rubbish heap. In the afternoon, they went to the river, where Charles and Miriam bathed and John caught leeches in a ditch with worms on a piece of worsted. After tea Miriam and Charles went up into the tree house again and John caught wood lice. There was a quarrel between Miriam and Charles "about nothing really," but they did not speak to one another over supper.

John was frightened of sleeping alone in a strange house, so a bed was put up for him in Charles' room. Miriam and Helen slept in the wing looking over the street.

Cousin Andrew, who had been given a week's leave, following his discharge from hospital, slept in the bedroom overlooking the garden which Helen later took as her own.

Helen and Andrew said good night to the children at half-past eight, pulling the curtains to leave a chink of light, because John was frightened of the dark. There was no sound from the room when Andrew went to bed at half-past ten.

John said that after they went out, Charles got out of his bed and came over and said, "Peter wants to play with you."

Asked who "Peter" was, John said he was a "make-up" boy Charles played with, when he was alone. "Sometimes he seemed more than a pretend boy," Miriam said, when she was questioned about Peter. "Charles said he was up there in the tree and used to talk to him, as if he was really there, which he wasn't of course, but it was frightening."

(I had completely forgotten about "Peter," but on reading these papers it came back vividly to me how Charles would say fiercely, "You *must* do it, you *must*. Peter says so," when he was playing these elaborate tying up games. I do not remember his ever speaking to "Peter" in my presence, but Miriam was right to say that it was as if "Peter" was really there.)

John said that he told Charles he was tired and he wanted to go to sleep and Charles said he was soppy, but went back to his own bed.

At dawn when the birds began to sing, he woke up and in the half-light he saw what he thought was a sack hanging from the beam in the ceiling and then he realized it was Charles and he screamed.

His screams brought Bessie Toole and Lizzie Allfrey running from the maids' room, to the north, and Andrew, followed shortly after by the frantic Helen, from Andrew's bedroom to the south. Charles' toes were only a couple of inches from the floor and eighteen inches away was a footstool on which he must have stood to put the noose around his neck.

Andrew, who lifted the boy down, claimed to have no clear memory of exactly what happened, but the cook and parlor maid agreed that Mrs. Scarlet screamed, "Oh, God! Oh, God! This is a judgment," and then she went into hysterics.

The body was cold and the doctor estimated that death by strangulation had taken place about six hours before.

There seemed to me little doubt that while her son had been hanging from the beam in the next door room, Helen had been with Andrew. There was no other explanation of "Oh, God! This is a judgment." I was, I confess, shocked; in that part of myself which preserved a childish reverence for what had appeared the cool, impregnable beauty of Charles' mother. But I could not condemn with my adult mind either Andrew or Helen for what must have been a passion quickened by the imminence of his death.

What I found surprising was the series of letters written by Helen to Oakes in what I could only imagine to be a distraction caused by her own guilt and her horror at the discovery of her son's perversity. She accused John Scarlet of having deliberately kicked away the stool from under Charles' feet; of being in fact a child murderer. The motive, she suggested, was the hatred planted in John by Ernest against her for marrying Albert and against Charles, because if he lived he would inherit Anglesey House and the Trust money.

These letters were horrible, the pen dashing madly across the page, the temporary insanity of grief alive in every stroke. They had been annotated by Oakes with question marks, exclamation marks, and "I wonder" or "Poor woman."

Those summer holidays which I had spent at Deal listening to the guns across the Channel, that might but did not blow my father to bits, had been the scene in Wilchester of what would have been a major scandal, but for the diplomacy of Mr. Oakes. I could see the gentle way in which he had calmed poor Helen down and prevented her wild accusations reaching Ernest. I could remember Oakes only as a cripple, a man all of whose emotions had passed through a filter of pain and so seemed weak. But I realized in reading the file how wise and sensitive he had been. And when I read the clipping from the *Wilchester Gazette,* I saw the triumph of his tactics. It read as follows.

TRAGIC DEATH OF WOLF CUB

Charles Kent Scarlet, 10-year-old Wolf Cub, met death by misadventure through his keenness on knots. Experimenting on the slip-knot, Charles stood on a stool and placed the noose about his neck. The stool gave way under him, with tragic consequences.

The Coroner, Dr. Starke Whyte, remarked in recording death by misadventure, "This only goes to show that keenness should be matched with caution. Cubs, scouts, brownies and guides, it must be emphasized, should try out their knots on *terra firma*" (Latin, firm ground, Ed.).

There was only one other entry for the year 1916. It was in Mr. Oakes's scholarly hand. It read: "September 1. E. Scarlet called. Wanted to know if adultery invalidated Trust Deed. Pointed out that adultery is impossible after death of marriage partner. *Quelle galère!*"

I was still thinking about this file, when the rector arrived. It was his habit to come to tea once a week. As his churchwarden, I had for years discussed the problems that worried him, without obtruding mine which had been comfortably manageable. Now was the time to make amends.

"You're looking remarkably well, George," he said, "better than you've looked for years. What's wrong?"

Martin Turner is a remarkable man of God. He has two voices. His own is rather gentle and indecisive, as befits a man who is truly humble. But when he is in church, whether preaching or praying or reading the lessons, he speaks with great authority. "That," he said, when I once taxed him with the disparity, "is the voice of God."

This assumption of his that something must have gone wrong for me to look remarkably well was delivered in his authoritative voice and it took me aback. "You sound as if you're glad," I said.

"I've been worried about you," he answered. "You've been jogging along, doing these books of yours—and they're jolly good books, in their way—but you've been getting further and further away from life. I don't mean contemporary life. You might have got closer to what you really need through a study of the *Thebaid*—or St. John of the Cross. But you've grown, if I may say so, too complacent."

"And so you're glad to see me worried?"

"No. Insecure. Insecurity is the whetstone of the spirit. What's wrong?"

I told him as briefly as I could the salient facts of the story which I have rehearsed above. "You see the quandary," I ended. "What am I going to do? I have recommended a house to a friend who doesn't believe in any form of life after death. And there may be a possibility that it's possessed by evil spirits. On the other hand the whole thing may be idle rumor."

Martin popped one of Mrs. Ambrose's grated cheese and tomato sandwiches in his mouth and as he chewed, he closed his eyes in what a stranger would have thought to be an ecstatic tribute to her sandwich-making but I knew to be prayer. He took another sandwich, but before biting into it, he said, "Aren't you asking the wrong question, George?"

"But what *am* I to do?" I asked. The terrifying thing about saintly people like Martin Turner is that they get such strange ideas in their heads.

"I don't see that you can answer that, until you know what God is doing with you—and Everness—and the Scarlets—and perhaps quite a lot of other people. To say nothing of Anglesey House." He put the sandwich in his mouth and chewed it with relish.

Martin had not allayed my anxiety. He had merely shifted its ground. I was, in fact, more deeply alarmed. I see now why. I had been a traditionalist by temperament. My English Catholicism had been the religious aspect of a love of the Western tradition or so my critics had maintained. I don't think this was true. As far as it went, my religion was quite sincere. But I was terrified of coming too close to God. The Church provided a comfortable intermediary between me and His dazzling love and glory. After death I might not be able to avoid seeing Him face to face, but for the present I was content with being able to see Him only through a glass darkly. "I haven't the foggiest idea of what you mean."

"My dear George," Martin said, "I'm afraid that I may hurt you, which is very distressing to me, because you have been such a loyal churchman—but haven't you ever wondered whether you used your piety as a means of cutting yourself off from the blinding vision of God? I have, constantly. Pharisaism is the professional disease of clergymen. But churchwardens are liable to catch it. It's very contagious."

"What are you trying to say?" I asked, only too aware of what he was saying and its truth.

"I don't pretend to know that," Martin answered. "But I am certain that you have been given a job to do, which is going to shake you awake. I envy you, George. It is going to be frightening—and wonderful. And I'll pray for you and be there when you need me." He stood up. "I'm late for Evensong." He snatched a last sandwich. "Have you ever thought what it *means* to pray, 'Thy will be done!'? That's the answer."

"I'd like to come with you," I said.

"Poor old Raikes would like that," Martin said. "He has to be there as verger, but he hates being all alone."

8

THE ARMORY OF UNBELIEF

It was too late to call Kit at his chambers when I returned from Evensong. I telephoned his flat in Wessex Place, but Sir Christopher and Lady Everness were dining out. The Hungarian refugee did not know at what time they would be back. I had the impression that she regarded the telephone with some apprehension as an intruder which could penetrate barred doors.

Remembering my own humiliations trying to telephone in other languages than my own, I tried not to frighten her by talking too loud or too fast, but fell into the error of articulating each syllable so distinctly that even to myself I sounded as if I was talking gibberish.

But somehow or other she gathered that when I gave my exchange as "Will-chest-air" I really meant "Wilchester" and that I wanted Kit to call me urgently as soon as he came in. She knew my name and I thought it probable that the Evernesses had told her about the house. But when I rang off, I was still uncertain whether I had made communication and how much of my message would get through to Kit. Had she even said that the Evernesses were out to dinner? Would they come back that night? Had they gone abroad? I did not dare to harass the Hungarian by telephoning a second time.

Yet I could not settle down to work after dinner. Since Miriam Schroeder's morning visit there had been such a succession of revolutions in my accepted ideas, of Helen, Charles, John Scarlet and myself, that to take refuge in working on my book appeared an act of escapism. Hadn't my lifework been precisely that? I had become so engrossed in the biographies of people I had never met that I knew worse than nothing of the lives and characters of those I knew personally. It was fantastic that in the course of all these years I had been so cut off from Wilcastrian gossip that I had never heard—or was it rather, taken in?—a hint about the real circumstances of Charles Scarlet's death. I, who prided myself on what I could read in and between the lines of holograph material, had been blind to the tragedy of Helen's life, even though this must have colored the whole of her relationship to me. How could I continue with a work which now appeared to be an unconscious pursuit of ignorance?

My thoughts turned to Kit's Buyermanship. It might be legitimate for him to dramatize the house purchase by running both the rival buyers. But it was not legitimate for me to be an accomplice. Honesty in my opinion was the best, because the most disarming, policy.

After Evensong I had told Martin, "I don't see there's anything more I can do than tell Everness the place may be haunted."

"Isn't that enough?"

"But he'll think I'm crazy."

"That's another thing you can do for him. Let him."

"*You* don't think I'm crazy?"

"You've told me enough to make me suspect you aren't," he said. "But this isn't my assignment. It's yours. The object of the exercise might even be to show you that in this matter you are a bit crazy. If so, it wouldn't be wasted."

Martin Turner's complacency irritated me. "It would make me such a fool."

" 'If the fool persist in his folly, he shall become wise.' " It was a favorite saying of mine, but I had always taken Blake to mean a real folly in which the fool persisted. But it could mean the opposite, just as "The path to wisdom lies through excess" could, or "Damn braces, bless relaxes."

I went to bed as usual at ten-twenty, after my nightcap (taken at ten). I fell asleep a few minutes after reading the customary chapter of St. Thomas à Kempis. But it was not my usual dreamless sleep. Partly this was due to the fact that it was a very hot night, partly to my carelessness in making my bed. I had as upper sheet one of the last that my mother had turned and instead of discarding it when the hole had appeared in the center, I thought that I could use it for a final week. But the principal reason was that I had denied any feeling about Charles' death. It was so horrible that I had even tried to impersonate him as "the Scarlet boy," as Oakes himself had done in his notes of the case.

In this dream I was aware of Charles as he had been during my childhood. So far I have made him seem a perverse little monster—but that wasn't how he appeared to me or indeed was. He was a most brilliant boy. I use the word "brilliant" deliberately. He gave off an effulgence, partly of the mind and partly of the spirit. He shone, as I imagine angels do. And so the dark fits of which I have written so much were all the more tragic, like a brilliant landscape plunged by stormcloud into shadow.

In this dream I loved Charles even more deeply than I had done when he was alive. He was all light, his own and Helen's, and all I yearned to be in my overcast self. He was one of the sons of the morning and he stretched out his hands and lifted me up. I could feel myself rising, transcendent, into that mid-space between earth and heaven (to use words which are geographically false about the spiritual universe) and as I rose the thong tightened round my neck and I was being strangled.

And as I was dying, there was suddenly an ambulance racing after me to bring me back to life and I did not want to come back, because being bodiless was so much easier, but the ambulance traveled so fast that the bell grew louder and louder until I was awake alive again, putting out my hand for the telephone receiver beside my bed, the hem of the sheet somehow tangled about my neck. "Hullo."

Kit's voice, slurred with drink, boomed in my ear. "Georgie Porgie old boy, you said to ring. Important, it says."

"Tomorrow." I said. "Can you meet me at El Vino? One o'clock."

"I shouldn't but I will." Suddenly his voice softened. "I didn't wake you up, old man?"

"I was sleeping. The sleep of the dead. One o'clock. G'night."

I turned on the light in order to remake my bed. It was past midnight. What an awful man Kit was to ring at such a time! And yet if he hadn't, I realized as I padded to the linen cupboard to get a new sheet, I might have strangled myself. The bloody man had saved my life. Perhaps.

As I waited to fall asleep a second time, I thought of a remark of Martin Turner's, which had always seemed to me overclever. "The great vice of Christians, us Christians, is to forget that every man, woman and child is an agent of God."

"And bird and bee and flower!" I said, carrying his argument to what I thought was the point of its absurdity.

"Yes," he answered gravely, "down to the last virus and the final antibody."

El Vino's at one o'clock is not the ideal place for a private chat. Discriminating wine bibbers from Fleet Street and the Law Courts begin to converge on it at 12:45 P.M. and do not dissipate till half-past two. The front bar is three deep in barristers and feature writers, free lances and leg men; and the back bar with its tables is crowded to seating capacity.

Knowing this, I arrived early enough to secure a small table for two in the corner, from which I signaled to Kit as he came purposively in at ten past one. His face appeared to me strained—he was a man who found it hard to work, except at high pressure—but the moment he saw me ten years dropped from him and he was the vigorous man of action.

He had with him a slim black brief case, which he propped against the wall. "Don't let me forget that." It contained the papers for the afternoon sitting of a breach of contract case, in which he was representing E.B.F. He was a brilliant company lawyer and my legal friends had often told me that if he had been content to leave politics alone, his fees could have run into six figures annually.

I knew immediately he sat down that the time was as unsuitable for my purpose as the place. His mind was occupied with the afternoon ahead and he was only giving me a fraction of his attention. "What I've got to tell you is important," I said, "but it isn't all that urgent. Would you like me to tell you about it later?"

He ordered a bottle of Chablis and half a dozen sandwiches.

"Tell me now," he said. "I dispatched this afternoon's business to the department of the unconscious on my way here. What's the snag with the house?"

"You remember that rumor Dawkins picked up about the place being haunted," I said. "It seemed to me ridiculous. But now I've made investigations, I'm afraid it may be true."

He leaned back in his chair, his eyes twinkling, his mouth twitching with amusement. "Really?" he said, or perhaps it was "Really!" Maybe both. "You fascinate me. Tell me more."

I am not a good expositor, except on paper; and my case was far from complete. I knew that I could prove nothing. It was rather like an archaeologist from a few potsherds trying to reconstruct a complete vessel, but more difficult. The curve of a lip, a fragment of base or neck enables anyone with a knowledge of geometry and the potter's wheel to reconstruct the missing fragments to the satisfaction of anyone else with similar knowledge. But behind my argument was a body of what I would call experience and belief, but what to Kit was superstitious nonsense.

Even if I had presented my story skillfully and without interruption, it would have carried no weight with Kit. As it was, distracted between eating, drinking, carrying on a light flirtation with the waitress and ruminating his legal arguments of the afternoon, he could give me no more than the indulgence of an amused tolerance. "I am most deeply touched," he said at last. "But you must see, my dear George, that though Anglesey House might be a dangerous residence for someone like yourself, as vulnerable to the assaults of the Devil as you are susceptible to the Divine afflatus, a stalwart rationalist like myself is immunized against the supernatural. We are the despair of Shaitan, who not having souls cannot lose them. The armor of our unbelief is impenetrable. Only those aspiring to salvation can be damned; while we, content within the limits of our life span, have only earthly heavens and hells." Rhetoric was his natural element and if I had not interrupted him he would have rolled on as long as a period by Sir Thomas Browne.

"Redemption is a common fortune which anyone can refuse to inherit," I answered in kind, "but immortal life is the condition even of those who are unprepared for it."

"If it comes, I shall be ready," he answered, "with a pleased surprise. Heaven may be the bonus dividend on the investment of a well-spent life, but I don't need posthumous rewards and punishments to teach me my duties as a civilized man."

We were getting so far from the threat of Anglesey House that I turned my attention to the sandwiches, letting Kit ride the humanist hobbyhorse of the moral superiority of agnostic man. It was as if we were talking two separate languages, each incapable of understanding the other.

Normally I would have made no attempt to find a *lingua franca*. Matters of faith cannot be resolved by human argument. But in this case, if I was right, danger might threaten some member of his household. "Does your wife share your views?"

"Nieves is a Catalan," he answered. "She considers my humanistic tolerance of all the vagaries of the religious impulse, Christian or otherwise, as the product of a sloppy nineteenth-century liberalism, which of course it is—but none the worse for that. For her, religion is the Roman Catholic Church as exemplified in the Iberian Peninsula, superstitious, reactionary, venal and power-loving. She is fanatically anticlerical, as intolerant of the Church as the Church is intolerant of people like her. To massacre every priest and butcher every bishop would be, in her opinion, too lenient a retribution for all the misery Mother Church has caused or condoned and all the ignorance and superstition she has spread throughout Iberia. Mutilation and slow torture would be necessary to wipe the slate clean, according to her; though in fact she is so gentle-hearted that she would help even a Jesuit in trouble."

"What about your daughter?"

"Rosa? We had a row about Rosa. When she went to school, she asked to be baptized. C. of E., of course. Nieves wanted to forbid it. But reason prevailed. I pointed out that unless Rosa experienced the vacuity of organized religion, she would feel spiritually underprivileged. As I see it, every child has to live through the spiritual evolution of the human race, the primitive animism of the nursery and the mystical ecstasies of adolescence. I couldn't have reached the maturity of my humanism without passing through those phases myself."

"What did you do about godparents?"

"The chaplain fellow—I suppose he must be your vicar or something—Turnbull, is it?"

"Turner?"

"That's right. Very sensible chap. He suggested a modified form of adult baptism, without godparents. And we undertook that she should be confirmed, when the time came. I was quite honest. I explained that I didn't think she could really lose her faith unless she had had it. 'And you're prepared to take the risk of her not losing it?' he asked. Of course I was. Some people are spiritual Peter Pans, like you, my dear George. It would be criminal to deprive you of your religious solace." He poured himself the dregs of the bottle and because he was ashamed of the insult he turned to the waitress and waved the empty bottle. "Another half, my sweet."

She nodded and he put the bottle down.

"Have you ever thought that Rosa is vulnerable?" I asked.

He looked at me with sudden anger. I could see by his eyes that the wine had taken effect. His was a frightening future. He was not an alcoholic, at least yet; but he had come to rely upon drink to keep him at that state of nervous tension where he functioned best. He was like a tight-rope walker poised between sobriety and drunkenness. One day something would go, his kidneys, his spleen, his liver, or if God was merciful his heart. "By God," he said, "don't you try that, George."

"Try what?"

"I know what you're up to, you and your bloody Jesus-creeping."

The waitress brought the half-bottle and showed it to him, but he didn't look at it. "Pour it, dear," he said, stripping a couple of pound notes off his wad. "And keep the change."

I put my hand over the top of my glass.

"For God's sake, man," he said, "you aren't the vicar's wife, or do you want me to lose this case this afternoon? Is that what you're up to?" He looked at his watch. It was ten to two. We had drunk fast, at least according to my standards; but I took my hand off my glass. I did not *have* to attend the British Museum that afternoon. "That house is lovely," he said. "It's what I've always wanted. You remember when I came down to stay with you and Mum and I were living in Colville Square. Well, I'm going to have it."

I remembered him so well, when he had graced The Chantry with his to me so august presence and we had swum above the weir and shot rabbits in the chalk pit with the B.S.A. air gun and walked along the North Downs and he had said in surprise because my country legs were so much stronger than his town ones, "I didn't realize you had it in you, G.G.," and we had crept under the netting to eat strawberries and raspberries with the sun on them and the curious shame he had about a brown birthmark between his shoulder blades which to me, because it was between *his* shoulder blades, was wonderful. I could see within the body of the bald distinguished Q.C. that honored schoolboy, with his passions and privations, just as I could feel within myself, beneath that recurrent throb in the left lung and the pain of the osseous spicules in the right elbow which I refused to have removed by surgery, the reverent schoolboy to whom Kit Everness was a hero.

One has these incongruities of time. That catchword "Be your age" seems to imply that one ought to deny all the other ages one has been, whereas age is the sum total of all one's ages. "Kit," I said, "I'm not trying to attack you. I'm just worried about your daughter."

"So am I," he said, "and I'll tell you why. She isn't very bright. She doesn't take after either of us. But she's a very sweet child. She'll be all right. She'll be all right, that is, provided somebody like you doesn't go putting damn silly ideas in her head. I'm not frightened of the house, but I'm frightened of you, George. Not you, but this religious bug you've got. I can see you snagging the whole thing up."

"I don't think that's very fair," I said, "considering that I've disrupted weeks of my working life to find you this house and further your rather shabby intrigues to buy it. But I can promise you that I don't want to interfere from now on. I don't want to meet your wife or your daughter; or for that matter you, if you ever buy the place." The rancor of the wine was working in me also. "I can tell you that the whole thing has been most distasteful. From now on, you're on your own. I want to have nothing more to do with it."

"Christ!" said Kit, "I'm late." He scooped up his brief case. "Pray for me on the way out. The Commissioners of Inland Revenue want me to win this case."

In a moment he was gone, leaving me an unfinished glass of wine and half a smoked salmon sandwich. I finished both and then walked to the lovely octagonal of St. Dunstan's in the Fields and tried to pray that he and Nieves and Rosa and I would do His will while the organist practiced a voluntary.

It wasn't easy.

9

A BUNDLE OF OLD LETTERS

Next morning Yerbury came to see me. He was a strange man who chose to cover his fine cranium in a National Health Service auburn wig but who refused to cover his gums in National Health Service (or for that matter any other) dentures. He had lost all his hair in his early twenties and felt that there was a sort of obscenity in baldness. But he had no such feeling about the loss of his teeth in his fifties.

He was, like most men in the secondhand trades, a shrewd operator, buying cheap and selling dear. When he told me that he could get the Danziger cabinet for me at thirty guineas, I knew that he had offered John Scarlet twenty for it. But I did not mind. It was worth forty to fifty to the right customer, who had the space for a piece of such a size.

I told Yerbury that the price was right and showed him where I wanted it placed. Obligingly he helped me to rearrange the room, moving my working desk from the window overlooking the garden up into the tower room, where I kept my files, from which I could see across the whole valley. It had long been my intention to have this as an alternative working place—and I could have fulfilled it sooner by buying some cheap desk for the purpose. But I had always put this off in the conviction that the Danziger desk would one day find the home which Helen wanted for it in my study.

To make room for it, I moved great-grandmother Waybridge's lacquer table from the corner into the window where the desk had been—a vast improvement for the appreciation of its pretty floral design of mother-of-pearl. The corner it vacated might have been planned especially for the triangular desk of Helen's. It gave me views from two windows, eastward across the garden to the cypress tree, and southward to the Roman camp on the hill.

I wrote Yerbury my check there and then. He operated on a slender capital, which seemed always stretched to the limit, and I did not want the piece to slip from my grasp at the last moment. "There's no need to do that, George," he said, once he had made sure that the check had been made out in his favor.

"It's for my own convenience, Nathan," I answered. "If I do it now, I shan't have to remember to do it later."

We were on Christian name terms, vaguely because "we both loved beautiful things," but I always had to remind myself that the name was Nathan, not Nathaniel or Benjamin or Nahum, because I privately thought of him as Yerbury.

As he took the check, he drew from his pocket a manila envelope. "As I was poking about, I found in the back of the desk a second secret drawer," he said. "There was a bundle of old letters, belonging to the old lady, I imagine. I suppose, strictly speaking, I should hand them over to John Scarlet. But knowing how you like documents, I thought you could probably make much better use of them."

"That depends. Are they interesting?"

"I just glanced," he said. "They only seemed to have a sentimental value. But then you've got the imagination. I envy you the way you can read into things like that and really make them come alive. I can do that with my stuff, furniture, curios; but not letters."

Perhaps I was unduly suspicious. Yerbury might have intended to give me the letters anyway; but I took them as a discount for cash. In a place like Wilchester, the private letters of the dead have a curiosity value, if they are revealing enough.

And these *were* revealing, as I saw immediately I began to

examine them, after Yerbury had departed promising to deliver the desk that afternoon.

The envelope contained what appeared to be one bundle of letters tied with pink tape. But when I undid this, I saw that there were two separate groups, the first and larger tied with faded blue silk ribbon and the second with the sort of silver string used for tying Christmas presents.

There were thirty-two letters in the first group, each in its envelope addressed in the same copperplate handwriting to Miss Helen Kent and with the same florid Edwardian penny stamp heavily postmarked. They had been numbered in sequence in what I could recognize from the later examples with which I was familiar as Helen's precise and scholarly hand. The address varied. Most were sent to St. Clare's, but others written during holidays were "c/o The Dean of Salisbury," "At the Lucknow Private Hotel, Lyme Regis" and so on. The date of the first sur-charge was February, 1902, and the last exactly two years later.

They contained, clearly, the story of her courtship and I hesi-tated before I began to read the letters, because relentless though I am when writing a biography there was no professional reason why I should penetrate these secrets.

I reflected that as Helen had wanted me to have the desk, she knew it contained these letters and so by inference wanted me to read them. They might modify my view of her—as, for example, Miriam Schroeder's remarks and the evidence of the file lent by Neville Fairchild had—but at least I could assume that these let-ters contained information which Helen wanted me to know after her death. This convinced me that the duty laid on me by Helen was to learn what they contained, even if I destroyed them later.

They were written in the rather stilted language common to the period, to which Albert Scarlet's patchy education gave a curi-ous twist. The first letter set the tone. It was on mourning paper with a thick black edge.

Anglesey House
Sunday night, late

MY DEAR MISS KENT,

I trust you will pardon me confiding to you an experience witch has ocupied my thoughts to the exclusion of all else, since it happened this a.m. But it is so strange that for reasons witch you will see hereunder I feel I must comyunicate to you forthwith.

Juring the Vicar's sermon this a.m., my thoughts were, as you may well think, much concerned with my beloved spouse, God rest her soul, this being the first time I was in His house since the burial this Wed witch I so understand was too harrowing for you to attend, you being so close. I felt her very close to me and to the children as we sat there, wondering what hope can the future hold when all seems dark etc.

Then as we were leaving, I saw you waiting there in the porch to say those few kind words witch mean so much and I noticed for the first time, my dear Miss Kent, how you are very beautiful. Of coarse you will think this extraordinary, because I have seen you so often during the last two years first as my little girl's good teacher who was so kind and came to tea and then as our kind kind guest, dear Miriam's best friend, my beloved spouse, during the holidays, with her sinking and sinking before our eyes. It was so aweful at the end, so weak she was and you so loyal, never dawnted. But it is God's Truth. I never looked at you all that time except you were Miriam's best friend and else you might have been the sideboard for all the notice I took. You must believe this, my dear Miss Kent.

But as I'm standing there, holding your hand and looking into your beautiful eyes, I hear Miriam's voice as plain as if she's there beside me, saying, "Bert, Bert, you and Helen must get married. I would like that. You two will be happy together and she will look after the children as sweetly as she looked after me."

This was an extraordinary thing, because it was what I never thought of but Miriam my beloved spouse put into my mind. I would not think of suggesting it on my own, especially so soon after my tragic loss, it would smack of unseemly haste, only it was Miriam's own idea, which you will appreciate makes the world of difference.

If not, can you see me writing this, my dear Miss Kent, even though seeing you now for the first time, so beautiful and good and kind.

Hopping you will forgive the forgoing in the spirit in which intended.

Yrs ever truely

ALBERT SCARLET

I was surprised at the wildness of Albert's spelling. I remember that he spoke a rough "country." But I had seen nothing from his hand before.

Helen had made no copies of her replies to Scarlet, but their gist could be inferred. Albert's second letter, for example, revealed that Helen regarded the precipitance of his proposal indecorous and that even if her dead friend considered such a second marriage desirable for the sake of her children, she, Helen, could regard marriage only in terms of herself and her husband and not in those of other people, alive or dead. She forbade him to mention the matter again, at least for a year.

Albert seized on the important point. Miss Kent had not rejected his proposal; she had merely postponed its consideration. He himself did not pay undue regard to social convention where the heart signaled clearly; and he was sure that Helen agreed. But he accepted her condition in the eager trust that after the lapse of a twelvemonth his suit would not be looked on with disfavor.

I found it an "extraordinary" correspondence with its motley of religious, emotional and literary clichés cloaking the rising passion of the elderly ironmonger for the young schoolteacher. Careful to preserve her reputation, Helen refused to visit Anglesey House; and Albert reproached her on her discreet chilliness whenever he met her at such public Wilcastrian functions as the Church Lads' Brigade Jumble Sale or Whist Drives in the Church Hall. They met clandestinely in London on several occasions, at the Royal Academy, Madame Tussaud's, the Natural History Museum and the Albert Hall, where Melba sang "Rock of Ages" and Albert ventured to place his hand on Helen's. These meetings served only to inflame the smoldering passion of Scarlet, especially when after the lapse of a year Miss Kent appeared more elusive than ever.

Like many self-made men, Albert Scarlet had a self-confidence founded on the visible evidence of his material success. During that first year, he had no doubt that after a decent lapse of time the penniless schoolmistress would come submissively to his arms. He was the sort of man who thought in terms like "She knows what side her bread is buttered"; and underlying his romantic feelings was the businesslike purpose of finding in his new wife a reliable housekeeper and stepmother for his children.

Helen Kent, on the other hand, was not so submissive as Albert's "beloved spouse" had been. She was prepared to accept Albert on her own terms, but what those terms were she only gradually revealed, partly, I imagine, by hints in letters and in the conversations held at the house of a Mrs. T. where they went ostensibly to play croquet or bezique and partly through the good offices of Mrs. T. herself, who seemed to have acted as marriage broker for the fun of the thing.

Albert's letters, the spelling of which had improved over the months thanks apparently to the schoolmistress's tuition, were still couched in the language of piety and romantic affection, but in each was embedded some concession or business proposition which he hoped would remove Miss Kent's reluctance to commit herself. The idea that Helen should take Miriam's place with the children was abandoned. As the courtship advanced through its second year, Albert urged that the children were growing up and would soon be leaving home. Ernest had already been working five years in the shop and wanted to marry Susan Tempers, the girl in the china department. She was a strong girl and hard-working, who would make a good shopkeeper's wife. Though they were young, there was no harm in starting young. They could live over the shop.

This still left Percy and Celia.

Percy, Albert suggested a couple of weeks later, would prefer to live with Ernest and Susan after their marriage. Being on top of the business, he could learn all its aspects far quicker; and also, they would be young people, all together. Celia, of course, was so devoted to Helen that she would be a positive help at home.

Albert was obviously more concerned for his delicate daughter than for either of his sons, but within a month he was writing to say that perhaps Helen was right that a finishing school in Switzerland would establish her health and teach her the accomplishments of a young lady. "A girl's education is her dowry, as you say." The letter ended with the hope that Helen would at last "name the day" on which she would make him "the happiest man in the world."

But Helen, having disposed of Miriam's children, seems to

have reminded him that she might have children of her own. What was to happen to them and to her, supposing as was probable Albert predeceased them? Albert replied in a letter singularly free from sentiment.

My dearest girl,

The points which you raised in Mrs. T's conservatory y'day I have considered carefully and reply as follows.

(1) The business, as I told you, belonged to Miriam, coming from her father. She left it to Ernest, Percy and Celia in equal shares as respects profits after my death, but till then only wages if they are working in it. There is nothing I can do about this and if they gave any children of ours a chance in the firm would depend how you all got on. Anyway I think you would prefer something more professional, even if it paid less, like the Church, remembering yr father.

(2) Anglesey House is mine. I bought it when I put two thousand pounds (£2,000) into the business for improvements. Miriam wanted it that way. She was v. strong on keeping the ownership of the shop in her hands; old Anglesey rubbed that in.

(3) Also I have capital of my own amounting at the moment to just under ten thousand pounds (£10,000). I would propose on our marriage to settle on you the sum of two thousand (£2,000) absolutely with the understanding, which I would get Mr. Grantley to draw up legally, that on my death all my capital should be left in trust to you for your lifetime and thereafter to our child—or if children in equal shares between them—absolutely. If we are not blest with children, the money would of course go in equal shares to Ernest, Percy and Celia or their children, if they have died before then.

I hope this reassures you that in the event of my demise you would not be left "utterly penniless."

I may add that I have been saving at the rate of approx. £350 p.a. and when the children are off our hands, this should be substantially increased, if we exercise thrift.

Yrs affectionately,
ALBERT SCARLET

The words "just under £10,000" had been underlined and in the margin Helen had penciled a note "£9,710 @ 5% = £486 p.a." The word "substantially" had also been underlined and in the margin she had placed a question mark and below it "£90–£110 p.a."

This letter was written in early November, 1903. Albert clearly expected it to be final. He had, as far as it was possible, dispossessed his children in favor of the woman he wanted as his second wife. There was nothing more that he could do, except to increase the amount of the marriage settlement, and to do this he warned might hamper him in future business deals, such as the acquisition of property, which might substantially advance their combined prosperity.

Yet still the schoolmistress wavered in a way that clearly drove the wretched man to distraction, because he could not understand or get her to tell him what further concessions she wanted. His letters increased in frequency and intensity of feeling. His handwriting, grammar and spelling deteriorated. He no longer regarded himself as an elderly man of substance offering the young woman of his choice the security of a good home. He was the lover driven half demented in pursuit of a woman who eluded his every attempt to grasp her and who became more desirable with every evasion.

The final letter was written on the second anniversary of his first outrageous proposal. In it, occurred this paragraph:

It wasn't true what you said this p.m., my dearest girl, and you know it. I never did love Miriam. It was the shop I married it was a busyness arrangement I could run it like nobody she knew could. You are the only woman I have ever loved, you are the only person in the whole world I care for, not forgetting the children, yes Celia too and I didn't want to have to say this, not to write it down, but you are driving me mad Helen I cant sleep I think I am going out of my mind. Dont you see what you are doing torchuring me like this. Oh Helen. I thought you were the sun but everything is darkness.

Helen had drawn a pillar in the margin of this passage and

written in small scholarly letters which made a strange contrast to Albert's wild copperplate. "Accepted A.S. 9/2/'04 H.K."

If Albert Scarlet and Helen Kent had been strangers, I would have read these letters as a delightful exhibition of Edwardian manners, typical of the human spirit wandering where it lusteth. There was poetic justice in the indecorous old satyr starting in pursuit of the chaste young nymph the moment his wife was buried and ending as the groveling victim of Venus.

But as one who had for years regarded Helen Scarlet as a woman set above others by the spiritual, mental and physical excellence with which my craving for perfection had endowed her, I was shocked, not by her refusal to marry until Scarlet had declared his love, but by her deliberate severing of all his other natural ties of affection. Celia, for example, never returned from Switzerland. She graduated from finishing school to a sanatorium in Davos. Helen had told me that Celia had inherited tuberculosis from her mother, but I could not help wondering whether that was the whole, or even the most important part, of the story. And the expulsion of the two boys from the family at so early an age—perhaps Helen could never have given Ernest and Percy the love and guidance they needed, but she might have made the attempt. Helen, that gallant old lady who had, apart from myself, been almost friendless in the last quarter of a century of her life, had created her own desert. There was no one else but herself to blame for those sterile years devoted to cultivating that lovely garden from which the world was excluded.

I turned my attention to the smaller bundle of letters. These had not been composed or kept with such care; they were not numbered, but they had been arranged in chronological order. They were all from the Australian cousin Andrew, written in indelible pencil, which when he licked it turned violet. His handwriting was as unformed as a schoolboy's, very simple and open-hearted. They were not good letters from a biographer's point of view. They did not express any subtlety of character. The first was written after returning from his first forty-eight-hour leave spent at Anglesey House. It was addressed to both of them.

MY DEAR COUSINS,

I do want to thank you for the dinkum time you gave me. I don't mind telling you I was pretty scared at asking myself, even though Mum said to do so, because I didn't know how you'd feel about a stray cousin arriving from down under. But it was like being home, it really was, you were so kind; and I've written Mum about the house, it is a beaut and so is little Charlie. I am so grateful and do you really mean I can come again, because I will, if you really mean it, but maybe you don't.

Thank you,
your affect. cousin
ANDREW CHARLES, Pte. A.Z. 279864

Helen had written back on behalf of them both to tell Cousin Andrew that he would always be welcome. The fact that she had kept that first "bread and butter" letter showed that there must have been a deeper undercurrent. The second letter was addressed to her alone.

DEAR COUSIN HELEN,

You won't know how good it was to have your cheery letter. I was afraid I might have done something wrong, because I enjoyed myself so much. That sounds silly. But life is very hard in the forces and it is like being in paradise to meet someone who is really kind and gentle. It meant so much. I felt I was in paradise. I see I've said that already. But it is really true.

Thank you.
ANDREW

Looking back, one is liable to get the age groups mixed. The date was early 1915. I didn't know Cousin Andrew's exact age, but it must have been between twenty-one and twenty-three. At that time, Helen must have been forty-one, old enough to be Andrew's mother, but young enough to be Albert's daughter. Albert had passed his three score years and ten.

There was a later letter written after Andrew had had his embarkation leave, which showed a total change.

My dearest Hell on earth, what do we care? what does it matter? We're all racing each other to the grave and I'll be there before old Albert. Damn him. Except if he hadn't caught you, I would never have met the only woman etc.

It must have been then that old Scarlet had summoned Oakes and written in the restrictive codicils about his wife's marriage. A letter from France, written after the old man's death, said:

I love my own Hell, which is so much sweeter than the one we're living in. You talk of your age and mine. Think of his and yours, sweet agony. I love, I Love, I LOVE you. . . .

Poor Andrew saw the shadow of death over them both, but in those days it was only the young male who suffered in war. She went to work in the convalescent hospital where Andrew was posted at her request. And he spent his final weeks of recuperation in her house, the weeks which ended in the suicide of Charles.

The last letter from Andrew read:

My dearest Helen, darling, I've called you Hell so often, as we lay in love together. But I don't dare now. Poor sweet, poor love. I knew always it was a dream. I don't think I will live through this show. I should have thought of this and gone down the whores of Lisle Street like the rest of the boys and got poxed up. What does it matter, poxed in the grave. But I love you. I love you. And he was in the room next door. I remember that, it was the first real time after the wound. Oh, God, your yearning! How you need to be loved! And he must have heard. That's the awful thing. He must have heard.

Written in the margin beside this, with rather less than Helen's usual command, was the comment, "Dear Andrew. Thank God he was not right in this."

There were only two other entries in this bundle. The mention of Charles' death in the local paper and that of Andrew's death in the *British Gazette,* where he was cited for a D.S.O. Against this last were two entries in Helen's handwriting. The first read, "If he had lived, he would have made a woman of me." The second was written many years later. "Thank God, he didn't. For both our sakes."

10

HARRY WAYBRIDGE

In disentangling the threads of this narrative, I find myself envying the writers of fiction. A novelist can invent his characters, allot them roles, circumscribe their behavior, see that they pull their weight or else sling them out of the boat. But I can only try to make sense out of what happened, describing each situation as it appeared to me at the time even though in retrospect I realize that I did not properly understand what was happening to myself and the others.

If the reader complains that he does not find the tidiness to which he is accustomed by the contrivances of novelists, I can only answer that this is how everyday life is, extremely complex and far more discontinuous than most of us realize. Problems arise; loom enormous about us. But before they are resolved, they disappear. People swim into our lives. We have expectations from them in which we are disappointed. But after they have swum out again, we discover that they have done something to us for us of a different nature. I do not mean that life is nonsense; merely that the sense which it makes is different from that which we try to impose in advance.

Sometimes this difference can be explained merely in terms of the interplay of personalities changing in a changing situation. But in this case I can only make sense of what would otherwise be the most extraordinary combination of coincidences by explaining the curious feeling I began to have about this time of being at the same time an agent and a patient (having for so long been just a spectator).

This may seem vague. I mean that there were certain things which I had to do, because of the unique position I occupied. But at the outset I was not qualified to do what in the end I was called on to do. I had to undergo in myself a change of heart before I was capable of what was necessary. Though I was in the center of the stage, I was not the dramatist in this affair, nor even an actor who knew his lines. I had wildly to improvise, unaware until it was over that there was any plot or coherent development.

The reading of those letters to Helen is a good example of what I mean. If I had known before Kit wrote asking me to find him a house what I did after reading those letters and the file which Neville had lent me, I should probably not have gone to see John Scarlet about Anglesey House. I would have written off the house with Helen and Charles Scarlet as aberrations of my long-protracted adolescence. If I had found out about Helen at any time before Kit had warned me to say nothing of the possibility that the place might be haunted, I would not have known how to act.

As it was, I was still puzzling what I ought to do, when I was distracted by the arrival of a letter from Cousin Harry to say that instead of arriving with his family at the end of June he would reach London airport alone next day and would like me to leave a message for him there to say whether it was convenient for him to come down immediately to stay. "I pray that you can give me house room, dear cousin. I have had a most shattering experience."

I telegraphed his flight to say he was always welcome and to telephone me what train to meet. People with large families say, "Relatives are hell." But they say it out of richness. An only child of a dying line, I know how precious are the ties of blood, that curious sympathy of the clan which lies so much deeper than compatibility of interest or temperament.

I had nothing in common with Harry, except that his mother was my mother's sister. He had gone to Dover College and distinguished himself as an athlete. As a boxer, he won the Public Schools Welterweight Championship. He was Captain of Football and Cricket at Dover, made a century for the Southern Public Schools and was given a job during the thirties in one of those firms that liked to employ young athletes for publicity purposes. He got his cap playing scrum half for England and for several years after water on the knee incapacitated him as a footballer, he played cricket for Kent. He was good-looking in a chunky, solid way, very attractive to women who had been married for four or five years and rather lazy, except on the playing field and in bed. He basked in the glory which as an athlete he won earlier and easier than professional men who had only brains and skill on which to rely.

When he was twenty-five he married the daughter of a wealthy paint manufacturer, whose game he slaughtered and whose fish he hooked when he was not hitting, kicking, catching or running after balls. He betrayed no interest in paint or any other sort of business. Games and the distinction of his prowess as an athlete were all he cared for. I met him once or twice during this period and found him intolerable. The sex idol of silly women. When his marriage produced a child, who became the focus of his wife's attention, he hung around bars for the admiration he could find there.

The marriage foundered in the middle thirties and Harry began what my mother called his "footloose career" by borrowing £300 from his mother to explore the commercial prospects of Central America. I remember his coming to The Chantry before he left, his almost Uriah Heep-like deference to my mother and the vague confidence in his nebulous plans. "Of course I shouldn't be going out without these agencies," he said, rather as John Scarlet might in his more modest way. "Then there are the opals. I shall be going to Guadalajara. The prospects are enormous. Opals, silver, oils." He had a wonderful historic innocence, imagining that the adventurers of the West from the time of Cortes onward had been unaware of fortunes to be made in Mexico.

We had what he called "the odd booze-up," two pints of old and bitter in the Wilchester Arms and two more in the Intrepid Fox, and I tried to tell him that Central America was hardly virgin territory for the merchant adventurer. But he would not listen, because he had invited me out in order to give me a chance of getting in on "the ground floor of the iguana industry." Fifty pounds invested in buying iguana skins for ladies' shoes and bags would double itself in three months. "They are crying out for skins in London," he said. But luckily I myself was crying out for fifty pounds.

This was the beginning of what Cousin Harry described as "the wanderings of a modern Ishmael." Ishmael, according to Genesis, was "a wild ass of a man." Though not very wild, Harry was a bit of an ass. Sometimes his schemes failed through lack of capital and at others through lack of persistence, but always they failed. He returned from Mexico without opals or iguana skins, but with a crate of avocado pears. There was a fortune to be made from importing this delicacy, he maintained. He was quite right, but by the time that money began to be made from the import of avocados, he had already lost money trying to import rugs from Bokhara, hummingbirds from South America and koala bears from Australia.

As a businessman, my mother maintained, he might have succeeded selling novelties from a tray in Oxford Street, provided that the succession of novelties was rapid enough to sustain his interest. But I believe that the truth was that he was not interested in these projected fortunes, the pots of gold at the rainbow's end. What he loved were the changes of scene, the new faces, the extensive exercise of charm. "In my beginning is my end" might have been his motto. He was like a person unable to finish a sentence. His projects ended in a row of dots, beginning afresh in a new city, another land and preferably a different continent.

He was as restless as Everness, but unlike Kit he had not found a profession to indulge the vice profitably. He had tried the United Nations Specialized Agencies, those asylums for spiritually displaced persons, but apart from sport he had no skills, no specialized knowledge, no grasp of foreign languages even. His general knowledge was all particular. He knew a man who could fix almost anything in Tampico, the best place for shark's fins in Kowloon, just the chap for a safari in Buganda. But of what makes the world go round he was still as ignorant as before he had gone round it; twice, once each way.

Though his life had taken on a pattern as regular as a Paisley shawl, he alone was unaware of it. Each hopeful start and hopeless ending were different from the others before. Fate was against him, he believed, not the nemesis inherent in his nature. And when he married the widow of an East African farmer, where he had been working as factor, he had succeeded in convincing me that he had turned over a new leaf on which would be written a pattern of success. His letters took on new confidence. His wife, Clarissa, was "the woman he had been waiting for all his life"; the two boys, his stepsons, were "lads to be proud of." The farm, the country, the stock, the game, the life were all that an immigration leaflet could promise. Harry, it seemed, had fallen at last on his feet.

Waiting for him at the station, I was apprehensive. Into what depth of depression would he have fallen after his sojourn on the high euphoric plateau? And would I, after the lapse of seven years, recognize him among the crowds poured out by the 5:20 fast from London? I need not have worried. Among the dark-suited, bowler-hatted, tightly-furled-umbrella-carrying season-ticket holders I spotted Cousin Harry fifteen yards away by his huge bush hat and walnut face. I had forgotten that his returns were always in the costume of the country of departure, as if to prove he had been where his letters came from. From Mexico he had come back wearing a *sombrero* and *zapatas,* with a *serape* in his suitcase, and my mother had declared that if it had been Alaska he would have sported snowshoes, a parka and fur mitts and cried "Mush! Mush!" to the porter.

As he drew close, bush pack over one shoulder and a hold-all in the other hand, I saw that he was dressed *à l'Afrique de l'Est* from top to toe, an open bush shirt in the neck of which his curly pectoral hair served as a choker, khaki shorts, knees burnt mahogany beneath more hair coiled like Dannert wire, short khaki stockings and tough sandals.

He did not for the moment see me, but came shambling on like a bull bison among a herd of sheep, patient, perplexed and out of place. I wondered whether it might be better to follow him out and greet him in the station yard. But his pale blue topaz eyes hardened. "Cousin George!" he bawled, dropping his hold-all in the middle of the stream of businessmen and clutching my elbows as if they were the handles of a test-your-strength machine. "Long time no see."

I was acutely embarrassed, especially when Cousin Harry, realizing he was causing an obstruction, swung round to apologize and clipped Randall Rushmore a left to the chin with his bush pack. ("You never told me," Randall reproached me later, "you were related to King Kong.")

Somehow I got Harry to the car and dumped his bush kit in the back and him in the seat beside me. "Aye, but it's good, Cousin George," he said. "Golly, it makes a new man of me to see you alive and kickin' after all these years. Lost a bit of the thatch perhaps, but just the same at bottom."

To have thought that Harry could ever be master of The Chantry was insane. I had forgotten what he was really like, persuading myself that his marriage had wrought a transformation. Nothing would change him. If he lived to ninety, he should be placed in his coffin, a cricket ball in his folded hands, a rugger ball at his feet and a willow bat by his side, ready for play on the Elysian fields, the moment he was issued with heavenly shorts.

I am sure that Harry's embarrassment was even deeper than mine. The Ishmaelite had a far deeper need for kinship and I was so inadequate a family for him to confide the inadequacies of his marriages to. He sat there with his hairy mahogany hands cushioned on the hairy mahogany knees, talking wildly about an interesting Ethiopian he had met on the plane who was seeking finance for the pisciculture of Lake Tana. "You know, knocking around like I do, you see These Possibilities." He looked at the suburban conglomeration which hemmed us in, like a baled-out pilot rounded up by the Home Guard. "You don't see it here."

Arrived at The Chantry, we made for the tray of drinks like two foreigners seeking an interpreter. Harry asked for whisky, "Scotch on the rocks." "There's a Clos Vougeot for dinner," I warned. "I prefer it with ice," he answered. "But if you haven't any . . ."

I gave him time for the whisky to take effect, then asked him about Clarissa. He was too deeply tanned to express emotion within the normal color range. His complexion took an ox-liver tinge. "Terrible," he said. "Terrible."

I had tried to ask the question in all sympathy; but I must have become for him all symbols of authority, father, headmaster, bank manager, commissioner of Inland Revenue. "You couldn't believe it, Cousin George, you couldn't believe it!"

At this moment Mrs. Ambrose came in to announce dinner, an excellent quick roast duck with peas from the garden. Harry welcomed the interruption. I imagined him poised over Africa and Europe wondering about this moment, the confession of the ultimate failure.

Over dinner Cousin Harry seemed to be trying to prove I was wrong in saying that he could not generalize. He talked about "the white" and "the black," "your Kikuyu" and "your Masai," "these Mau-Mau bastards," "the average colored" and "those damned Reds masquerading in Whitehall as Conservatives." It spoilt a good wine and a better meal to see between the pectoral and the cranial bush the Sahara of Harry's face where nothing grew but hatred and prejudice. If I had never met him before, I should have lost my temper. But poor Harry, the wild ass of a man, who had been trying to find in opals, hummingbirds, iguanas and marriage the magic he had found in youth on playing fields and lost in middle age, filled me with a sadness which was perhaps a reflection of my own.

The green salad and the Brie were perfect. "Why did it bust up?"

"I am a gallant man," said Harry, finishing his glass of wine. "Besides I look for the best. In you, Cousin George. I look for the best in you."

This seemed to be a hint that I should produce my checkbook. "What went wrong?" I refilled his glass, but this time with a Mâcon.

"I don't like to be used," he said, "to be used and . . ." he fumbled for a cliché, "and then tossed aside like a worn glove."

It was strangely appropriate. He was like a worn glove, kid. But I said nothing. I waited for the defensive confession of failure. It was very simple. Clarissa liked factors. It was her money that had bought the farm in the first place. She had taken Harry as her lover when her husband was still alive, which was understandable to Harry. What he could not accept was that when he became

Clarissa's second husband, the new factor should become Clarissa's second lover. "It's so damned unfair," he said.

"Mightn't her first husband have said the same thing about you?"

"But he was impotent," Harry answered. "That was quite different."

"I thought you said that there were two splendid sons."

"Golly!" he said. "You're right. This is something I hate to say. But I believe that I'm married to a B-I-T-C-H."

Harry was not a person from whom one could expect a coherent statement of affairs. In the course of the evening a collection of facts emerged, as oddly assorted as the contents of a schoolboy's trouser pockets. It seemed to me at first that as Clarissa's husband Harry was in a strong position. He could insist on the discharge of the new factor or at least on his wife's fidelity. If Clarissa refused, he could divorce her and claim damages for the alienation of his wife's affection. "No," Harry said, shaking his head, "I couldn't do that, old boy."

I tried to reason with him. Harry Waybridge might imagine himself as a Sapper or John Buchan character, but the fact was that he had been deprived of his security as a farmer and deserved compensation for his loss. I considered that he was making too much of his gallant scruples, until at last he said uneasily. "It isn't quite as simple as that Cousin George. You see, I don't want poor Gwyneth's name dragged through the mud."

It was the first time I had heard the name of poor Gwyneth, but gradually it emerged that she was the wife of the neighboring farmer, "Who, not to put too fine a point on it, is ... well, an S-H-I-T-E. Of the first water, the very first water." Harry plucked nervously at the hair on his knee in rather the same way that people when embarrassed pull stuffing out of the arms of padded chairs. "I used to jolly poor Gwyneth along, just to help her keep her pecker up. And Clarissa took a dim view. She's got that sort of mind. I saw the only thing to do was to pull stumps; the only gentlemanly thing."

A cynical part of myself interpreted this as Harry's euphemistic way of saying that he had so fouled his nest that he could never return there, but I am sure that such an idea never occurred to

Harry himself. In the quixotic world which he inhabited, he was a perfect gentle knight; though I suspect that lurking deep in his unconscious he had his Sancho Panza.

11

COMPARATIVE MAGIC

Though Harry had no friends, he had a large number of "contacts" listed in what he called his Doomsday Book, a fat exercise book bound in black morocco, with an elaborate system of cross references, according to names, countries and subjects. Until he showed me this, I had not understood the operation of what I had always considered his "genius for acquaintanceship."

"It's really very simple, old boy," he explained. "People are very lonely. I s'pose, lonelier than they've ever been—with all this globetrottin'. Ships that pass in the night, yer know." He put on a pair of heavy horn-rimmed spectacles, which were strangely out of character with his bush rig. "Now supposin' I have a noggin with a chappie in the Metropolitan in Cairo. We make it an evening, exchange cards and promise to look one another up sometime somewhere. Well, this chappie thinks no more about it. But I make a few notes." He turned up the Cairo page. "Here we are. 'Metropolitan Bar. Prosser, Douglas Edward, see London, E.C.' Turn to London, E.C." He handed the book to me, pointing to the entry.

I read: "PROSSER, Douglas Edward. 'Doug.' Hates Duggie. 15 Hog Lane, E.C.2. Tel MINcing Lane 73490. Pickles, sauces. Prosser's Paste. S.5, '49 Cecil, curvature of spine. H. Teddington. Hobs. Butterflies, outboard motor boats, fishing (not fly)."

"There's also a cross reference under Pickles," Harry said, "just in case I forgot where I met him—which I don't usually. The names are my difficulty. Look up Pickles under P."

It was a fascinating book, like an index to Burton's *Anatomy of Melancholy*. Under P I saw Photographic equipment, Porterage (Kilimanjaro), Peacock's feathers, Pearls, Pig iron, Paradise birds of and Psittacosis (Parrot disease) before I found Pickles. There in addition to Prosser was a reference to Frank D. Zucker of Cleveland, Ohio.

"That's the beauty of the system," Harry said, when I asked about this. "It almost does the thinkin' for you." He took the Doomsday Book from me. He found the full entry under Cleveland. "I always do the main classification under Home Town," he said. "It gives what the Yanks call the sense of togetherness. Here we are. 'Zucker, Frank D. Met Havana Country Club, June '37. Stomach ulcers. 2 s, younger Carl no good. Daughter Frieda, m. Schumacher Public Relations N.Y., favorite but sterile. Adopt? Twice divorced. Catsup, Zucker's Chili Sce. pickles ass. Zucker's Saucery Inc., 1759 W. 15 St. Tel. ad. Zucksauce.' Rather an old entry of course. The way he knocked back Daiquiris, probably the sons are running the business now."

"Am I to understand you put two and two together and make . . . well, a livelihood?"

"I've got a sort of flair, yer know," Harry said, removing his glasses. "I'll give Prosser a tinkle. He won't know who I am from Adam. He was pretty pickled by the time I dumped him in Shepheard's. But when he finds out how much I remember about that evening, how impressed I was with his knowledge of butterflies and I ask how Cecil is and know that he's sixteen now and how's his spine, then he'll feel that he really made a friend that night, someone who cares for him; and he'll invite me to lunch, which I daresay will be a jolly good one, because he can charge it up to exes and he likes his fodder. And then I put up the question of marketing Prosser's Paste in the U.S. Maybe he already does, in which case he merely thanks me for a kind thought. But if he hasn't exploited the American market, then I write to my old friend Carl Zucker sending him a sample of Prosser's Paste and recalling old times. Maybe nothing comes of it. But I've strengthened two friendships. I've tried to be of use."

If I myself had evolved a system like Harry's, I would have become a hypocrite, a cadger or both. I am morally too self-conscious. But Harry, oozing innocence like a scoutmaster, could convince me as he had himself that this type of *savoir survivre* was a form of social service, a mission to lonely businessmen.

And since his mission took him daily to London, renewing contacts, I blessed his absences, retiring to my tower room to take up the work which had been so curtailed since I had received that first letter from Kit Everness.

The tower room had the advantage that I could not hear the ringing of the telephone. Mrs. Ambrose had instructions not to summon me, unless it was the BBC, but to make a note of all calls and when I could call back.

On the third day of Harry's visit, however, Mrs. Ambrose paid her annual pilgrimage to Sandown Park. All morning I heard a noise like water in my ears which might have been the telephone ringing downstairs. And as I went down to eat the cold salmon, cucumber salad and the excellent *sauce mayonnaise à l'Ambrose,* it began to ring again.

It was Miriam Schroeder, speaking from a callbox. "Oh, George, I've been trying you all morning. It's happened. What you said."

"What did I say?"

"After the surveyor's report, Dawkins withdrew the offer. And then what do you think?"

"John said he didn't feel very well."

Miriam laughed. "He's feeling wonderful. That supermarket idea of yours, I think it's going to work. No, Dawkins had put in another offer for two thousand five hundred. It's absurd."

"With the ghost? Too high, you mean?"

"Don't be absurd. You don't believe that nonsense, George."

"It isn't impossible," I said. "I have an open mind."

"Well, she hasn't seen it, your friend," Miriam said.

"The ghost?"

"No. The house, silly. What I want is if you could bring her down to view on Saturday afternoon and then on to John's to tea."

"But I have a cousin of mine staying with me. He thinks he's Ishmael, but he's more like Esau."

"Bring him too," Miriam said. "Karl has hair on his shoulder blades. They can compare notes. I thought he was attractive in the High Street."

It sounded like an undergraduate sex rating. "Attractive in the High Street." But that was jealousy. Mine would be "Acceptable in the dark." If as high. I said, "I don't know if Nieves can manage it. I'll call you back. This evening, some time."

It was a difficult situation, since I hadn't ever met Lady Everness and I did not want to ask her down, in view of what Kit had told me. I decided that I would ring Miriam that evening and say that I hadn't been able to reach Nieves.

But the moment I put the telephone receiver down, the bell rang again. It was Christopher. "I thought you worked at home," he said. "The office has been trying to get you all morning. Dilettanting with your noisy typewriter, I suppose? What's the news on the Scarlet front?"

I could picture him in his chambers, pouring the last of a half-bottle of champagne into his glass to give him the life he needed to carry him through to the afternoon session. But his voice was so infectious that I couldn't do anything but relay Miriam's message. "They want me to show Nieves over the house on Saturday afternoon and then take her on to potluck with the ironmonger for tea," I said. "My cousin King Kong is staying with me, but they've asked him too."

"That's splendid," Kit said. "She was planning to see Rosa on Sunday. Could she sleep with you on Saturday night?"

"Could she *what?*" I asked, compelled into his game.

"Or with King Kong?" he said. "I've forgotten your sleeping arrangements, ha! ha!"

I felt as embarrassed as I had at the age of twenty when people talked about "flirting" and said "top hole." "I am sure that Mrs. Ambrose would come in to sleep for the night," I said, "but isn't all this rather ridiculous? Could you both come?"

"I'll pick her up on Sunday," he said. "Tell you the truth, I've been worried about this week-end. I've rather a difficult case for Monday. I'll get a Godfrey Davis car, if you could give her lunch. You won't be the loser."

"For God's sake," I said, "I'm your friend, not the head waiter in the Savoy."

"I'm sorry, Georgie Porgie," he answered. "This is the call to Lagos I've been waiting for. Thanks a lot."

The telephone went dead. I felt very angry. It was bad enough for Kit to presume on my friendship, but downright insulting to pay me for it. My irritation spoilt my appetite.

Just as I was finishing my meal the telephone rang again. It was Nieves Everness. Like most Spaniards, she spoke a harsh English, ugly in its distortions. But she seemed possessed of a greater sympathy than her husband, Keet as she called him. It was a *sinverguenza* that Keet should impose on my hospitality, she said, and she became so angry with him that I was forced, quite sincerely, to say that it would be a pleasure if she would stay Saturday night. From being the reluctant, I found myself becoming the almost overeager host, pressing her until she made the suggestion that instead of putting me to the inconvenience of asking Mrs. Ambrose to cook the dinner and stay overnight, she should bring with her Magda Kovacs, the Hungarian refugee, and "all what is necessary for the *comida.*"

Out of natural conservatism I demurred, but agreed at last, thinking what a deliverance it would be from a week-end alone with Harry Waybridge. The conflict of personalities might be awkward, but I was absolved of responsibility. Everybody was self-invited and I could sit back enjoying the play as a spectator.

By the end of Saturday luncheon, I found myself praying for their early arrival. Perhaps if I had been a novelist, I would have taken a delight in the study of my Cousin Harry, noting his obsessional routines. Like many men of weak character, he cultivated personal rituals as its substitute, explaining these to me in great detail as if he was initiating me in the mystic path which had made him the man he was. He smoked a tobacco called Three Nuns, which he always bought in two-ounce tins. "Only way to keep it fresh, old boy." This tobacco was cut into little rings, like some form of *pasta*. He took these rings and rubbed them in the palm of his hand until they had lost their shape. "Frot well," he said, "that's the secret of a good smoke." In his case there were others. He was a "wet smoker" and instead of placing the tobacco directly into the bowl he put it in a circular piece of paper, which he twisted round at the top, so that it resembled a minuscule plum duff, and thrust this twist downward into the bowl of a curved pipe. It seemed to me strange that he should choose a pipe of this shape, if he had a tendency to dribble down it. But there it was. "It makes for chin comfort," he explained, "and when you take up pipe-smoking, there are two things to watch. See you have a fish-tail mouthpiece. Gives you a cool smoke and prevents cancer of the tongue. And make sure of the dottle trap." He proceeded to demonstrate this filthy contraption, convinced that because he preferred a pipe I should soon follow his example.

"I always use Swan Vestas," he said, "the best match on the market. Twice the price, but the cheapest in the long run." He struck one and set fire to the white bundle bulging from the bowl, and holding the pipe in one hand with the other he swept the incandescent fragments of tobacco from his shorts the moment they landed. "Of course a pipe's a man's smoke," he said, but it sounded more like a distant branch-line engine tackling an incline as he puff-puff-puffed infuriatingly away in his armchair.

He was puff-puff-puffing away and telling me the way he shaved himself each morning, when I heard the Godfrey Davis car drive up. He was still wearing his bushman outfit. When I suggested he might like to change, he'd said, "This suits me fine, Cousin George, it suits me fine."

As I went downstairs to greet my guests, I reflected that it did not suit me so well. As my cousin, my resident guest, he was in a way an extension of myself. Trying my hardest, I was a rather dingy type (though I had been careful to dress in a way which was a sartorial denial of any affinity to Harry). I saw Harry as a double satire on myself, his hirsute mahogany health pointing the balding bister of my unhealthy (but studious?) head, his boy-scout rig the outward and visible sign of my middle-aged immaturity. "Dear me!" I thought in the hall. "If I prayed hard, would they be removed like mountains?"

Mrs. Ambrose came from the kitchen at the jerk of the bell. She'd been lurking there like a hungry spider. "Don't you trouble," I said.

"It's no trouble, Mr. George," she said, "you'll be wanting a hand with the cases."

I was angry with her because she was taking the visit of these two ladies as if it were a violation of her rights, a threat to our *liaison de cuisine,* the more angry because I knew that there was no reason why it should be and yet it undoubtedly was. It was intolerable not to be able to entertain two strangers without one's cook silently taxing one with infidelity.

They were standing together, the chauffeur with their cases at the foot of the steps. I did not know who was who, until the one on the right, black-haired with a fleshy face in which were set a pair of large dark eyes and a big red-painted mouth smiling, introduced the other as Magda Kovacs.

Madame Kovacs was also black-haired and dark-eyed, like Lady Everness, about five foot two; and yet the two, even at that first moment, were in utter contrast. Nieves seemed to me violent, the prey to emotions, anger, jealousy, hatred, love; Magda Kovacs more controlled, not necessarily feeling less but the mind intervening between the emotion and the response. I liked them both immediately, especially the Hungarian, partly I think because they were so unlike the women in Wilchester. And any shyness I might have had was dissipated by the discomfiture of Mrs. Ambrose on being introduced.

Nieves was an amusing contrast to her husband. Instead of classifying things as characteristic of "the habitat of the Grantley bird," she was interested in them for their own sake. She stopped on her way up the stairs to examine the Chinese blue china pillow, which while too recent to be a collector's piece is nevertheless extremely pretty.

My pleasure in her admiration was marred by apprehension that Harry, hearing their voices, would come out and meet them casually. If he did so, he would engineer some excuse for coming with us to Anglesey House. Though I had thought of them originally as foils to Cousin Harry, he now appeared as a blight on what might otherwise be a delightful week-end.

I had not known how they would want to sleep, so I had made up two beds in the southeast bedroom and also one in the slip room leading off. The position of Madame Kovacs was equivocal. She was at the same time the Evernesses' friend and their cook. Just where the boundaries between these two relationships lay had been impossible for me to determine in advance. But now I realized that both my alternatives were ill-chosen. I should have given Nieves the southeast bedroom with one bed and Madame Kovacs the equally large, though less sunny, northeast bedroom. Women normally are no more anxious to share a bedroom than men are; and I had forced Madame Kovacs to choose the dressing room, thereby emphasizing invidiously the inferiority of her position.

I do not want to overstress the ineptitude. Magda Kovacs covered up her embarrassment immediately, saying that she loved the small room and how beautiful the view was; and yet I felt that she had been hurt and was sorry to have been the cause of it. She had, I suspected, already been hurt more than enough in life.

They said that when they had unpacked, they would like to look over Anglesey House. I showed them the door of the sitting room and said that I would wait for them there.

Cousin Harry, whom I had left in his bedroom composing a letter to Mr. Zucker, had drifted back into the sitting room and was clearly waiting to meet the two ladies. But with a firmness which surprised him as much as it did myself, I drove him out, saying that I had private business to discuss with them and we would pick him up at four o'clock to take him out to tea.

Mrs. Ambrose brought in a tray with hot coffee and milk in thermos flasks. "Well, I suppose you won't be wanting me any more, Mr. George," she said ominously.

"No. Thank you. Not until Monday." My resentment of Mrs. Ambrose was really a resentment at the narrow limits which seemed to circumscribe my daily life. My rooted existence had grown pot-bound.

I told myself it was absurd to be making so much of a visit from two women of Kit's household. Had I reached the follies of the grand climacteric that I should be so disturbed? Or was it the realization that I had wasted the best years of my life falsely romanticizing a woman old enough to be my mother? I did not know, but I knew that the scruples about the Evernesses buying Anglesey House had disappeared. Perhaps those scruples merely cloaked my misgivings about having Kit and his menage in my home town. The word menage aroused a distressing suspicion that the relationship between Magda Kovacs and the Evernesses might be more intimate than it appeared. From his conversation,

Kit appeared to have small regard for the virtue of chastity.

As I showed them over Anglesey House, I watched the two ladies carefully, trying to detect from the way they treated one another, what their respective relations might be to Kit Everness. But I could make nothing of it.

I found I no longer thought how wonderful it would be if someone restored the place to the grace and glory which it had had in my recollection of Helen Scarlet. I thought instead how splendid it would be if Kit bought it and Nieves and Magda realized its possibilities; what a different place Wilchester could be for me with them in the town. In fact, during this day the needle of my interest which had always been veering from the present into the past now swung into the future. I began to look forward.

It was only when I came to the room, now unlocked and emptied of its lumber, which had been Charles' bedroom that I recalled its tragic associations. *There* was the beam from which the rope had hung; not a sign on it of course. There was a cupboard under the eaves, which I glanced into. But it was very dark and I could see nothing. I did not know, anyway, what I was looking for, if anything.

The place felt cold to me and I went into Helen's old bedroom, which Nieves had already earmarked for her own. She was sizing the room up, trying to imagine how she would have it made over. I could understand why Kit had come down himself in the first place and emphasized that the price for the house must be reasonable. Nieves had obviously no sense of money. She had set her heart on the house and would have offered on her husband's behalf any price to get it. Her imagination was already running amok. She was going to do this and that, knock windows out here, block doors up there and make them somewhere else.

Out of loyalty to Kit I began to put the damper on her enthusiasm. When the deal had gone through would be time enough for her to become engrossed in planning. Then I noticed that Magda Kovacs was taking my side and with a subtlety I lacked she would take over my ideas and reinterpret them in a way which would achieve the same effect without making it plain that we were trying to save Kit from the effects of Nieves's wild extravagance. I wondered whether it was possible that Kit, engrossed in work, had failed his wife emotionally, and she was trying to take out of him in money what he had not given her in love.

Whether that was so or not, Madga and I were drawn together in a tacit alliance against the follies of her extravagance. I had never felt so in accord (and so immediately) with any woman before and the fact that all our exchanges of sympathy were unspoken and in the currency of the Evernesses made the friendship the more exciting for being devious.

I took them through the garden, showing them what riches of perennials were still struggling to survive beneath the weeds. Whether they would ever recover I was not so certain. The lilies were strangled in bindweed and the rank ground elder was tangled in the roots of almost everything. Couch grass had overrun the paths and fought with plantains, willow herb, cow parsley and dandelions for dominance.

Even the steps of the terraces were hidden in weeds. Helping the ladies up what had been steps, I grasped their hands. From Magda I received a pressure which at first I thought was merely a firm handgrip. But on the second terrace I looked into her eyes and saw it was deliberate. On the third I gripped her hand so firmly she grimaced. We were, delightfully, conspirators.

"Lady Everness," I said, "you must not show John Scarlet that you want this house."

"But I do," she answered. "And please call me Nieves."

"If you want it, point out everything that's wrong. Or say nothing. That's even better."

"Yes," Magda said, "say nothing at all."

So we said nothing when, having picked up Harry Waybridge, we reached Kohi-noor, Kitchener Crescent. To my surprise John Scarlet had recognized the importance of the occasion by handing over the shop to Lucy Worplesdon. Though it was a sweltering day, he was wearing a heavy gray suit and black boots. He greeted us as if he had been caught *flagrante delicto*. "It is most decent of you, most awfully decent of you to come to this 'umble abode," he said, gingerly extending his hand as if expecting that it would be savagely wrenched off at the wrist and tossed into the front garden of Shangri-La on our left or Journey's End to our right. In introducing Nieves, I compromised by calling her

Nieves Everness, sinking my voice on the surname. John was far too shy to notice, but Miriam, who was hovering, registered that at least the name was different from the Mariposa she had been expecting. But I brought "her friend Madame Kovacs" so quickly up behind that Miriam had no time for reflection.

The meeting between John Scarlet and Harry Waybridge was as impressive as a public monument in the nineteenth century, symbolizing the abstracts of that era, "The Spirit of Commerce and the Spirit of Empire." "This is a real pleasure," Harry said. "Mr. Scarlet. I've heard so much about you from my cousin and I was wondering if you were related to Bob Scarlet of Bulawayo. Met him years ago, when I was bushwhacking."

John disapproved of corporal punishment in any form. "Not to my knowledge, no, definitely not to my knowledge. We Scarlets don't hold with whacking, us Scarlets, I mean."

There was discussion as to whether tea should be served "in the lounge or on the loggia," the "loggia" being a bit cut off from the sitting room, or "lounge." As tea had already been laid outside, it was agreed that the loggia was a perfect idea and John Scarlet proposed that we should "make a tour of the estate, ha! ha!" while his sister made the tea. The estate consisted of two herbaceous borders four feet by fifteen, two lawns eight feet by fifteen and a crazy-paving path down the middle three feet by fifteen. Beyond that, screened by rambler roses from polite view, stretched the vulgarities of the "kitchen garden," twenty-four feet by twenty crammed with rhubarb, beet root, runner beans, etc. "Give me a hand, for God's sake, George," Miriam muttered.

"Where's Karl?" I asked in the little overheated kitchen.

"He went out, down to the river to bathe," she answered. "They're not on speaking terms any more. Anyway, how did they like it?"

"They were taken with its possibilities," I answered, "but they know what it will cost. And I warned them that John had the most exaggerated ideas."

"But he hasn't," said Miriam. "That's what makes Karl and me so angry. He sees the sale of the shop getting him out of his fix and he doesn't care about Anglesey House. He wanted to write to that awful man Dawkins and accept. Just to get enough to keep the creditors quiet."

"You mean the supermarket scheme is going ahead?"

"It was Mr. Rushmore's idea. Turn the shop back to front. You know the new through road is being driven through North Street and the new car park will be right opposite the North Street entrance to Scarlet's. It's one of the most valuable sites in town. We may get £50,000 for it."

The dark figure of John Scarlet appeared in the sitting room across the passage. He had exhausted the conversational resources of the estate. "Go to him," Miriam muttered, emptying the water she had used to warm the teapot.

I went into the sitting room and put my arm round his padded shoulders. "Miriam tells me you've high hopes of the redevelopment scheme. Congratulations."

He wrung his hands. "Nothing definite. Nothing definite," he said. "One mustn't count one's chickens when they're all in one basket, eh?" He laughed, finding his nervousness had minted a new adage. "Rather neat, that."

He wanted to take me onto the loggia to help him with the guests I had brought. But I held him back. "I did not know until just the other day," I said, "but even so late I want to sympathize." He looked at me, fear like a fever flush touching his white cheek with a patch of red. "About what?"

"Charles. I never knew you were there, when he hung himself. It must have been terrible. I'm sorry." Perhaps in the subliminal abyss, I had desires to test or taunt him. Consciously I only wanted to sympathize. But in his dark eyes I saw the fears and suspicions dart like bats disturbed by an explosion in a cavern.

Miriam passed us with the teapot and hot-water jug. "It's all ready," she said. "Your guests are waiting."

They were not waiting. Cousin Harry had mounted his rostrum and was delivering a lecture on Mau-Mau in particular and African magic in general.

He continued throughout the meal. Even if he had been aware of the undertones, it would have made no difference. He wanted to impress the ladies with something new out of Africa. "Your white man has a most unholy respect for your African's juju," he said, surveying the tea table and deciding that the sandwiches which had been prepared by Miriam were more to be trusted than the tired "fancies" from the cake shop. "Take the Taskers' kid, Jimmy, for instance."

I suppose that I ought to have changed the conversation, but I let Harry take the Taskers' kid, Jimmy, because I could see that Harry was rapidly erasing the good impression which he had made on Nieves and Magda with his he-manliness. It was one of those stories which proliferate among East Africans; a dismissed servant, a white cock found with its throat cut on the steps of the veranda one morning, a week later the marmalade kitten, which was Jimmy's pet, hanging from a rat snare tied to a nail beside the front door.

Harry was a poor narrator, but his only reaction when he saw the interest of his audience flagging was to say, "Well, to cut a long story short . . ." and make it longer still. A pregnant rat was found dead on the veranda, strangled with a fiber thread. The Taskers became alarmed, but none of their servants admitted to seeing any stranger and the police reported that the servant who had been dismissed was back in his village sixty miles away. I knew what the dénouement would be. The morning after the pregnant rat was found, Jimmy was ill. There were scratches all up his arm, which festered. He ran a high temperature. He grew delirious. Tasker was frightened, because no dressing seemed to relieve the infection. He put the boy into the station van and drove him to the nearest hospital, which was a hundred and forty miles away. His wife went with him. They decided on the way that they couldn't stand the country any longer. If the boy recovered, she would take him back to Camberley by the next plane and Tasker would follow as soon as he had sold the farm. When they reached the hospital and took off the dressing, the wounds had completely disappeared without a scar. They felt very foolish and went to stay in a resthouse overnight. They reversed their decision and next morning the wounds were worse. But when once again they reverted to the plan of leaving, the boy recovered immediately. They flew out on the next available plane.

"I suppose Tasker sold the farm at a loss," I said.

"Lost thousands, poor devil," Harry said. "Hard-earned savings and all that." He took another tomato sandwich. "He'd made a killing on the Stock Exchange before he went out."

"Excuse me, please," Magda Kovacs said. "My husband was

a medicine, I mean doctor. I do not believe this. In Hungary are villages, very very backward. There is the wise woman . . . they think yes. But it's not true. This is superstition."

I looked at her, thinking that her lack of English was like a stammer. There was much more she could have said, but language was a gag on her intelligence.

"Hear! Hear!" said John Scarlet, grasping a plateful of castle cakes smeared in red jam and sprinkled with coconut. "This is the twentieth century," he said, thrusting them toward Harry, who looked at them and said, "No, thank you."

"It depends where you are," Miriam said. "In Africa it's juju, in the West Indies they call it obeah, voodoo, shango. But it works. I know. I've seen a dozen cases."

"Only if the victim believes," said Nieves. "That is fear. Fear works."

"I think it is more than that," I said. "There *are* unholy places." I was thinking of the Vale of Tempe in Hadrian's Villa, which I swear is still the haunt of pagan gods. "You can say they belong to the childhood of mankind. But that childhood is repeated in every human life. We've all known such places."

There was a silence in which the noise of cars racing down the by-pass came to us like a series of sighs. John Scarlet had relinquished the plate and sat with his fingers interlocked looking down at them. "Surely you can remember at least one, John," I said, "from when you were a child."

John Scarlet looked up at me with a strange expression in his eyes, as if it were not me he saw, but a ghost—Miriam's witch in the cupboard beneath the stairs, perhaps, or the Scissors Man.

"No, Mr. Grantley," he said firmly, "no! Not one!"

12

SURPRISES

The first surprise was when Magda asked me if on our way home I could point out where the church was. I had assumed, because she was a refugee under Kit's care, that she was some sort of Hungarian Communist, believing in the Marxist-Leninist gospel according to Imre Nagy. Though I had noticed a thin gold chain around her neck, the cross itself was hidden by her dress. "You want the Roman Catholic church?" I asked.

"No," she said, "I am Lutheran."

"Then I can take you," I said. "There is Communion at eight or the Sung Eucharist at nine-fifteen." I myself prefer the Sung Eucharist as a rule, but I was so excited by the thought that if the Evernesses took Anglesey House there would be at least one adult Christian to keep an eye on Rosa that I was quite indifferent which she chose. "If they sing well," she said, "I like the Sung Eucharist."

"They do."

I prefer to walk to church, because it gives time for the collection of thought. But walking down to St. Luke's next morning, I spent my time interrogating Magda—or rather, prompting her to tell me her story.

She and her husband had been as opposed to the Communists as to the Horthy regime, because each was a different expression of the same tyranny. They were Christian Socialists who felt that in the national rising there was at last a hope for freedom and social justice. Her husband, being a doctor, had not fought; but he was killed by a stray bullet, when dressing the wounded in a street in Buda. Her son, a student of eighteen, had fought until the collapse and then fled with her to Austria. He had been killed by a mine on the frontier. "I wish I had died too," she said.

I find as I grow older that my ability to judge the age of those younger than myself grows worse and worse. I had imagined Magda as a young woman, thirty at the oldest. She shook her head. "I am forty at the next nativity." It was hard to believe. There was not a gray hair on her head and the lines about her eyes were only those of a woman whose face is more than usually expressive of emotion.

I felt in the presence of her loss utterly inadequate to give her solace. My own life, so humdrum, so free from tragedy, appeared to me worthless and superficial; and when I said, "You are still young; there is so much to live for," I realized its inanity even before she said in a flat voice, "Is there?" Her life had been laid waste by the loss of what I had been too selfish—lazy? work-busy? or divided—ever to gain. Together we knelt, the devastated and the fallow, at the altar rail.

Father Martin as usual went down the aisle and greeted the congregation going out of the porch. I introduced Madame Kovacs to him, as someone who might be coming to live in Wilchester if my friends bought Anglesey House. He shook her hand. "I most earnestly hope you will," he said.

Magda was puzzled. As she went away, she said, "He spoke as if he meant that. Why?"

I had been struck by the same thought. It was not a casual piece of clerical politeness. "I'm sure he did mean it," I answered. "But he might find it difficult to say why." Martin had the faith to say outright things which came into his head out of the blue, because, he maintained, they usually made more sense than what he worked out on his own.

"It is the first time since three years," she said later.

"What is?"

"That I go to the sacrament *with* someone."

There is, or at least can be, something additionally sacramental in taking the Host together with another person. I grasped her arm and gently pressed it. I had tried to make the Communion for her to be relieved of her grief. "It is much longer than that since I went with someone."

"But they are all your friends, your people," she said. "Me, I am a foreign woman, a stranger. And if they did know, it would be 'the woman who makes the goulash.'"

I asked her why she stayed with the Evernesses, cooking, when she could have taken a job with the BBC.

She did not answer, did not seem even to be listening, just kept shaking her head. But I persisted, feeling how wrong it was that a woman as young, as intelligent, as vigorous and attractive as she was should keep her eyes fixed on the past, however rich life had been when those she loved were living and however tragic their passing.

Suddenly she stopped and looked up at me. Her face was contorted with emotion. "You know what I pray," she said, "each night and morning. 'Let me die, oh, God, if it be Thy will.'" She turned away and started to walk off, dabbing her eyes with a handkerchief.

I followed her a few paces behind, until once more in self-control, she turned and waited for me, wryly smiling. "I'm sorry, my friend." She grasped my hand. "Till then, I cook. And very well. You see today." Her face was transfigured with the appearance of pleasure like the sun breaking through cloud onto spring pastures, and we walked, hand tightly pressed in hand, myself at least too happy for words.

But suddenly she jerked her hand away. Randall Rushmore and his two little girls had emerged from the Jubilee Gardens on their way to Matins. I was not to be disgraced, she explained later, being seen holding hands with Lady Everness' cook. From the slight wink which Randall gave me as he approached, there was no question of disgrace.

I introduced them and asked Randall if he would be free for a drink that evening at six. Though I did not know how it would fit in with the Evernesses' plans, I wanted to sound him out about the supermarket scheme for Scarlet's. There might be planning permission snags which Miriam, fresh from the West Indies, knew nothing about. He said he would love to come, if he could bring the two girls Dot and Carrie as their mother was away for the week-end.

Dorothea, who took after her mother, was a lumpy child of thirteen with a mass of unruly hair, a body too long for her legs and large feet. She had very fine teeth and beautiful eyes, which seemed to be looking out of her body as from a jail. Caroline, who was two years younger, was her father's child, slender, alert and charming, with the confident shyness of a deer.

I saw to my surprise Magda smiling at the elder child. She made some remark and Dorothea's face lit up with animation. "Why don't you bring them both to tea?" I asked. "There are plenty of strawberries, if you don't mind the bother of picking them."

"*Bother!*" said Dot.

"Can we eat some as we pick?" asked Carrie.

"Perhaps two, each," I said. "And there may be another girl to play with. I'm not sure."

The five-minute bell began to toll from St. Luke's and the Rushmores rushed. Magda turned and when Dorothea waved to her, she waved in reply. The longing—for motherhood? or just anybody to love?—was so transparent that if I had been a younger man, I would have been frightened, I thought. But now it seemed to me tragically beautiful.

"We must go home," she said. "I must cook."

"No," I said, "I want to show you the lilies in the gardens." I took her hand again. "They are beautiful."

"The cook must cook."

"I want to talk about Rosa. I am worried."

"But you don't know her."

"I know Anglesey House," I answered. "I'd be worried for any child there."

I really was worried, but my mood was such that I would have pretended any anxiety to have held her with me a little longer. Thank God, I could not see myself. If I had, the middle age of my body would have killed the youth in my heart. I took her, almost dragged her, to the place in the lake where the lilies spread either side the little paddling beach. There is a stone parapet there to prevent toddlers walking into the lake and drowning themselves. We sat on this and I told her simply what I knew about the Scarlet boy and the rumors running through the town. "It's probably pure imagination," I said. "Perhaps I ought not to have told you, in case the fear spreads by telepathy." This puzzled her, until I put it in simpler terms.

She said, "This is in your mind. It is not in my mind. Do not worry."

I saw two swans making toward us, one of them coming fast with quick strokes of its webbed feet like a destroyer, the other cruising sedately behind. "What a pity we have nothing to give them!"

Magda opened her bag and took out a little packet of biscuits. (This bag of hers, I found later, contained things against almost any common occasion, a habit begun as a doctor's wife and continued as a refugee, scissors, Elastoplast, half-inch bandages, sweets, an iodine pencil.)

She broke one of the biscuits and threw it to the first swan. He gobbled it greedily and hissed for more.

"No," she said, "you wait." Her sympathies went to the slower swan, just as they had gone to Dorothea.

"Give him another bit," I said.

She threw the swan a crumb which he was too proud to notice, but which some tiny fish fry fought for. Then the second swan arrived and she threw half a biscuit to each of them. "Look!" she said. "Oh, look!"

On the back of the second swan were riding two gray cygnets, so recently out of the egg that they were little balls of down, like a baby's puff except for the spade-black beaks and the tiny black webbed feet. As the mother bent to eat her piece of biscuit, the two babies came careering off her back as if it were a helter-skelter. They bobbed and jerked in the water picking at the sinking crumbs.

It was wonderful. I had never seen this before. By the time one has reached one's fifties, most things of that sort have been observed. It was like a revelation.

The two parents were feeding ravenously, completely ignoring the cygnets, snapping up the big pieces with sharp forward thrusts of their beaks, while the babies, so soft and delicate that they did not seem real, scavenged the crumbs which eluded them.

Suddenly from between the folded wing tips of the mother appeared for a moment another little black beak. "Magda, look! Look! There's a third." I used her Christian name instinctively. But she did not notice.

She paused with the last biscuit in her hands, the swans hissing forward at her like blackmailers. And there, sure enough, between the wings appeared the little black beak, the boot-button eyes, the downy head and struggling wings, the feet wildly clambering until they raised it out of the cavern made by the mother's wings and tail, the runt of the family, the little gray Benjamin of cygnets. He crept forward over his mother's back and when he reached the hissing neck, he put down one webbed foot as if to test whether the water was too cold and down he slid beside the others.

Magda split that last biscuit into tiny pieces, trying to feed this Benjamin. But the others were faster. She only succeeded in getting a few fragments to it. And then in despair she tossed the last piece and the little one darted his beak forward and snapped it up.

Magda looked at her watch. It was half-past eleven. "Oh, George," she said. (So she had noticed my use of her Christian name.) "The cook must cook." She held out her hand for me to pull her up. "Is it always with you like this?"

"No," I said, "only with you."

And so we walked back, quickly, in silence, and apart.

My second surprise was Nieves. Kit so dominated me when we were together that I had assumed that he would dominate his wife. But when I told her of the meeting with Randall Rushmore, she did not say that she could do nothing in Kit's absence. She picked up the telephone and called Miss Binks, the headmistress of St. Clare's, to announce, with a sublime disregard for exeats, that she had had to change her plans and would be taking Rosa out all day and could she be sure that the child would be ready in half an hour? Knowing Miss Binks, the headmistress, I thought how valuable it was to possess a title, even Socialist-conferred. "And Rosa can play with the two little girls, while we talk about the house," she said. "And perhaps they can be friends. Poor Rosa. We have traveled so much. And it is not easy for her to make friends."

Magda had disappeared into the kitchen and Harry was exercising himself on the hills. Like many athletes, he did not feel well unless he expended enough energy to prostrate the average sedentary man. He ran a hundred yards and then walked a hundred yards covering immense tracts of country, but oblivious of everything except the tingle of well-being in his body.

Nieves asked me if I would drive her over to the school to fetch Rosa for luncheon and though I had been thinking of putting in an hour's work, I readily agreed because I was curious what sort of woman could hold a man naturally as unfaithful as Kit.

Not that we talked of him. Nieves's imagination had been playing with the possibilities of the house and garden during the night. She hadn't slept until after midnight for thinking of it and had woken early to draw alternative plans. She talked of knocking the whole ground floor of the garden wing into a studio fifty feet long, of roll-away doors disappearing behind bookcases, of painting on the panels of the doors designs which would give to each room when the doors were drawn out an entirely separate character, of having the opportunity at last of trying her hand at sculpture.

Though Kit had spoken of her work indulgently as if it were a hobby, she was intensely serious in her attitude to what she regarded as a vocation to which family life was subordinate. Whatever her art was like, there was the authentic ring in her saying, "The more I learn, the more I know nothing, nothing." Perhaps her attraction for Kit was her egocentricity, or it would be truer to say "articentricity." A woman dedicated to his career or comfort would have made him feel captive. He flourished in the freedom of neglect.

She said nothing about her daughter until we were driving up the long avenue of poplars leading to the school. "Keet worries about Rosa, but I say she is an artist. You tell me later what you think."

I protested that I knew nothing about the young, of what sort of man the child might be the father; and I was glad that I had done so when I saw that the middle-aged auntie of a schoolgirl standing on the front steps was Rosa Everness. Kit was right to be worried. Something, I suspected glandular, was wrong with the child. She was enormous for eleven and her movements seemed to lack the co-ordination that one might have expected even in a child as adipose as she was. I could see no trace in her of either parent; she was like a monstrous changeling, already rather hairy about the chins. The smile with which she greeted her mother was unconfident, as if it were an expression tried on to see if it worked, but which could rapidly be superseded by some other if it failed.

I glanced at Nieves as she bent forward for the child to kiss her through the open window, before getting into the back of the car. I expected, foolishly, to see on the mother's face something of the pained surprise I felt on seeing the unfortunate child for the first time. But there was nothing surprising apart from a certain off-handedness on both sides, which might have sprung as much from mutual confidence as coolness.

Nieves introduced me as a friend of Rosa's father who had kindly asked them to stay for the day. "But I thought . . ." Rosa said, unable for the moment to suppress the shadow of disappointment.

"Magda is cooking us a wonderful meal," said Nieves.

"But we won't be *alone,* Mummy." Her voice had an accusatory whine.

"I expect you would both like to travel in the back together," I said, "so you can talk." I resented having spoilt the child's day without being warned that I might be doing so. If they were going to have a row, let them have it out together in the back.

I thought for a moment that Nieves was going to refuse. A quality she shared with her daughter was obstinacy. But she shifted onto the back seat and on the way home I could hear Nieves trying to interest Rosa in the house and the little Rushmore girls and anything else that might distract her from not being able to spend the day alone with her mother. My sympathies, I admit, were with the child. Being childless, I had the naive idea that parents should and could find their children interesting. But Nieves confessed to me later that though she had felt a deep maternal love for Rosa, as a baby, at this stage of her development the child bored her to distraction. The mother's boredom only made the daughter worse. She kept asking questions, prefaced by an infuriating "Mum-mee." "Mum-mee, why didn't Daddy come too?" "Mum-mee, will I be a day girl soon?" "Mum-mee, can't I go to another school?"

I drove rapidly back to The Chantry, anxious only to be delivered as soon as possible from the misery on the back seat. Going up the hill to the house, I saw the khaki figure of Cousin Harry. I hooted as we passed and he broke into a run. Sweat was streaming down his face and the bush shirt clung to those parts of his back which were not cushioned with hair. He gave no sign of noticing us, he was so wrapped in the exercise of the splendid machine that was his body.

As we entered the hall, he came padding up the steps behind us. "Fifty-seven, fifty-eight, fifty-nine. Now for a good cold tub. Sixty-three, sixty-four, sixty-five."

"Mum-mee," asked Rosa, "is that an African Daddy's rescued?"

The syntax of Magda's excellent meal was ruined by moods

and tenses. For one thing she refused to eat with us, saying with some justice that it is impossible to eat a meal and cook it. For another the quarrel between mother and daughter, while not erupting, kept rumbling on seismatically. I thanked God for the presence of Harry, whose ignoring of tensions relaxed them. He had a repertory of tricks which could be performed at the luncheon table, a special way of lifting an inverted glass between finger and thumb, an elusive manipulation of wiggling middle fingers which kept Rosa puzzled and giggling, an ability to produce strawberries from Rosa's ear and then make them vanish by legerdemain. As an accomplished child, he entranced his less accomplished spiritual coeval.

Nieves and I watched, fascinated and grateful at the way these two brought out in one another qualities which I, at least, had suspected in neither. By the end of the meal Harry was a god and Rosa his devotee. Nieves sat back relieved of her responsibility. But I remained on tenterhooks because each dish which Magda produced, perfect as it was, displayed more clearly her self-wounding abasement. The soufflé was served as, so to speak, a delicious insult. I tried to catch her eye to recall with a glance the pleasure which I could have sworn that we had shared that morning. But she was like a fury, powered by unhappiness.

After the meal was over, I went into the kitchen and asked if I could help her with the washing up. "No! No!" she said. "This is what I came to do and this I do."

"But, Magda!" I pleaded.

"Go away," she said. "In God's name, go!"

I went, knowing that she was on the verge of tears and nothing I could do or say would at this moment help her.

The others were in the garden. Harry was teaching Rosa how to make a cat's cradle. Though the rest of her body was so clumsy, she had competent hands; not those long slender fingers which are popularly supposed to be artistic, but the stubby, certain practical hands which most manual artists have, except musicians. She picked up the threads of the cat's cradle in a way that I have never succeeded in doing. Nieves leant toward me, holding her coffee cup. "Don't worry, *Jorge mio*," she said.

"Worry?"

"A worry is like a clock. The big weight. You put it more this way, the more it goes the other. Magda is all right. Okay."

There was something in her way of saying "Okay" which repelled me; the Spanish accent made it sound so common. But I could not restrain my curiosity. "Is she always this way and that?"

She shook her head. "You made her very happy. So now she's very sad."

"I'm sorry."

"Why sorry! Life is the happy and the sad. Magda comes back to life."

I was terrified by the way she said this. There are moments between individuals which are precious for their own sakes but it is quite wrong to think that these stake any claim upon the future. That is the knotting of the sentimental net which catches most men in marriage. I was too old, too bald and ugly to be caught in that way in the mesh of my own fantasy. "Do you know how to play croquet, Rosa?" I asked.

"What's that?"

"I'll show you, if you help me." I caught her anguished look toward Harry. "Uncle Harry played croquet for England, didn't you?" I asked, winking.

"No," he said, "old boy. But I did win the championship in Kashmir in '38. Not that I approve of the game. It's not really cricket."

"Hence the name, croquet," I said.

The croquet set was kept in the summerhouse. It must have been, I realized, almost thirty years since it had been opened, but the balls and mallets had been oiled before being put away and were in surprisingly good condition, though the hoops had deeply rusted where the paint was flaked. As Harry was putting them in place, I went back into the house and asked Magda if she would make a foursome. She pointed to the piles of washed plates, pans and silver. I took a drying cloth from the drawer and in three minutes we had finished them between us. "This is not work for you," she protested. "Not for you either," I answered. "But we're both doing it." I thought that this was part of her self-imposed penance of being the cook; but I found later that it ran contrary to her Hungarian view of the sexes. Men did not help with household chores.

"Have you eaten?" I asked.

"A little. To cook takes away the hunger."

She had had nothing since the night before, apart from the tasting of dishes and sauces. "What shall I cook you?" I asked.

I meant it, because I am a good cook for one person. But the threat was enough to induce her to make a rye bread and cheese sandwich. "Forgive me," she said.

"Why?"

"I was bad, bad, bad." Her hatred had now turned in on herself with the force which had been turned against us.

I took her hand. "You and I will challenge Harry and Rosa at croquet."

She nodded happily. But of course it wasn't as simple as that. Magda the cook retired upstairs and it was about twenty minutes before Magda the croquet player came down again, by which time Harry and I had succeeded in teaching Rosa and Nieves the rudiments of that most savage of Victorian games.

One learns a great deal about human nature at all games but I think croquet is the most revealing, especially in a double partnership. Harry was the strongest player and little Rosa the weakest. Magda and I tried to help one another through the hoops, having banished Harry and Rosa to opposite ends of the lawn. But Harry far more subtly kept our balls in play to help him to get his own and Rosa's through the hoops. Despite Rosa's difficulty with her mallet, they won three games before the arrival of Rushmore and his children. I admire anyone who does something, even the simplest, with grace and skill. Harry's positioning, his calculation of angle, strength and spin were superb. His Doomsday Book was an attempt to reduce life to the same principles, but unfortunately it was played with people, not balls.

I had expected that the arrival of the Rushmore girls would make Rosa's day. That was a great mistake. The child who had looked forward to a day with her mother had readjusted herself, thanks to Harry's tricks and charm. But now she was suddenly asked to readjust again and this time to two little girls, who were united in their resentment at being invited out to tea, not because they were wanted but because they could not be left at home in their mother's absence. The two sisters, close together, approached Rosa like a pair of dogs being introduced to a cat.

Croquet was impossible. Rosa had been carried on Harry's skill. With three children playing, it would collapse under the slowness of the play and the heaviness of mallets.

I took Rosa with me to collect three enameled bowls. Strawberry-picking was an activity they could indulge in with as much or little camaraderie as they chose. "I don't know what Dot and Carrie are like," I said to Rosa. "But I thought that if you *are* coming to live here, you might like to see who there is to play with."

Rosa did not answer. It was probably too adult a way in which to put the idea; possibly even, she had not thought of friends as the subject of her choice—she was not a person who could pick and choose, and even if she had been, her parents had never stayed anywhere long enough for a friendship to be established. "I've never picked strawberries," she said. "Do they grow on bushes or what?"

I took the children to the beds and told them that for every strawberry they put in their bowls, they could eat one, provided that at the same time they nipped off the runners. The two Rushmore girls moved quickly into the attack under the netting, but Rosa, apart from nibbling a strawberry or two, wanted to know about the runners and why they had to be nipped off. I explained about the strawberry spreading either through the seed of the fruit or by the runners; and the way the strength of the plants went into the runners unless they were nipped. "My mother used to say it was a race between the fruit and the runners and I had to help the fruit win," I said.

Rosa found a long runner and nipped it off. There were two plants already on it with roots and it was still running. She held it in her stubby practical fingers, touching the small leaves and the tiny thrusting radicles. I have said that she was an unattractive child, but the look of wonder in her eyes as she held it up and said, "How does it know when to stop and be a new one?" was so innocent that she seemed in some transfigured way beautiful. She pulled a dark strawberry and picked out one of the straw-colored pips with the end of her nail. "If I planted that would it grow into a strawberry plant?"

I said it would have a better chance if a bird ate it and the seed passed through and she bit off half and threw it toward a robin which was outside the net, but he flew away. "You'd better hurry up or you'll never fill your bowl," I said, looking at the other two who were already halfway down their rows. "It doesn't matter," she said. "You go and talk to Magda. I like to look."

Kit arrived soon after five. He had a bottle of Pimm's No. 1 Cup. "Dispense with the borage and all the other garden produce," he said. "On the rocks will do me."

He towered above Randall, greeting him rather as a colonial bishop might a shipwrecked sea captain. (It was a peculiar quality Kit had of being able to come into a room, or in this case a garden, and make everyone already there feel as if it was *they* who had just arrived, the gift of vicarious hospitality.) "I am so glad you were able to come round, my dear fellow," he said. "Grantley has so celebrated you that I began to suspect that you were fabulous, like one of the characters out of Lemprière's *Classical Dictionary*, like the Minotaur or that clever chap whose name eludes me who built the labyrinth he lived in, I mean the Minotaur, not Lemprière."

"He is nice, Keet," Nieves said. "Nobody pays you nothing to be bloody pompous on Sunday."

Kit put his arm round Nieves's shoulder and kissed her smackingly on the brow. "My Spanish mistress of the double negative, where would I be without your innocent obscenities?" He turned to Rushmore. "You must forgive my wife, if her language occasionally blisters your eardrums. English is not a real language to her. Catalan—or even Spanish—yes. But English is a joke. She could sign a contract with the Devil in English, because nothing said in English means anything serious. I do hope, if you have been discussing Tumbledown Towers together, you have been talking Catalan."

"What Lady Everness said to me in English made excellent sense," Randall said, stiffly.

I took the bottle of Pimm's and went into the house. It was far too early for me to start drinking, but I could foresee an early row between Kit and Randall unless I could mellow both of them. I poured Randall a much stronger drink than Kit, but topped them both to an equal level with Graves. As I put in the ice, I heard someone come in and looked round. It was Magda. "Please, please," she said. "They are quarreling. Kit is so *silly* when he drinks."

I turned and saw her just behind me as I was picking up the tray. I put it down and kissed her.

It was a light kiss upon her forehead, almost a brushing of the lips.

"No," she said, shaking her head.

I mumbled an apology. The impulse, which was one of pure affection, had for the moment mastered me.

She reached up her hands to my face, drawing it down until our lips met in a slow searching kiss. "Like that," she said and turning away she took the tray up and carried it out of the room. Over her shoulder she said, "Your mouth has lipstick."

By the time I reached the garden, it was too late to rescue the strong drink I had prepared for Rushmore from Kit's grasp. I raised the subject of the supermarket.

"I can't see any reason why it shouldn't go through," Rushmore said. "The whole of North Street has been scheduled for commercial development and if John Scarlet will hold on till he gets his price, it should be worth all of fifty thousand, maybe more. He's on the lucky side of the street."

Kit looked puzzled at the apparent change of subject. "Lucky side?"

"The other side is being compulsorily purchased at valuation," Rushmore explained. "But the south side property will rocket."

Everness still had not understood the connection between the sale of the shop site and the price of Anglesey House.

"To hold off his creditors Scarlet needs ready money quick," I explained.

Kit nodded. He looked at his watch. "Time for one more," he said, "while you two girls get packed. Then we'll take Rosa back and head for home." Apart from kissing Rosa when he arrived and telling her that the painting she was doing with my watercolors was pretty he hadn't said a word to his daughter. He drained his glass and handed it to me. "A lovely cool drink." He turned to Rushmore. "And if we get the place, Mr. Rushmore, can I rely on you to translate my wife's dreams into a reality I could afford? I don't want just a pretty set of plans with attractive estimates and then a bill at the end which is twice as much again. I want you to see the work through from beginning to end...."

I fetched Kit his second drink and then wandered off to warn Rosa that it would soon be time to go. She was on a seat by herself, oblivious of the lesson which Harry was giving the Rushmore girls in how to construct a blind for bird-watching out of bamboo. She did not raise her head as I came up and I looked at what she was painting. It was an idea derived from the bed of Peace roses a few yards away, but she had been defeated by the extraordinary delicacy of their coloring and given them carmine blooms instead. And to give the picture a center of interest she had painted in the figure of an old lady, obviously an afterthought because the shape of the rose trees could still be seen through her dress. One could not see the face, which was hidden by a big floppy man's hat. She had treated this figure very interestingly because it was outlined in a sort of cloud of light blue merging to pink, producing a strangely imaginative effect in the garden scene.

"Who is that?" I asked, pointing to the figure.

"Her?" Rosa said. "She's the old lady. Would you like to keep her?"

"I would," I said. "She reminds me of my mother."

She tore the sheet off the sketching block and handed it to me. "It's thank you for telling me about the strawberries."

I told her that it was nearly time for her to go and her face clouded with displeasure. She stood up, knocking over the jar of painting water. "Oh, Dad-dee," she wailed as she ran toward her father. "Dad-dee, we don't have to go yet, Dad-dee."

13

OBJETS TROUVÉS

I was surprised at the smoothness with which the purchase of Anglesey House went through. It was bought in the name of Nieves Mariposa (alias Everness). The purchase price was about midway between Dawkins' presurvey offer and his postsurvey offer. There was no stipulation about "subject to survey," which deluded John Scarlet and the Schroeders with the impression that they were dealing with a thoroughly unworldly artist. This made me feel morally less insecure, though of course the only people capable of being swindled are the dishonest.

Kit's influence put the searchings through on a high priority. Contracts were exchanged in the record time of three weeks with completion in another fortnight.

I heard that when Miriam discovered that my painter friend was really the wife of Sir Christopher Everness, she was furious. But by that time, she and Karl were settled in Mill Hill. John Scarlet bore me no apparent ill-will. He had the money to keep the financial wolves from the shop and Bardsley & Beard were briskly playing Universal Markets off against Super Foods.

For a time Harry talked of "going in" with John Scarlet. "All he really needs is contacts," he explained to me. But the enthusiasm died when he found an "opening in nonferrous alloys" in Birmingham with a chap who had been "rather under the weather in Dar."

"What *are* nonferrous alloys?" I asked.

"Well, you know," he answered, "they leave the iron out. It gets so rusty. There's a great future in them, especially in rainy climates."

"I suppose there'll be 'a certain amount of initial expenditure.'"

"As a matter of fact, old boy, there will," he said, looking his bush kit over. "I mean, these aren't precisely the togs for non-ferrous alloys."

I knew that in his wardrobe there were two good lounge suits and in his chest an adequate supply of shirts and socks waiting for him to disguise himself again as urban man. I waited for him to ask for a hundred pounds, ready to counter with fifty. He asked for a couple of hundred and I settled for seventy-five. "I think this is The Real Thing, Cousin George," he said, watching me make out the check. "This is what I've been working up to." His face shone with dedication. "Hopkinson's a brick."

Mrs. Ambrose was very sorry to lose Cousin Harry. He had always cleaned his shoes every morning, or rather his sandals. He had a method. It took a long while, because as he explained leather is alive and needs feeding. While his sandals were having their breakfast, he would help Mrs. Ambrose wiping up mine. "I shall miss Mr. Waybridge," she said, "he's such a practical gentleman. If only he'd stayed in one place, he'd be a millionaire by now, but he was bitten by this wanderbug when he was a boy."

She liked Mr. Waybridge better than she did what she called my "sudden new friends," by which she meant Kit, Nieves and Magda. She had gone round the kitchen on the morning after they left, clucking like an old hen. The tea things had not been washed up, because of Kit's sudden urge to go back to London, and the "bain Marie" whatever it was had been left dirty too. "I suppose everybody has her funny ways," she muttered, producing a bottle of powdered paprika, "but will we be wanting this?"

I said we might.

"In that case I s'pose I ought to screw the top on proper."

In her quiet way she had come to assume certain proprietorial rights over my life in the years since my mother's death and she resented encroachment. "It's all so very different from what it was."

It was delightfully different, especially when work actually began on "Tumbledown Towers" as Kit nicknamed it. By then Frisk had had her litter, five pups of which two were bitches, and I would take her down to Market Street every morning to see how the work was going ahead, because though Rushmore was in charge of works, he could not give it daily attention.

But there was a peculiar thing. Frisk would never go into the garden even when that hen house beneath which she had been trapped had been dismantled and burnt. She remained in the little back yard outside the kitchen door perfectly content until I came to take her away. And once when I tried to take her into the garden on collar and leash, she dug her four paws in and had to be dragged and the moment I let her go, off she streaked to her station outside the kitchen door.

We fell into a sort of routine. Nieves would come down most Thursdays, this being a day when Rushmore did not go to London. (It paid him not to work every day in London, because he could charge fares and part of his rates against office expenses.) At weekends, sometimes Nieves and Magda came and spent Saturday night and were picked up on Sunday by Kit, at others they all came down on Sunday and we either had a cold luncheon at The Chantry or went to eat at the Wilchester Arms. Rosa, who accepted me as "Uncle George," was given a liberal allowance of exeats.

I ceased to notice how strange she was; saw only her desperate need for love and her almost equally desperate gratitude when one succeeded in giving it. This wasn't so easy as it might seem— because she had dreamy fits, which were hard to penetrate.

I had a feeling, perhaps vain, that Nieves wanted to make me her follower, not because she was attracted to me or felt that I was attracted to her, but because the conquest of an old friend of Kit's might provoke in her husband an ardor she knew was dying. But when I made it obvious that I had no feelings of the sort she tried to foster, she insisted on bringing Magda down on Thursdays also, on the ground that it was her whom I preferred.

Though this was true, I was embarrassed—even though I knew the motives prompting Nieves. The confirmed bachelor, faced with a choice of "either . . . or," instinctively vociferates "Neither," and the attraction which I felt toward Magda was counteracted by terror at the thought of joining my life irrevocably to anyone's at that moment, when the pleasure of a present meeting or anticipation of a future one was dominated by fancies of what marriage might hold.

Magda was given once a week what she insisted in emphasis of her domestic status on calling "an afternoon off." And either I would meet her in London or she would come down to The Chantry so that we could spend these times together. We discovered that we had a basic cultural sympathy though our reading did not coincide. She was a great admirer of the Germans, Hölderlin, Rilke and Stefan Georg, whose real qualities I missed through my inadequate knowledge of the original language. In the same way, she found it impossible to appreciate Blake, Hopkins, Eliot and Dylan Thomas, whom I admired.

But we did not talk a great deal about the arts. We were content with familiarizing one another with the coinage of our personal lives. She told me a great deal more about herself, her parents, her husband, her son and also other men in her life than I told her about myself and my affairs. This was partly because she had more to tell, but also because I am by nature reticent, far more so in speech than I am in writing. As a Lutheran she did not go to confession; and I have always found that those who do not have the solace of this discipline, have greater need to unburden themselves.

I talked to her freely about Helen Scarlet and about my father and mother. But I told her nothing about Elizabeth and Weeny or Adrian, because they were people whom it was quite possible that she might meet in Wilchester, nor about other sinful relationships, which were past, repented of and pardoned. They were no cause for pride or publication. (Nor were they in my view the worst of sins. Sexual lust, when shared, is a companionable sin far less corrosive than envy, sloth or pride.)

Magda, of course, was curious about Helen Scarlet. Budapest is so much closer to Vienna than Wilchester is. I could see her weaving Freudian fantasies about me, even when I assured her that though Helen had been a great friend, she had never been a *grande passion.*

She asked me whether I ever regretted not having married. I answered that I regretted most of all having no children I could call my own, and how I envied even a person like Miriam

Schroeder the joys of being a grandparent. "It is not too late," she said.

"Would you marry a man who would be in his seventies before your child was twenty-one?" I asked. "If your husband lived that long?"

"Perhaps. It depends."

"On what?"

She shrugged. "Many things. Does he love me? Do I love him? If he died, could I support his children? Other things too."

As we were talking I thought of Albert Scarlet's letters to Helen Kent. How different his lusty confidence was from my hesitation, and Magda's warmth from Helen's coldness! But there was the same tentative higgling, though in different terms. Was there ever a marriage of true minds in which the impediments had not been carefully weighed beforehand?

We were having tea under the cypress in The Chantry garden. Our conversations in the past had revolved around this point, but keeping at a safe distance as on the outer edge of the marital maelstrom. But suddenly we had been swept dangerously close to the vortex. I say "we" deliberately, because I am certain that Magda was as apprehensive of me as I of her as a possible marriage partner.

"What other things?"

She looked into her teacup.

"Say what other things, Magda." I thought of my self-centeredness, my emotional sloth, my dowdy body.

"Can you give a woman children?" she asked, still looking at her tea. "Can you do it, George?"

I burst out laughing. Balding, hideous, middle-aged, dentured, dull, sprouting hair in the wrong places, selfish, silly, complacent, slack-bellied . . . I could have gone on with the list all afternoon. But not impotent! not sterile! no, by Adrian! no!

At that moment I saw Mrs. Ambrose coming from the house, followed closely by Randall Rushmore. A moment later Magda saw them also. I wondered whether she felt as great a relief as I did at the interruption and if so, whether for the same reason. That force sweeping us both toward the vortex was, I believe, no more controlled by Magda than by me. We spoke together, like two people about to be overwhelmed by an experience that would probably be a disaster, desperately trying to get to know one another better before the force beyond our control took complete charge of our destinies.

We both greeted Randall effusively, as if he were a rescuer. He was puzzled, because he sensed that he had broken in on some scene where he should be unwelcome. In fact, he told me afterward that Mrs. Ambrose had not warned him that I had a guest. I did not doubt him. Mrs. Ambrose regarded me as a middle-aged simpleton who had fallen into the toils of a foreign adventuress who would wreck our firmly established *liaison de cuisine.*

I told Mrs. Ambrose to brew more tea and bring another cup and saucer. Then I asked Randall how things were going at Anglesey House. "Or wasn't it about this you wanted to see me?"

"Oh, it was," he admitted. "But I wonder if I ought . . ."

"You can trust Madame Kovacs."

"It's not a question of trust, not in that sense," Rushmore said. "I'm afraid she might think I'm being silly."

"Whereas I wouldn't?"

Mrs. Ambrose brought the fresh tea and the extra cup, together with a plate of sandwiches. Randall waited until she was out of earshot before he began to talk.

"I think we all agreed that there was something rather chilly about the garden wing of Anglesey," he said, "not the southern end, but the part connecting it with building on the street."

"Which you attributed to the thinness of the walls, low ceilings and small windows," I reminded him.

"And the terribly drab interior decoration," he added. "That most of all. Chilliness is not just a matter of temperature or drafts; it is a state of mind, induced by the cubic complex of color and proportion."

Seeing Magda's bewilderment, I said, "Don't worry. That's a quotation from one of his lectures."

"As a matter of fact, it is," said Randall with a deprecating laugh, "but none the less true for being glib. But the extraordinary thing is that though we've completed the upstairs bedrooms in the garden wing, in a way that theoretically ought to make them gay and warm and delightful, the middle two aren't—especially the one that used to be the lumber room. There's something wrong."

I glanced at Magda. We had talked over the suicide time and again but she agreed with Father Martin that there was no point in going to meet trouble. It was enough to cope with it when and if it arose. I made a little movement of my hand to counsel silence. Though one could not inhibit telepathic transmission, I wanted neither of us to plant ideas deliberately in Rushmore's mind. "What d'you think is wrong?"

"You know they say in the town the place is haunted?"

"But do you believe that?"

"Ogthorpe's foreman does. Me, I've never tackled a haunted house before. But I know one or two architects who have—Sir Norman Richardson, for example, and, as one of my colleagues said, Richardson's got his feet on the ground, all four of them. It's possible. I won't go further than that."

"I don't see why you've come to me. Sir Christopher is surely the person to approach. If I tell him, he'll just tell me not to be a bloody fool."

Randall laughed. "That's what he's told me. I suggested that while he was having the place disinfested of rats, he might get Martin Turner to exorcise the place; you know, quietly, no fuss. 'My dear fellow,' he said, 'don't be a bloody fool. I'm the Honorary President of the Rational Truth Society. Just imagine a gossip writer getting hold of that story!'"

I turned to Magda. "You understand?" Though she had grown used to my way of speaking, she sometimes found it hard to follow strangers. She nodded and said, "In Buda was one psychic, Aladar Mikes, very clever. You give him an object, a ring or something, and he tell you all."

"But that is Buda," Rushmore said.

"And he is dead," Magda added.

"It's an idea," I said excitedly. "We've got somehow to convince Kit. . . ."

"Or rather find out for ourselves," emended Randall.

"Yes, find out for ourselves. Psychometry might do it, if only we can find the right object. Something belonging to Charles Scarlet." I thought of the games which Helen had kept in the desk drawer. But they were useless. She and I had played with them too often after Charles's death. "I looked around in that lumber room. But I couldn't see anything."

"Yerbury cleared the place out," Rushmore said. "That was part of the bargain. He had to take the junk as well. The only thing he missed . . . well, they certainly didn't belong to Charles; though it was in the cupboard under the eaves in that room. Wait a moment, I'll get them from the car. They're rather interesting."

While he was away, Magda asked me if I knew a psychometrist. I didn't; but I vaguely remembered Martin Turner talking about a friend of his, an archdeacon, who was interested in psychometry; somewhere in the Midlands or the North.

Randall came back with a brown paper bag. He opened it and was going to take out whatever it contained, but I called out, "Don't!" If we were consulting a psychometrist, the less contamination of objects the better. I passed him a clean handkerchief.

He emptied the bag on the grass. There were two spurs, a child's judging from the size, very rusty. He passed me one in the handkerchief, laid it on my lap and then put the other on the table in front of Magda. "I don't know the age of spurs, but they must go back a hundred and fifty years."

They looked to me earlier, at a guess late seventeenth or early eighteenth century. Rust had eaten into the shank and the teeth of the rowel. But where the rowel revolved on the axle pin, its color was not rusty but almost black with dirt. I took the handkerchief from Randall and holding the spur in it with my left hand, I began to pick at the dirt with the small blade of my penknife. The dirt was grease which had hardened and darkened with age. But it came away easily. I spun the rowel round on its axis with the tip of the knife. "What do you both make of that?" I asked.

The axis had been worn in the first place, we all agreed. It was pitted in some places with rust but elsewhere it was unrusted and almost bright. From the dark grease round the axis of the other spur, I judged that its condition was the same.

"I do not understand," Magda said.

"It seems obvious to me that somebody found these spurs rusted up," Randall said, "then he—or she—broke away the rust till the rowel wheel was running and greased it to prevent that happening again."

I nodded. "Do you know an analytical chemist?"

"Several," Randall said.

I took some letters out of my pocket and chose a couple of envelopes into each of which I put samples of the grease from the second spur (the grease from the first being scattered on the lawn). "Can you get two separate analyses of this, each for age and nature?" My hunch was that Charles found the spurs somewhere about the house and used them as properties in his pleasure-pain games. What I was really interested in was the age of the grease; to ask what sort of grease it was was merely a control to test the reliability of our expert evidence. "Don't lose them, for God's sake." He put them carefully in his pocket. "You quite sure there was nothing else, Randall?"

"Nothing of the least interest," he said. "There was some very old harness stuff, absolutely rotten, straps you know. And an old footstool with one leg missing, riddled with woodworm."

"Where is it?" I blamed myself for not searching that cupboard thoroughly. "What have you done with it?"

"I told the men to chuck it away."

I jumped up. "How long ago? Will it still be lying around? When are the dust bins emptied?"

"There aren't any dust bins," Randall said. "They've been burning the stuff. There was a great blaze going when I left."

"Oh, my God! Maybe it's not burnt yet, though. Let's go round and see."

"Aren't you taking all this a bit too seriously, George?"

"It's either got to be taken seriously or not at all," I answered. "Anyway, I want to see what you mean by the chilliness of that room." I would have taken Frisk with us, because I have a great belief in the sensory perception of animals, but the poor dear was then too occupied with the duties of maternity to be disturbed.

The men had knocked off work by the time we reached Anglesey House. The bonfire was smoldering, a heap of white ash over red-hot embers, edged round with unburnt ends of planks, like a huge gray dinner plate with an untidy design on the rim.

Randall saw it at once, one uncharred leg projecting upward on the edge of the fire. He raked it away and we doused it with water from the rain butt. It was still recognizably a piece of footstool leg, but, as Randall said, the effect of great heat on psychic sequelae was anybody's guess. I lifted it with two sticks and dropped it in the tin we had used for dousing.

"If we hadn't come immediately, it would have been burnt to cinders," I said, feeling the need to make the point against Randall—or perhaps to prove to myself that I had not been too fussy.

We went up to the ex-lumber room. I found it hard to appreciate what Rushmore meant about his decorations being calculated to make the bedrooms gay and warm and jolly or whatever it was. They made me as depressed as being in an *espresso* bar, those awful "contemporary" papers, looking like advertisements for Byrrh or enlargements of the spirochete under a high-powered microscope. "I want to look in that cupboard," I said.

The door of the cupboard had been left undecorated on the instruction of Nieves, who proposed to paint it as if it were a window, looking out on what she had not yet decided. Randall produced a little flashlight from his pocket. "I wanted to persuade them to insulate with fiberglass," he said, "but neither of them has realized the basic principles of thermal conservation."

I crept through the little door, flashing the light around. It was an extraordinary sensation, literally like walking from the twentieth century to the eighteenth by taking a single step. I could hear Randall and Magda in the room for a moment, but then as I began to creep on hands and knees across the rafters—no chill here! it was stifling beneath the hot tiles—their voices died. There were vast tangles of cobwebs under the roof in which hung the skeletons of spiders who had died before the papery fly victims of the webs which had survived them. There was a chirping of birds somewhere very close, either inside the roof where I could not see or under the jut of tiles and gutter. But this live sound did not recall me to the present. It was a sound that had been going on for hundreds of years. I would have heard it if I had been living when the Spanish Armada had been sailing up the Channel to its destruction or when the Cavaliers and Roundheads fought for Wilchester or the streets rang with the relief of the Restoration. There would have been just such a tragic beat of a fly caught in an obsolete cobweb.

I knew that the last person, apart from Ogthorpe's men, to

have crept under these eaves was Charles Scarlet. He was inquisitive. His knees knelt where I knelt. If I wanted his pure spoor, it was here.

I flashed the little torch across the lath and plaster. A bat's bones lay bleached, everything that was edible stripped by the creatures that came and went in this part of the house which was not used by the creatures who had built and cared for it. But there was no sign of Charles, not a marble or a button. Only a buckle of brass, covered in verdigris, and the tag of double-sewn leather. I picked it up in my handkerchief and put it in my pocket, resolved to tell the other two nothing of it because of my fear of its possibly spreading abroad through telepathy.

I heard Magda call me, so close in space and yet so far away in time. "George! George! Are you all right?" Her voice sounded frightened. "What's wrong, Magda?" I called.

As I backed out, I thought how ridiculous it was not to tell them about the buckle. If I was afraid of their telepathy to other people, there was equal reason for me to be afraid of my telepathy to them. These so-called "scientific" tests between human beings were impossible and designedly so. There was always the element of faith, based on the balance of evidence. The more you narrowed down the margin of faith, the more you narrowed down the evidence, in matters of the spirit. "What's wrong, Magda?" I repeated, as I saw her face, white, her body tense.

Before she could answer, I felt, though I was streaming with sweat from the heat of the roof, a sudden intense cold. I thought at first that this was caused by the difference of temperature in the cupboard and in the bedroom. But as I stood up I realized that this was contrary to the law of nature. The hot air should properly be flowing from the cupboard into the bedroom at the upper levels of the cupboard doorway where my head was. But this was not what had happened. What I can only describe as "a body of cold air" had entered the cupboard as I was crawling out, chilling my face and scalp as much as my hands, which were resting on the floor. It took only a moment to pass, but it made me shudder in its passage.

"*You* felt it," Magda said.

I looked at Randall. "What about you?"

He shook his head. "What was it?"

"Cold," said Magda. "Like the deep freeze, moving."

14

THE SENSITIVE BRICKLAYER

I said good-bye to Magda at the station, having secured a promise from Randall that he would have the fat from the spurs analyzed without giving any clue to where it had been found. And
for the whole of that evening, though I tried to work, I thought of
little else but the events of the day.

Yet the next morning after an unusually sound sleep, I had lost
what the Freudians call the "affect" of that experience in the Scarlet boy's bedroom. I could remember what had happened, but I
could not *feel* it. I think I lack spiritual memory. Martin Turner,
who lives continuously in the dimension of the spirit, is physically forgetful, because I suppose he is physically not all there.
But I am seldom there spiritually and as soon as I come back to
the physical world, I begin to doubt. Our experiences at Anglesey
House appeared to me completely unreal.

Yet the moment I finished breakfast, I received a telephone
call from Father Martin. "I want you to come straight round,
George," he said. "I don't know what you've been doing, but I
have a very strong sense that you ought to meet Augustine
Mills—the Archdeacon of Yarborough. He spent the night with
me and he has to leave in a couple of hours."

I felt suspicious, remembering Norman Newman-Turner's
mot, "He has the habit of putting two and two together and making the Kingdom of Heaven."

Father Martin cut through my havering. "I don't know how,
but I am sure that this is part of The Plan."

"What plan?"

"He can advise you about what's wrong," Father Martin said.
"And if I was still in the Army, I'd say 'This is an order!'"

I went round to the rectory immediately, taking Frisk with me in the car. She had decided that it was time that the puppies were weaned.

Archdeacon Mills was a short, very broadly built man in his late fifties. His head, set on his shoulders like a child's plasticine figure almost without a neck, belonged to a man several times larger than he. He had a very wide mouth, rather grim at rest but engagingly humorous when he smiled. When he laughed, it was as if a bull were roaring in his chest—altogether rather disconcerting.

"I'm sorry to have so little time," he said, "I have to be in Guildford by noon." He stuffed a small ball of tobacco into the bowl of a pipe which was almost completely carboned up. "Turner has given me the background, so all I want are the later developments."

I was mildly surprised that he should know that there were later developments, but I told him as briefly and clearly as I could about the *objets trouvés* and the sensations of cold in the lumber room. "Rushmore is getting the grease from the spurs analyzed," I said, "but I want to get the *objets* to a really competent psychometrist without meeting him or giving him any telepathic clue to what they might be."

"Now I understand," Mills said, slapping his knee. "You're exactly the person *I* want, and I believe I've exactly the man *you* want."

"I don't want a professional psychometrist, if I can avoid one."

"You want Percy Smith," the Archdeacon said. "He has the gift and he doesn't know what to make of it."

Percy, it appeared, was a Yarborough bricklayer, a working man of no very high intelligence, but whose family had a tradition of churchmanship. His father was part-time organist in a small village outside Yarborough.

Percy had discovered that he had powers of second sight. He frequently knew what was going to happen in the future, especially when people were going to die. There was a different color round them, he said. (He had never heard any talk about "auras.") He also found that when he was given objects belonging to other people, he could say what the people were like and describe important things which had happened to them. (Once again, Mills was convinced, he had never heard about psychometry.) For quite a time he had thought that these gifts of his were shared by other people. It was only when friends and workmates came to consult him about their problems and to offer him money for his advice that it was borne in on him that he was different from other people. Even so, being a naturally incurious man, he would have thought nothing more of it, if the vicar of his father's village had not come to hear of Percy's powers, "not the most intelligent priest in the diocese." Percy had been solemnly warned about the dangers of witchcraft and necromancy and been thoroughly alarmed by a sermon preached ostensibly about the Witch of Endor, but actually at him. He had been placed in an agony of mind, coming to suspect that he was possessed by evil powers and feeling the more distressed because he did not believe that there was anything wrong in what he had done.

"Luckily I came to hear of it," the Archdeacon said. "I've seen Percy several times and I have tried him out on several occasions, at first with packaged objects which I knew something about and later with objects wrapped up by other people and which I knew nothing about. Of course you can explain everything by telepathy, if you want to. When A passes a package to B, he may at the same time telepathize its contents to B's unconscious, which in its turn conveys it to the sensitive; or A may communicate directly with the sensitive at a distance. I don't suppose we shall ever understand exactly what happens. But all I can say is that Percy seems to have extraordinary powers."

"What powers?" asked Martin Turner.

"Powers of extrasensory cognition or perception—call it what you like. He has told us a lot about these objects which we know to be true, plus a lot which may or may not be true—our own knowledge is insufficient to check."

Martin was uneasy. "Are you right to encourage him in such practices?"

"If he has a gift of extrasensory perception," Mills said, "it's neither good nor bad—any more than exceptionally keen hearing is. It may be dedicated to God or, if you deny it that outlet, to the Devil."

"But it *is* a gift of God," I suggested. "No positive faculty is spiritually evil as such."

"The visionary mystics had extrasensory powers; and that's what comes from their dedication to God, surely," Martin said.

"One of the things." Mills had a subtler mind than Turner. "The mystical vision is a combination of holiness with extrasensory powers. Percy isn't a holy man and yet he does see things. Perhaps the dedication of his gift might be scientific, so that we can learn more about its nature; it isn't supernatural, it's just paranormal. In the way an artist's discrimination of color can be paranormal."

"I don't agree," Martin said. "These 'sensitives' like Smith see and know things which ordinary people don't. The artist merely has an abnormally fine perception of what all but the blind can perceive in lesser degree."

"How d'you know that?" asked Mills. "Haven't you ever, driving a car, known that there was something round the bend? When you go into a room and know immediately that something is wrong, what tells you?"

"Intuition working on sense data," Martin said.

"Intuition, telepathy, extrasensory perception—mayn't they be three different theoretical labels for the working of the human spirit in everyday life, the contact between man and man which is a lower term of the contact between man and God?"

Martin Turner shook his head, smiling. "You're not going to convince me that I see auras."

"If you don't, lots of people do, without realizing it," Mills said. "Looking blue, seeing red, being in a brown study, being in the pink, giving someone a black look, turning green with envy . . . aren't those 'aural' metaphors?"

It was an argument which I had heard before. "That doesn't work out, if you study what 'sensitives' say about auras," I said. "Their color ranges mean quite different things to each of them—and none of them correspond to the popular emotional-color metaphors."

Mills laughed disconcertingly. "I know. I was trying to shake Martin's complacency. I'm not really sure about auras, except that some people see them. Percy does, but of course it may just be a sort of 'color feeling'—which you'd get with someone without the intellectual equipment to analyze emotions or states of mind."

"I hope you haven't talked like this to Yarborough," Martin said.

"But of course I have," answered the Archdeacon. "I wouldn't have anything to do with this sort of thing without the Bishop's blessing. The Church is right to regard Spiritualism as a heresy which has arisen among those who have repudiated God and yet cling to the belief in an afterlife. But the Church isn't without blame. Either psychic phenomena are fraudulent, in which case they should be exposed; or they are genuine, in which case they should be studied, explored and, if God wills, explained."

My heart warmed to Mills. It was the first time I had met a priest who had any time for the paranormal. The business of a parish priest, the struggle to keep things going, the constant round of services, the visitation of the sick, the ravages of the death-watch beetle, the bickering of parishioners and recently the Christian Stewardship campaign keep him too busy to think about what is a minor problem in any one parish, though of considerable importance taken in aggregate. It needed an arch-deacon with a roving commission and more flexible duties to tackle it.

I told him that I intended to collect my three groups of objects (the footstool leg, the straps and the spurs; though I had been careful not to specify to him what they were) in three identical shoeboxes. I would have someone wrap and tie each box and a third person number them, 1, 2 and 3. I could not conceal their differences of weight without introducing counterweighting material which might prejudice the test. He was to place them all on a table and push them across to Smith, noticing as he did so the number on the wrapping. Smith could lay his hands on the top of each box, but might not place them at the sides in case he tested them for weight. Mills was not to open them; I would seal them with my signet ring; but he was to send them back unopened, together with a transcript as accurate as possible of what Percy said about each of them.

"Aren't you making rather a business of all this, Grantley? You know I'm not a Harry Price."

"Christopher Everness would have trusted Harry Price, as 'the great skeptic,' more than he would you," I said. "My job is to give him whatever the scientific facts may turn out to be. And he'll challenge your transcript, if he has half a chance."

Mills wrote a form of speedwriting, which he had used on other tests with Percy. But he proposed to employ the tape recorder, which they had just bought for recording cathedral services for the bedridden, provided that I would supply the tapes. "You must have a tape recorder for your work," he said.

The idea had never occurred to me, but I promised that I would get one, thinking that if I did so I would not have to render unto Caesar quite so much as he would have taken otherwise because it would be useful for timing my broadcasts and for recording interviews.

And at that point the Archdeacon rose declaring he would be late for Guildford unless he started at once. "By the way," he said, "I shan't be able to see Percy for some weeks, because I have a rather unpleasant assignment in Italy. But I'll write you as soon as I'm back."

It was three weeks to the summer holidays and Nieves planned to move in a week before they started even if the house was not finished. I had hoped to present my report to the Evernesses before then. It would be so much easier to have the place exorcized before they took occupation. But Mills brushed my fears on one side. "The old lady seems to have lived there for years without coming to any harm," he said. "You've only to advise them to shut that room up for the time being."

"And if I do, Kit will make it his own bedroom."

Mills exploded with laughter. "Couldn't be better. And even if you get the tapes before then, don't produce them until they're really needed."

I found it impossible to induce any shopkeeper to part with his shoeboxes. They are used apparently year after year until they are worn out. But from the stationer's, I bought three identical boxes, each of which I wrapped in new brown paper in exactly the same way and tied up with white string carefully using the same number of knots. I left them on the table in the hall and the next time Magda came to visit me, I asked Mrs. Ambrose in my absence to shuffle them around in any way she wanted.

She looked at me curiously. "Are you feeling quite well, Mr. George?"

"Of course. I've never felt better."

"And supposing I don't want to shuffle them around in any way?"

I realized that she thought I was going crazy. "It's just an experiment," I said. "Somebody says he can guess what's in these boxes. I want Madame Kovacs to number them when she comes this afternoon. But if I knew what was in each box and what number she had put on, then this man might be able to find out by reading my mind."

"Couldn't she move them around?" Mrs. Ambrose asked.

"I'm going to ask her to do that, before she writes the numbers, as a further precaution."

"I should've thought you were too old for parlor games like that," Mrs. Ambrose said. "You're growing rather queer these days. I don't know what's happening with all your new friends, Mr. George. Really I don't."

But she agreed to do it and that afternoon we dispatched the three boxes in a large parcel to Yarborough. As packing inside the boxes, I had used plain crumpled typing paper and both Magda and I had worn gloves throughout the operation. I felt that it was too much to ask Mrs. Ambrose to put on gloves and since she did not understand what the experiment was about, she could hardly create any interference.

It wasn't until we were back at The Chantry that I realized that Magda was against me. I had been telling her of the analysts' reports on the grease on the spurs. It was mutton fat, both agreed. About the age they were less certain. There were so many different factors, such as comparative heat and cold. One said "not less than 25 years, nor more than 60." The other said, "I should say this was mutton and not lamb fat. I guess 1915–18, but that is based on the greater likelihood of there being mutton fat at that time. Might be as early as 1905, or as late as 1928. An admixture of iron filings, rust and various vegetable and mineral dusts."

This proved to my satisfaction that it was Charles who had found the spurs, freed the rowels and smeared them with mutton fat to prevent their rusting up again. I suspected that he had found them after I had gone for my summer holiday to Deal. I was sure that otherwise he would have shown them to me.

I had expected that Magda would be as excited by my discovery as I was. But though she did not interrupt, I could feel her impatience beating up at me like the heat of a radiator. As we got out of the car, I said, "I'm sorry. What have I done wrong?"

She did not answer. She ignored my outstretched hand and began to walk toward the house and when she heard me following, she broke into a run. "Magda! Magda darling!" I called.

"Go away! Let me alone!" She made for the house as if it was a sanctuary.

I followed, my heart torn with uncertainties and fear. I had done something wrong, but I had no idea what it was. I did not want to catch her up until my mistake was clearer to me, but I was afraid to lose sight of her in case she might disappear from my life in one of those capricious fits of hers.

As I reached the hall, she was running up the stairs. I saw her face, looking agonizedly down at me as if I were what she was fleeing from. Till that moment I had taken a complacent pleasure in her company; I enjoyed, I delighted in, being with her. But it was not till I saw the possibility of that pleasure turning to something negative—indifference, antagonism, even enmity—that I realized I was in love, that after having for so many years resigned myself to the acceptance of lovelessness, an emotional frigidity which I could not try to thaw without doing violence to my nature, I was at last most agonizingly ensnared.

Who she was, what she was, what sort of life we would give one another, I did not care. As she ran up the stairs, weeping, I knew only that whatever chance on earth I had of male fulfillment lay with Magda. And I was terrified. I had been snug so long, cushioned against the buffets of life. I was almost as frightened of the possible heights of ecstasy as of the abysses of despair.

Old Frisk came out from the kitchen begging for her meal. I went back and fed her, and looked at her litter in the basket. Rosa had loved the puppies and I thought how nice it would be to give her one of the bitches in return for the bitch that Helen Scarlet had given me when I was about Rosa's age.

I didn't want to go up. I wanted to put it off. I was afraid. I felt

I was going mad. To imagine that Magda could possibly want to marry me was lunacy; and it was equal lunacy to imagine that if she did, I could make her happy. I did not want to be put in the position of being either rejected or caught. That was the point we had reached, the showdown I had been trying to postpone.

If only I could induce her to come down, I might delay it a little longer; and though the suspense was intolerable, I felt its resolution either way would be even worse. I tried to will her to come down; but I was even more conscious of her willing me to come up. I refused. I played with the puppies, trying their teeth with bone-shaped biscuits.

Then I suddenly felt that Magda's despair with life might make her want to kill herself and I stood up so quickly that Frisk scuttered away from her bowl in fright. I ran to the stairs. "Magda!" I called, "Magda darling!" I had thought that while she was upstairs she could not escape me, because I had forgotten the other way out. She did not answer. I ran up the stairs two at a time. Before I reached the room, I could see the scene, wrists cut, the dark blood welling out.

I flung open the door. She was lying on the bed, her face sunk on the pillow, her black hair splayed across it. I had not realized how small her body was. "Magda!" I knelt down beside the little bed. Her face buried deeper into the pillow. "Please, please, my darling!" She turned her head away. I kissed her hair and stroked it, trying to make contact. But she was drawn away from me into some inner world of grief. "I love you," I said, "I love you. But you could not possibly love me. And yet I want to marry you. Could you? Could you bear to have my children?"

Her hand grasped mine and held it tight.

"I've never loved anyone in my life like you," I said.

She muttered something into the pillow and was shaken with sorrow. I could not hear what she said. I bent forward and whispered into her ear, "You are my heart's delight, the light of my life. Could you marry me, Magda?"

"Your friend's cook!" she said.

"The person I've been waiting for these thirty years," I whispered.

She turned her face round and I was looking into the eyes of a suspicious stranger. She put her hand out and stroked my cheek. She ran her fingernail down my nose, along my lips. "My darling George!" she said. "You know I love you. From that Sunday. Lie beside me. Dearest, lie beside me."

And I lay beside her and kissed her and explored the wonder of her body and I could feel my passion rising as strong as ever and hers straining toward mine, sweeping in from her pelvis. And her mouth and my mouth sought one another more hungrily and she became wide-open to my will. I could do with her what I liked. And then I suddenly understood the biological purpose behind all this, in its own way as calculated and instinctual as Helen Scarlet's need for financial and emotional security. And I went dead.

"Oh, please, please," she said, "please finish it."

But though I wanted as much as, perhaps more than, she did, I could not do it. In a sense she might be right to want premarital assurance of my potency, but my spirit rebelled. Marriage is a sacrament, which is desecrated by such lack of faith. "Do you want me as a husband," I asked, "or as the father of your children?"

"I want . . . I want . . . oh God! I want!" She pressed toward me, trying to kindle what she thought my coldness.

I pushed her away, holding her by the shoulders, looking her straight in the eyes. "Listen, my love. I can give you babies. All you can bear. I know that. But not before marriage. You've got to take me, you understand. Me for myself. In sacramental marriage. Not a stud animal."

I was shouting. I could see the violence of my emotion reflected in the change in her expression. "You know?"

I nodded.

"Oh, my God!" she said, bursting out laughing. "My God!" I thought she would never stop laughing. But at last she looked at me. "You got a bastard?"

"I said I had no child I could call my own," I said.

"The English phlegm!" Once again she went off into a fit of laughter. "And with this bastard, you still want to marry this 'bloody foreigner,' dearest George?"

"If you will take this bloody, balding bachelor."

"Why? Tell me why?"

And so at great length—indeed for the rest of the afternoon—I told her why I wished to take her to my wedded wife, to have and to hold, for better for worse, for richer for poorer, in sickness and in health, to love and to cherish till death did us part, according to God's holy ordinance.

Before she left that evening, we went round to ask Martin Turner to put up the banns. There was one thing on which she was adamant; she must leave the Everness household before they moved into Anglesey House. She rightly foresaw the possibilities of ugly gossip and we talked about the advisability of special licenses or being married at her church in London. I persuaded her to wait a day or two. Kit and Nieves regarded her not as their cook but as a friend; and sure enough, that very evening they rang up to congratulate me and to say that Magda had agreed to let them hold the wedding reception at Anglesey House. A new cook had already been found, a Cape colored refugee, whose husband would do the garden when he wasn't editing his monthly propaganda sheet.

I had expected from Kit some heavy badinage, but both he and Nieves sounded genuinely delighted. I asked him as tactfully as I could how Magda was placed for money, what Nieves thought she would need for clothes and other expenses. But he brushed my inquiries aside. "Don't worry your head about that," he said, "it's already taken care of."

I found later that Kit's first reaction on hearing Magda's announcement was to fling his arms round her and give her a hearty kiss; the second was to retire to his study and come out five minutes later with a document for her to sign. It was a receipt for £250 as compensation for dismissal without notice. "You know I'm mean," he said, "I never make a gift if it is possible to claim it as legitimate expenses."

I thought it was typical of the man who had haggled so deviously with John Scarlet. I did not realize until later that the receipt was not for presentation to his accountant. Kit knew that Magda would never have accepted so large a sum as an outright gift.

15

A RUM TAPE

This is not the story of my marriage, though I have not been able to exclude it entirely, because as Father Martin pointed out it formed part of the large design deployed through the Scarlet boy. I had thought of myself at the outset—and indeed for years before—as the disinterested spectator, who for that reason saw more of the game.

I discovered the moment that my engagement was known—and it was through Wilchester by bush telegraph within twenty-four hours—that I had been regarded for years by my fellow Wilcastrians as an eccentric recluse and not—as I regarded myself—the one balanced and objective man in a curiously distorted community. People with whom I had been on nodding acquaintance for years accosted me in the street—as they had done previously after my single disastrous appearance on television—and wrung me by the hand as if I were a leper released at last from lifelong residence in a leprosarium—or, a more grisly thought, like lepers welcoming me at last to their community. Husbands and wives whom I had always regarded as peculiarly ill-matched congratulated me on having realized that the purgatory of marriage was better than the hell of loneliness.

I had never felt lonely, though I had come to feel sere and unfulfilled. Magda restored my innocence, made me young again, refreshed each minute of each hour. I was, if the metaphor may be forgiven, like the driver of a hearse who having crept at funereal speed through the limits of the city reaches the open country and belts along full speed toward the crematorium.

These dreary men and women, my contemporaries with

nothing to look forward to except their golden weddings, saw in me a chance to exercise their matrimonial wisdom. As they had endured the diaper years, looking no doubt with envy on me, they took pity on me with what I found an irritating complacence. "You may find," said one, "romping is rather exhausting, at your age. But then your wife is younger, isn't she?"

Cousin Harry wrote from the Midlands to say that he had seen it coming. "I knew you were both 'round the corner' and I suspected it was round the same corner." He added, "It seems there's rather a glut in nonferrous. But I ran into a bod in the Feathers here—which has the best draught Bass for miles around—and confidentially he has something cooking in Karachi. So Ishmael may be off again."

I found old Newman-Turner most sympathetic. He and his wife Hedda were two of the few guests I chose to invite who were not Christians. "You know, George," he said, "considering that God Almighty only had one of Adam's ribs to work on, He made a wonderful job. Of course there are lots of bits missing. But when you think of the materials, it's marvelous."

My whole life changed. I was going up to London to see Magda at Wessex Place, or Nieves or Kit. Magda, or Kit or Nieves or two of them or all were coming down to The Chantry. Mrs. Ambrose was in a fury. There was too much work. Her midday racing was upset. Our little gastronomic excursions together were ruined.

Mrs. Ambrose appeared red-eyed in the mornings. She snapped at me. She did not want any morning conferences, any post mortems on her efforts. Her standards lapsed. She ruined sweetbreads, which as well as being the most delicious of the offals, are also the most difficult to sabotage. She became aggressive, moody and destructive. She had probably learned from her mother that the way to a man's heart was through his stomach and the shock of finding that this was not so was too much for her. I had sensed that something was not quite right by many little signs but I did not become fully aware of it until after a visit to London I presented her with a pound of squids which I had found in an enterprising fishmonger's. I was explaining to her the very simple method of making *Calamares en su Tinta,* when she picked the lot up and dropped them on the floor at my feet.

I looked at them. They didn't look nearly so delicious on the Marley tiles. Then I looked at Mrs. Ambrose.

"If they're as easy as all that, Mr. George," she said, "you can bloody well do 'em yourself!" Then she burst into tears.

I picked up the squids, the ink sacs of some of which had been injured by this violent treatment, and then I consoled Mrs. Ambrose, who when she stopped weeping admitted that the extra work of entertainment had been too great a strain on her.

I promised to get her "rough help" and found her a delightfully scatty woman called Mrs. Jelly, who, I thought, could be no challenge to Mrs. Ambrose. But Mrs. Jelly proved to be above herself. She was, said Mrs. Ambrose, "as common as dirt" but she didn't realize it. She was in fact the most engaging of simpletons, a cockney from Bermondsey, who had married into the great Jelly family which has spawned all over Surrey. She did everything wrong but in such an endearing way that one had to admit it was right so as to keep her happy.

Her husband kept turkeys and every morning she would bring me a turkey egg. "You'll need that, duck," she said, slipping it on the breakfast table in an International Stores bag. "Nothing like a turkey's egg to keep your cocker up."

At the end of the week when she received her wages, she produced a miniature bottle of gin. "You're going to have a lot of expense, love," she said, "so you'd better 'ave a drink on me."

Mrs. Ambrose was outraged. She said that Mrs. Jelly was inefficient and impertinent. Every morning Mrs. Jelly would arrive with her old oilcloth bag stuffed with things to cook, beet roots and rabbits and pigeons and lettuces. "We ain't got a fridge," she said, "it'd all go bad. Would you like an 'are? Jelly loves an 'are."

"Where do they *come* from, Mr. George?" Mrs. Ambrose asked. "I could never look Mrs. Grantley in the face if you come up on a charge of receiving stolen goods." It was her desperate fancy that somewhere beyond the grave she would be called by my mother to account for her stewardship of me. "Jelly's nothing but a poacher and they're trying to drag you in, you mark my words."

Mrs. Ambrose did not dare to attack Magda, but I knew that she was preparing to give notice using Mrs. Jelly as an excuse. It gave me a wonderful sense of relief. A few weeks before I would have regarded the loss of Mrs. Ambrose as a disaster. Now despite her cooking I was glad to see her go. Dear, inefficient but loving, earthy Mrs. Jelly was a symbol of the new life. I accepted Mrs. Ambrose's resignation with appropriate regret, gave her a present which agreeably surprised her and asked her if I might call on her in case of need. We both knew that I never should, but it eased the break of an odd relationship which had lasted many years.

There had to be a change. The kitchen and washroom, which had done for Mrs. Ambrose, had to be made over to Magda's liking. And we arranged for the changes to be made during our two weeks of honeymoon in Florence and Assisi.

It is no part of my purpose to describe our wedding or our honeymoon. The reception showed Kit at his most generous and charming and the honeymoon reassured Magda—and me after years of desuetude—of the vanity of her fears. That is, of course, a typical British understatement. A world of joy opened up, the more dazzling, because I had re-entered it so late. With Elizabeth X I had been dallying merely in the antechamber of Venus.

On the day we left Assisi, we received a letter from Nieves one paragraph of which struck our self-absorption. "I am glad you will be coming back soon. We like this house. But I am worried about Rosa. She will not play with the Rushmore girls. It is always Charles. Charles and Peter. All the time. But I never meet them. You know who they are, *Jorge mio?*"

This was the Tuesday morning. We were booked to go on the night train, but I immediately wanted to catch an earlier train, if we could. There were no reservations. I rang round all the agencies. It was the same story.

Magda lay on the bed. "You worry too much. Relax."

"We've just relaxed."

She held out her arms. "Relax again. It's good for you."

We relaxed again and it was very good. But all that day I was filled with guilt that my happiness had made me forget the dangers that might threaten Rosa Everness in our absence. The name Peter especially alarmed me and I kept praying that nothing would befall Rosa before we reached Wilchester.

By the second post arrived a letter forwarded from The Chantry. It was from Mills and was brief. It said:

DEAR GRANTLEY,

I have only just heard from Martin Turner of your marriage. I wrote him because I was surprised to receive from you no acknowledgment of the tape I sent you last week by registered post. I do not know how long you are going to be away; but I trust it will not be too long a honeymoon. This matter is urgent.

Yrs p.J.C.D.N.

AUGUSTINE MILLS

The moment we reached The Chantry, I telephoned Nieves. "Is everything all right?" I asked.

She replied in Spanish. "Everything is good," she said. "And it will be nice to see you."

I heard Rosa's voice in the background, "Mum-mee, who is that? Who're you talking to?"

"Bueno, a las seis y media?" Nieves asked.

I looked at the clock. It was six. I had hoped to play the tape through before she came round. But there was no time. *"A las seis y media."* My fantasy of evil had been all wrong. There were no ghostly hauntings, no elemental concentrations. Nieves had not sounded scared.

While Magda set herself to unpacking, I undid the tape and threaded it on the recorder. I am not a handy man, but I found it was extremely easy even for an ass like me. Then I opened the letter enclosed in the parcel.

DEAR GRANTLEY,

I think I ought to explain the circumstances of this session with Percy. It was the first time I have ever used a tape recorder myself and the first time Percy has worked to a microphone.

The session was held in my study, which is not a soundproof room; and foolishly I had taken no precautions to exclude extraneous sound. You will hear certain "noises off" during the reading of Object One, which will be intelligible only if you realize that my house is on a main road and there is a bus stop outside,

*that the downstairs toilet adjoins the rear of my study (I feel that
this might have been put more delicately!), that in the middle of
the reading of Object One my daughter put on the Eroica Symphony and toward the end Yarborough rang me about a matter
that brooked no delay.*

*These factors explain why you may have the impression at the
outset that you are listening to the sound track of a Marx Brothers
film. Listening to it bore in on me how insensitive I had become
over the years to the row invading my privacy.*

*The quality of the tape improves after the reading of Object
One. But I suspect that the most valuable material, if any is such,
is contained in that first hectic reading.*

*I shall be most interested to hear from you whether Percy has
been of any use. And if so, the degree of accuracy he has achieved.*

Yrs p.J.C.D.N.

AUGUSTINE MILLS

I tried the tape to find if it was running correctly and then
switched it back to the beginning, as I heard the doorbell ring.
I overshot the mark, and had to rethread, by which time Magda
had brought Nieves upstairs.

I had expected, though I don't know why, to see more visible
signs of anxiety or distress on her face and was almost disappointed that she should appear so calm. Apparently what worried them was that Rosa, normally a difficult child and constantly
demanding parental attention, had suddenly become extremely
docile. She was *too contented*. She resisted any suggestion that
other children should be asked round to play and when Nieves
had insisted that she accept an invitation to tea with the Rushmore girls she had made a display of temper which was so violent
that even Nieves was shocked. Yet left to herself she played con-
tentedly for hours in the garden, reluctant to come in to meals
and running off immediately they were over.

Nieves might have paid no attention, thankful for being given
the opportunity for painting the panels in her studio, if it had
not been for Kumari Ramratan, the Cape colored refugee who
said that on several occasions, mostly in the garden but also once
and twice in the house, she had heard Rosa talking. It was not,

she said, the conversation of a lonely child talking to herself. It seemed like one half of a real conversation, always she thought with the same person, somebody called Charles, though there was mention of somebody else called Peter whom Rosa wanted, but wasn't being allowed, to meet. Nieves said Mrs. Ramratan compared it to listening to one end of a telephone conversation, the other end of which was audible to Rosa but not to herself. The pauses were of that sort of length and Rosa made no attempt to impersonate the imaginary creature as children usually do with pretend playmates.

Even so Nieves had not paid much attention to Mrs. Ramratan until Kit had suddenly remembered that the Scarlet boy had been called Charles, or some name like that.

"I thought Kit did not believe in that sort of thing." I could not resist my dig at his rationalist connections. But Magda turned on me angrily. "He is Rosa's *father*." To her it was logical that a man should throw his beliefs overboard if he saw his child threatened. There was no inconsistency.

Kit, who arrived some ten minutes later, having caught an early train and found his wife was at The Chantry, was quite aware of the inconsistency. "I don't believe you," he said. "It runs contrary to all my experience and beliefs. But something's happening to Rosa which I can't explain—I don't know whether it's a bad thing, because she seems happy enough—but I'm willing to examine any working hypothesis."

"What about the Rational Truth Society?"

"B—— the Rational Truth Society," he said. "It's the truth part I'm interested in and if it isn't rational, then I want to find out what it is. What's your explanation, George?"

I told him I had no explanation, but I explained what Rushmore and I had found in the house, the intense concentration of coldness Magda and I had felt.

Nieves interrupted. "I felt this too. But not just in that room. All over the house and in the garden too, even when the sun is shining."

"You did?" Kit turned on her angrily. "Why in heaven's name didn't you tell me?"

"To make you laugh?" Nieves asked.

"But I've felt it myself. Only I took no notice. Thought it was imagination. Besides it's so small. I feel it with my hands but not my face."

"My God!" The exclamation slipped out and Kit immediately asked, "What, George?"

I wouldn't explain—at least not yet. They were receptive. It might antagonize them if I suggested that Kit stood head and shoulders above the Scarlet boy. Instead I told them about the analysis of the fat on the spurs and showed Kit the two reports. "I think it's a reasonable deduction that those spurs were found by a child sometime between 1900 and 1945," I said. "That child freed the rowel wheels, greased them and hid them away, perhaps because he felt rather furtive about the uses he made of them."

"All right," Kit said, "let's say it was the Scarlet boy, but where does that get you? We're not in a court of law, thank God."

"Maybe we aren't in a court of law," I answered, rather smugly, "but for my own satisfaction I don't like jumping to conclusions. I'll spare you the arguments why I think it must have been Charles who found the spurs. The point is that we have three objects, the leg of the stool which I believe Charles Scarlet stood on when he put the noose round his neck; a pair of spurs which Charles found and played with but which belonged to some child born over a century before . . ."

"Who is Peter, I suppose you'll say." Kit couldn't prevent the skepticism breaking through.

"*I* don't know," I answered. "That's your suggestion. All I know is that it must have been a child, because they are child's spurs. And finally there is a fragment of strap, which I suspect was the stirrup strap belonging to the spurs and which was so perished that I don't think Charles ever played with it—though he may have handled it." I intentionally went very deliberately. With his quick brain Kit presented me with the conclusions I wanted him to draw long before I had given him the evidence on which I based them. He was so used to manipulating people under cross examination that he did not suspect (or was it, care?) that he was being manipulated. "And so you are going to submit these objects to some professional psychometrist, who will present us with the solution?"

"I *have* submitted them to an amateur sensitive," I answered. "What the readings are, I don't know myself. They're on that tape. But before playing it, I want to explain the conditions under which the reading was made." I told him about the boxes, the numbering and showed him the Venerable Augustine Mills's letter.

"Augustine Mills," he said. "That rings a bell. Wasn't he in East Africa?"

I didn't know, but I described him physically.

"It's the same man," Kit said. "Very intelligent—within the limitation of his religious blinkers, I mean." (I found out later, as I suspected at the time, that this meant the Archdeacon as a Christian had said something of which Everness approved as a politician.) "He may grind slowly, but he grinds exceeding small, eh?" He paused waiting for me to grasp the pun on the Archdeacon's name. Then when I did not laugh, he suggested a drink.

"No! You drink too much! Wait. Listen." Nieves spoke with an authority which surprised me and Kit obeyed with a submission which surprised me even more. I realized that his marriage was a *terra incognita* not recorded on the charts of his public life—a thing which as a biographer I should have known all along. The secret of her power over him was that she was never impressed or overawed.

"Let's listen to this bloody tape then quickly," he said. "Start it up, George."

I arranged the numbered boxes on the table beside the recorder and switched the key on to Play. "Hello," Mills boomed. "This is just a test before Percy comes, so that you can adjust the volume. God knows whether he'll be able to manage the mike. The first box I am going to give him is the one marked Number Two. I think you had better open it now to see what it is. The second box I shall give him is the one marked Three and finally the one marked One. Remember Two, Three, One. I shall let the tape run for thirty seconds after this, because I shall start by testing Percy and I don't want him to hear any of this when I reverse for testing. Over."

I asked Kit to unwrap Box Number Two. It was the stirrup strap, the object which interested me least, because it was so remote that its psychic associations must surely be dissipated. "You found this under the roof?"

I nodded. "And as I was coming out, the cold thing passed me, going in." Could It, I wondered, possibly have been hurrying in to see what I had found?

Kit dropped it back into the box as if it were something rather grubby; and I put the lever back on to Play. After what seemed an interminable time, Mills said, "This little box here is the microphone. I don't want you to pay any attention to it after we have found the best place to put it. I'm going to try it on these books here and I just want you to say something." There was a pause, then Percy's voice said, "What am Oi going ter say, Mr. Mills? Oi doan like that tichy thing. Would it give me a shock if Oi touched en? Oi got nothin' ter say."

"Splendid," said the Archdeacon. "Now we'll run that through and you'll hear what it sounds like."

Almost immediately afterward, because the tape, of course, did not record their running it back and listening, came Percy's reaction. "I diden know I talked that broad. Diden sound loike me, not what Oi sounds to meself; and comin' out of that box, right back at yer, it's . . . it's loike it's mimickin'." Percy sounded ruffled as though his own voice had been making fun of him, but Mills smoothed him down with an explanation about the *objets* and not lifting them and not worrying to say anything if there wasn't anything to say. "They may be empty for all I know."

"Oh, no," said Percy, "I beg to differ, Mr. Mills. There's some-then' in thissere. Um. An's old. 'S real old. Um."

The quality of his voice changed. He was still talking as broad, but it became sleepy and slower and the background noise, because of the silences, became more insistent. "An' it's young, too. A boy. A long-ago boy!"

There was the clunk of a chain, the sound of rushing water followed by the inexorable filling of a cistern, through which it was possible only to hear fragments of what Percy was saying. We were all leaning forward over the table. Kit clicked it into neutral. "Run it through again, George. What did you get of that?"

I had caught something about "the ole devil" and what I thought was "Poppa trancing." Kit thought it was "proper trouncing." On the second run-through, I agreed with him. There was also a phrase which might be "this strap," but I pointed out it might also be "this trap." I wanted to arouse doubts before they occurred to the others. "What an ass Mills was not to tell people to use the other can!" Kit said.

There was a lucid interval in which we plainly heard, "Just for spite! The silly little fool. To kill himself for spite. As if that wasn't what the ole devil wanted!" Then there was the sound of squealing brakes, a car horn hooting and the noise of Mills pulling the curtains to cut out the street noise. The only phrase which emerged from this was "pore little bastard." It was as if Percy were watching something, as on a cinema screen, and all he could do was to comment on it. It was hard to visualize what he was seeing.

Mills seemed to realize this, because he broke in with the question. "Who is the boy? What is his name?"

"Ingleside!" said a voice, which must have come from Percy but bore no trace of his accent. "They call me Peter Ingleside. But it's his name; but he isn't my father and that's why he hates me. And her too. He hates—"

And then the Eroica Symphony swelled into a crescendo and Mills muttered, "Oh, my God!" And the little-boy voice went on half-drowned in the music, babbling about hate and Her and his Real Father. "Deborah! Deborah!" boomed the Archdeacon. "Turn that thing off! Please, turn it off at once!"

The music stopped. But immediately the telephone bell began to ring. It went on clanging and clanging with the little-boy voice faintly audible between the rings and then Mills's voice bellowed, "This is Yarborough 2256. Can you ring me back? Oh, it's you, Charles, forgive me." There was a click on the tape and then Mills's voice said, "I'm sorry, George. That was the Bishop and I had to switch off and by the time I'd finished, Percy had dried up. We shan't be interrupted again. I've told the exchange to hold all calls. I ought to have done all this before. In a moment, we shall be starting on the next *objet.*"

I switched off.

"My God! I hope Mills can run his church more efficiently than this sort of thing," Kit said. "I suppose you'll say that Ingleside was the nearest he could get to Anglesey."

"You open the next box," I said. I went over to the bookcase containing the run of the *Surrey Archaeological Society Quarterly*. I found what I wanted in the 1936 volume, an article I had written called "The Inglesides of Wilchester."

"This one's the footstool," Kit said, "what's left of it."

I marked the passage with my thumb nail and handed the book to him. He read aloud. "The name of Anglesey, common today in Wilchester, Chipstow and Sodbury, seems in the course of time to have gone through a series of different spellings. Though finalized as Anglesey in the second half of the eighteenth century, perhaps as a result of the desire to associate themselves with Brigadier Thomas Anglesey who distinguished himself under General Wolfe scaling the Heights of Abraham, one finds in previous documents members of the family subscribing themselves variously as Englesey, Inglesey and in the seventeenth century more commonly as Ingleside or Engleside. What is now known as Anglesey House in Market Street, Wilchester, was until 1726 described as Ingleside House and thereafter appears as Angelside. Englesea and even Inglesey according to the caprice or literacy of the rating clerks continued until the year 1810, when its name was finalized."

I had completely forgotten this little piece of research completed nearly a quarter of a century ago. Though it was, I suppose, possible for Percy Smith to have fished it out of the pigeonhole where it lay forgotten in my memory, it certainly had not been transmitted consciously by me. Kit looked shaken. "Do you know anything about an illegitimate child called Peter or a suicide?"

"I can't remember anything," I said, "but if I ever discovered a thing like that, it would either be in that article or in my notes, up in the tower room. I'll check them through sometime."

The second reading was uninterrupted and far easier to hear, but to me it was disappointing, because I had hoped it would contain the clue to what had happened to Charles on that last fatal night. Percy spoke throughout in his own voice, but more slowly than usual and with a greater license than he would have allowed himself in front of the Archdeacon, had he been in full control. After Mills told him to place his hands on the parcel and to remember not to lift it, there was a silence which lasted for thirty-six seconds. Then Percy said, "It's a bitta wood . . . a bitta wood, carved. Parta somethin'. A woman liked it. An' ailin' woman. Little dumpy thing she is, sittin' by the fire wi' a rug round 'er legs. Got 'er feet on it. Stool's what it is, 'cos 'er legs is so short. An' this geezer! Cor, what a flamin' face. Cheeks like bloody rump steak! Warmin' 'is arse in front of that ruddy great fire! An' she cryin' 'er eyes out."

Mills explained at the end of the tape that he had asked Percy if he could explain what he saw, instead of just commenting on it, as he had done in the first reading and this seemed to carry over into the reading. It was as if he were looking through a window at the scene and describing it to us, who couldn't see. "Laidly little thing, she is. Doan' care a tinker's cuss for 'er, 'e doan'. An' she know it. Stands there warmin' 'is arse and waitin'. 'When you turn yer toes up, laidly old bitch,' 'e's thinkin', 'there's a warm piece waitin' to lay in your bed.' "

After a silence of over a minute, Mills said, "That seems all there is coming through from that, so we'll try the last packet." Kit switched off and said. "For God's sake, let's have a drink, all of us."

As Magda fetched the glasses, Kit said, "Where does that get us? Precisely nowhere."

"It convinces me that Percy really has a gift," I said. "I thought it was the footstool Charles stood on—and maybe it was. But it was Miriam Scarlet's footstool, Albert's first wife's. She was the person it was really associated with. And Percy picked up what I can imagine was the most important moment at the end of her life when she realized that Albert was only waiting for her to die before he started courting her friend Helen Kent. It would explain why she willed all her money to her children after Albert's death instead of leaving it to him absolutely."

"That would be to avoid death duties."

"Not in those days."

Magda brought the Pimm's No. 1 Cup, which I had not touched since Kit brought it that Sunday. As I made them each a drink, Nieves said, "He has a gift, this man, I think. But what of Rosa? Does it help? I don't see."

Nor, for the love of God, did I. Yet, we were getting somewhere. Whatever else Percy might be doing, he was teaching us a common language. A fortnight ago, it would have been impossible for us to listen to this fantastic tape and try to disentangle what was significant from the flushing of a lavatory and the hooting of a horn.

"My dearest spouse," said Kit, his forensic flow restored by a deep draught of Pimm's, "we are like keen amateur photographers poised over the hypo bath—or whatever keen photographers poise themselves over—watching the development of some very old film on which the emulsion has run. A pattern is beginning to emerge. What it is, is not yet plain. There must follow—correct me, if I am wrong in my dark-room discipline, George—the fixing and the positive printing, with no doubt here a masking and there an enlargement, before we can be in the position to know—if then—what the bloody hell it's all about."

I switched the recorder on to Play. Mills's voice said, "You were much better that last time describing what you saw."

"Oi do 'ope thissun be aloive, Mr. Mills," Percy said. "Oi doan loike that dead stuff. It gives me the creeps."

"Why?"

" 'Cos it's loike a stink. It wears off."

"A stink?"

"This lot was a stink. Like a muck 'eap. But not now. Not any more, much." There was a change perceptible in his voice. "Except kids. All this stuff is kids." Suddenly, like a wireless set warming up his voice zoomed into full volume. "Aye, it's all mucking kids and Oi doan loike un. Up to no good and mucking kids up to no good is bad. I doan want this, I doan want it. Keep away, you bleedin' devils. Tell 'em, Reverend, tell 'em to KEEP AWAY."

"*Retro me, Satanum.*" I could hear Mills muttering, "In the name of the Father and the Son and the Holy Ghost, good Lord deliver us, good Lord deliver us!" And, though it may have been my imagination, I could feel the easing of the burden of evil which we had gradually been laying on the shoulders of that sensitive bricklayer.

"Thank God you done that, Mr. Mills," Percy said. "They was after me proper."

"It's all right, Percy," the Archdeacon said. "There's nothing to worry about any longer. I want to thank you, because there's somebody who may be in great danger."

"I know that," Percy said. "But doan ask me ter do this again for 'er or anyone else. See. I won't do it, Mr. Mills." There was real fear in the man's voice. He was panting, almost whimpering. There was the click of Mills switching off and Kit snapped the lever into neutral.

"He knew it was a girl, it was Rosa."

"You don't *know* that, Kit," I said. "You wouldn't take that as evidence in court."

"Don't be a child, George," Kit said. "The presentation of evidence in the court is rehearsed as elaborately as a play. This is the real thing." He ran it through a second time. "You see, he said 'for 'er.' He knew it was a girl."

"A female."

"Oh, for God's sake!" Kit took his glass over and poured himself out another Pimm's. "I go all the way with you and then you call me back. What *do* you want?"

"God alone knows," I said.

Then the telephone rang. Magda answered it. "It's Kumari, Nieves." She held the receiver toward her. "Something's happened to Rosa."

16

FELO-DE-SE

Kit pushed his wife on one side and took the receiver. "What's happened, Kumari? Is she hurt? . . . But she can't have 'disappeared.' Even if her bicycle is there, she could have gone for a walk. She could have gone to see the Rushmore children. . . . No, don't ring the police. My wife and I will come round straightaway." He put down the receiver. "Rosa has 'disappeared,'" he announced, putting into the last word a skepticism to hide his anxiety. "Kumari and her husband have searched everywhere, but there's no sign of her." He finished his drink at a gulp.

"Shall we come too?" asked Magda.

"Of course not. Rosa doesn't like the Ramratans. She's probably piqued at being left alone with them." He opened the door for Nieves and followed behind her. "She's probably hidden herself to give us all a scare. Or she's gone out for a walk. Did you tell her not to go out by herself without telling someone, Nieves?"

"She knows that."

"That daughter of yours knows nothing, unless you tell her. And even then she forgets five minutes later."

I knew that he would refuse any offer of help at the moment because it would admit that the situation might be as serious as he secretly feared. So I told him to let us know what happened and if they needed either of us, we would come round immediately.

As we went back into the house, I put my arm round Magda. "Can you believe there are people drinking Campari in the piazza at Assisi, my heart?"

She squeezed my hand. "It's like another life," she said. "Perhaps we should not have gone away. I am afraid for Rosa."

I was not afraid. I did not see what intricate purposes were being pursued. But in what had happened so far there was already so much evidence of design that it was little tax on faith to trust in future revelation.

Over a simple supper, we could talk of nothing else but the Evernesses and the tape. I told Magda of my suspicion that what I had hitherto thought of as "the cold elemental" might have the shape of a little boy, either Peter Ingleside or Charles Scarlet. She nodded. "I have thought the same, but to Kit it was right to say nothing." Then she added, "This I do not understand. We feel this coldness. But Rosa is different. She sees Charles. She talks and plays with him. Why?"

I did not answer. I was thinking that what was wrong with Rosa was that she was, in popular parlance, "not all there" or more precisely not all *here*. It wasn't surprising. The Evernesses had dragged her around the world. They had never stayed long enough in any place for her to take root. Instead of friends, she knew only acquaintances in hotel lounges or schoolgirls whose engrossments with one another made her separateness sharper. She needed some attachment to this world if she was to be diverted from the world of Charles and Peter. If we gave her one of Frisk's puppies, it might keep her amused until after the exorcism.

That I should think "after the exorcism" shows how far we had progressed how fast. I had been puzzling how to persuade the Evernesses to try exorcism, but now they were so alarmed I knew they would try anything. Whether it would work was another matter. I had heard more accounts of failures than of successes and most disconcerting of all, the half-success of a priest who exorcised a poltergeist from a house only to take it back to his vicarage from which he could induce no other priest to exorcise it. I did not like to think of Martin Turner being saddled with Charles and Peter for life.

We were both waiting for the telephone to ring. We were too restless to settle to anything in this our first night home together. After we had finished washing up, Magda suggested that we should ring Nieves to find out what had happened. But I disagreed. If and when the Evernesses had news, they would call us. If we wanted an excuse to see what was happening we could easily take one of Frisk's puppies down later in the evening. But first I wanted to see whether I had any material on Peter Ingleside in my Anglesey file.

I took Magda up to the tower room. She had said that she would like to help me with my research work and it was a chance of showing her my system of filing and indexing, which was almost as thorough as Harry Waybridge's Doomsday Book.

But Magda was far too unsettled to take it in. With the door open she was listening for the telephone. So when I had found the Anglesey box, I told her to go down and I would join her as soon as I had looked through the envelopes to see whether there were any which might contain relevant material.

The difficulty for the research worker is to remember the wealth of material which he needs to collect for the preparation of even a short article. For the time of writing it remains in mental suspension borne up by the play of imagination; but how soon afterward it all collapses into a heap of paper! It was many years since I had worked on the Angleseys; and indeed I should never have done so if Helen Scarlet had not passed over to me the papers which were in her possession. I had returned them later because of the outcry which John Scarlet had raised, not because he was interested in them himself but because he resented anyone making something public from his private family papers. Anything which might be of interest, however, I had photostated before I passed the papers back.

As I fingered the envelopes which were arranged partly chronologically under the different heads of families and partly under general headings, such as "Anglesey House, Family Tree," I tried to think what might give me a clue to Peter.

There was no overt reference to any suicide in these papers. Of that I was convinced. It was not something which I could possibly have overlooked. But of course it was not a subject that in most families is bandied about. Silence proved nothing.

I opened the family tree envelope, a large one containing on folded paper the tree I had compiled and enclosed in a rubber band the documents on which I had based it. I unfolded the tree on the desk, feeling, I must confess, a certain thrill of pride at the neatness and thoroughness of my work. As my father was never tired of saying, "A thing worth doing is worth doing well," and I had done this thing so well (drawing green lines under the names of those who died beneath the age of twenty-one) that it was the matter of a moment to discover that the eldest son of William Ingleside, born May 7, 1698, was named Peter and had died on August 18, 1709.

The date in August may have been sheer coincidence. The eighteenth was the day when Charles Scarlet hanged himself. I don't believe in astrology. But it was odd, odd enough for me to consult the photostat of the entries in the family Bible. And there was William Ingleside's handwriting, powerful though ill-formed, white script on black paper in the photostat, with the heavy entry underlined "F.D.S. Aug. 23," after the date of death, August 18. I remembered having been just vaguely puzzled by this entry when I read it years before. But when one is writing the history of a family, there are so many deaths of the young that one is not curious.

Now I suddenly felt that thrill of contact which is the joy of research. I could see William Ingleside's writing on August 19, the date of his son's death the day before. It was shaky, perhaps with grief, or just shock, or even fear. But when he wrote *"F.D.S. Aug. 23,"* it was bold, assured, vindicated. I could see what had happened. The boy had killed himself. There had been an inquest. And the verdict was *felo-de-se.* Suicide. The father was exonerated; or rather the putative father, if Percy was right.

I looked at the date of William's marriage. I could have kicked myself for my insensitivity in the first place. I hadn't done my work well, only neatly. William Ingleside had underlined the date on which he married Harriet Squelch, *September 27, 1697.* And he had also underlined at the same time the date of Peter's birth. There was the same savage stroke under each, of a man who had discovered that he had fathered a bastard.

It looked as if Percy Smith had been right—or Peter through the medium of Percy—but William Ingleside had through love or hate driven Harriet overhard. After Peter, she had borne eight children (only three of whom survived) before her death three months after Peter. It was, if ever there was one, a case of murder by childbirth. Within two months, William had married again.

I know that in these matters there is no possibility of mathematical proof; but there was certainly a balance of probability in favor of Percy's psychometric reading being right.

I didn't know what it meant then—I'm not even certain that I know now—but I was sure that the two child suicides were in active conspiracy to induce Rosa to join them in whatever child hell is reserved for prepubertal self-destructors.

I put the photostats back in the envelope and folded up the family tree. I ran down the stairs. "Magda!" I called. "Magda! I've found it. Percy was right about Peter Ingleside."

She was waiting for me on the landing. She had discovered something too and was on her way up to see me.

Then the telephone shrilled. She turned and ran back into the sitting room. The standard lamp was on by the Danziger desk. It threw the twilight into darkness. I could hear the voice—it was Nieves—but not what she said.

"No, of course, she hasn't come here," Magda said. "We would have called." She cupped her hand over the mouthpiece. "They want to call in the police."

I took the receiver from her. "Don't call the police, Nieves," I said. "This is something they don't know anything about. It won't get you anywhere."

I heard the noise of squabbling and then Kit came on the line. "What the hell are we to do then?" he asked. "She's gone, man. She's disappeared. God knows where she is."

"I've found out something," I said. "There was a Peter Ingleside. And he was a bastard. And he killed himself, when he was eleven years old. In 1709."

"You fool!" He was shouting. "What do I care who killed themselves in 1709! Where's Rosa?" He waited for me to answer. "Where is she? Tell me that!"

"I don't know," I said. "Give us time. For God's sake, give us time."

"We've got no time to give you," he said. "What's happened to her? Where on earth can she be? You got us in this mess. Where is she, man?"

The accusation was so grossly unfair that I didn't trouble to answer him. "Look, we'll come round right away. Don't do anything till we arrive. Four brains are better than two."

"We've searched everywhere," he said. "What can you do? She isn't here."

"Don't worry. It's going to be all right. I know it's going to be all right, Kit."

"How d'you know?"

How could I answer that? I knew because we were all puppets in a drama designed by God Almighty. But I couldn't say that to Kit. It would only convince him I was dotty. And perhaps I was. The borderland between religious insight and hallucination was so ill-defined. "You must have faith."

"In what? You?"

"In God."

"Oh, Jesus Christ!" He slammed down the phone.

I looked at Magda. She was lovely in the light. What a homecoming! "We've got to go. I'll get one of the puppies in case."

She picked off the desk the watercolor which Rosa had made in the rose garden the first afternoon she came to The Chantry. "Look."

Suddenly I saw the picture for what it was, a faithful if crude picture of what the child had seen that afternoon. The old lady imposed upon the roses and surrounded by a strange light was not an afterthought for the sake of the composition, whose resemblance to my mother was fortuitous.

No, this was what Rosa had seen. This was what Miriam Schroeder had meant, when she said, "Has anybody ever suggested that The Chantry is haunted?" and Mrs. Ambrose meant, when she said my mother was still benignantly around. The odd quality which Nieves had detected in Rosa was not aesthetic. The child was simply clairvoyant.

"Rosa is like Percy," Magda said.

If Rosa is like Percy, I thought, then we are dealing with someone who is innocent, but with a very special gift which makes her peculiarly vulnerable to evil spirits.

"But Rosa isn't evil," Magda said. "She's lost, and lonely; but she isn't evil." What she said followed so completely on my thought that I looked at her. "Did I speak aloud just now?" I asked.

"No," she said. "But she isn't evil. She just sees. She sees your mother. She sees Charles. Anybody who's around."

The telephone rang again. I picked it up. "You haven't started," Kit said accusingly. "I thought I would miss you." His voice was thicker. Whatever he was drinking was beginning to take effect.

"We're just on our way. Has anything happened?"

"This is Nieves's idea. It may be nonsense. She said as you played here when you were a child, you might have ideas where a child would choose to hide." I knew he meant that as I played with Charles when he was alive, I might understand where Rosa might play with Charles dead. "I'll try to think," I agreed. "We were just going when you rang. We'll bring over one of the puppies. When we find Rosa, it will make her happy."

He laughed savagely. "How d'you know you'll find her?"

"How d'you know you'll win a case?"

"I don't, ever. Not till it's won."

Magda said, "I want to speak to Nieves."

When she got on to Nieves, Magda said, "Have you any paintings which Rosa has made? Since you went to Anglesey House. A lot? Can you find them? Good. We see you soon."

It was something I hadn't thought of. If Rosa painted what she saw, she had probably painted the clue to where she would be. But would she still be alive there?

As we drove round to Anglesey House, a new and frightening thought struck me. We had been considering that we were dealing with the spirits of two little boys who had killed themselves—to my mind forlorn little figures, children for whom the strains of life on earth had been too much. Could it be far worse than this? Had Peter Ingleside and the Scarlet boy been possessed by evil spirits who had gained dominion over their souls?

17

ABOVE THE ADULT WORLD

It was a horrible thought. I'd been imagining Charles as I knew him, vicious maybe but in spirit still a human child, lonely in limbo, seeking his release. And Peter Ingleside the same, a little boy obsessed with punishments and driven in his desire to escape from those of this earth into the long agony of those beyond. But this might be something of which I had read as happening only to the living, a case of "overshadowing." It had actually occurred once in my presence, when as an undergraduate I had visited Glastonbury with Michael Lessing, a young physicist.

We were walking in the ruins of the church, trying to speculate what had been the limits of the little wattle church built by the companions of St. Philip the Apostle in the first century A.D., perhaps the most ancient Christian church in England, when suddenly Michael's voice and subject changed. He began to talk with passion of the venerable Abbot Richard Whiting and his fight to prevent the dissolution of the Benedictine Abbey of St. Mary. "They quartered him," he said, "and there—" he pointed as if the buildings were still intact—"they fixed his head above the Abbey gate." It was not Michael's voice—much rougher and more robust. Nor, as I looked, was it the way Michael held himself. It was the manner of a bigger man, still blazing with anger as

172

if this incident had happened yesterday, not nearly four hundred years before.

And so he continued, talking of Whiting executed for "diverse and sundry treasons" consisting in the defense of the property consigned to his charge from the hands of greedy robbers, as if he had known and loved and venerated the Abbot personally.

It was the eeriest experience in my life, as if I had fallen through a pocket of time into the sixteenth century; and I walked beside him, not daring to speak but nodding my head from time to time.

Then as we came outside the walls, as suddenly as he had changed, Michael was himself again, except that his face was as gray as bleached oak, and he said, "My God!"

"What happened?" I waited. "What became of you?"

"I think I was 'overshadowed.'" Despite his German name, Michael was half-Welsh and more than half a visionary. "By a monk. He was all around me, George. I could feel his cassock brushing my legs." And then he looked at me very strangely. "Did I say something?"

I was so alarmed that I tried to make light of it. "You must remember."

"I remember that I was very angry and sad. Or *he* was, rather. But I don't know what it was all about."

I told him what he had said and he looked still more shaken and puzzled. "Who was Whiting?" he asked.

This was the only case of overshadowing I had ever had experience of. It remained something completely outside everyday reality and I have no theory which will explain it or explain it away. It was there like a great hole torn in the fabric of the commonplace through which anything might come. What that might be I had not the slightest idea. If a Benedictine monk of Glastonbury could remain earthbound nearly four hundred years in his agony of righteous indignation at the execution of his Abbot, by what powers of evil, humanly adult or demoniacally malign, might these suicidal children be overshadowed?

As I drove through Wilchester, I cursed myself for my complacency. I had thought of the whole thing as a divine drama through which I could ad-lib my way like an amateur. I realized that however desirable it might be to place upon God the burden of guidance, there were times when one must follow that guidance at the speed of lightning. Rosa was in terrible danger, a danger in which I had placed her through my sluggish confidence that God would do all the hard work.

I jumped the lights at the intersection by the Odeon cinema. It was dark now. There was no moon. But thank heaven it was not yet closing time for the pubs. The High Street was half-asleep. I hooted as some ass drew quickly away from the curb. I swung round and then branched right into Market Street.

I clutched Magda's hand. "Pray God, we're not too late."

"I pray," she said, "all the time. I am frighted, George."

I was "frighted" also, as I turned off the main street up the cut to Miss Spreckles' School of Equitation. If Magda felt it too, my instinct wasn't wrong.

We went in by the back way. Kumari Ramratan opened the door. "Good you come quick. It's bad—real bad."

"Where are they?"

"The studio. I show you."

But we pushed past, down the corridor and to the left into the garden wing. It was an extraordinary thing. Despite all Rushmore's efforts to change the spirit of the house by decoration, the house was still curiously the same—curiously chill on that warm summer evening.

And there was Nieves in the room which she had tried to convert to her studio, with all those personal pieces, the fragments of root which nature had fashioned into sculpture, her paintings, the Mexican masks. She and they and Rushmore had changed nothing—it was still the place I had known in Helen Scarlet's day—and what I thought was her cool atmosphere probably dated from long before that.

Kit had a full, dark glass of whisky in his hand. His head was lowered, his eyes bloodshot, like a bull in the ring softened up for the kill. "You've come."

I turned to Nieves. Like many emotional women, she was at her best in a crisis, cold-resolute and keen as Toledo steel. "No paintings," she said. "But on the walls of her bedroom, yes."

"That's a lie," Kit said. "They can't find them. There were dozens of them." He shot the accusations like mortar bombs out of the dugout of his intoxication. "They don't know. They don't *know.*"

Mrs. Ramratan had followed us into the studio. "There was a cardboard folder. Many, many drawings, crayons, paintings. But we can't see no place."

"I should have thought, Nieves," Kit said heavily, "that as Rosa's mother, you would—"

Nieves cut him short with a stream of Spanish, in which the word *"borracho"* was repeated frequently.

"Could I see the paintings on her bedroom walls?" I asked.

Nieves seized the opportunity gratefully. Things were bad enough without drunkenness and squabbling.

Going up the stairs, she grasped my arm. "It will be okay? *Jorge mio,* you believe that? Truly?"

"I pray it will."

"You know what?" she said. "I pray too. Me, the anticlerical of anticlericals, I pray."

She opened the door of Rosa's room. The walls had been rendered white a few weeks before, but already one side had been defaced with pastels, an abstract or rather symbolic composition consisting of an enormous tunnel, the mouth of which was brilliant with sunlight, with bright green grass and a puppy in the foreground crouched down looking into what might be a huge rabbit hole stretching away into deeper darkness. And then in the center a red glow such as flames might make reflected on the walls of the tunnel, but not seen directly because the fire itself was round a bend. As I went closer, I saw that on this red reflection, in a darker shade of red, were shadows such as might be cast by figures dancing before the fire between the flames and their reflection.

I thought, if a psychoanalyst was looking at this, he would immediately talk about the return-to-the-womb fantasy. But my mind went rather to the ultimate *reditus ad uterum,* suicide.

It gave me a terrifying vision of the state of the child's mind. That brilliant sunlit circumference did not matter. The only thing which was interesting was what lay round that bend in the tunnel, the reality of the shadows and reflected flames. It wasn't vicious; but it was fascinated. Curiosity was the chink in the armor of her innocence.

"What do you think?" Nieves asked.

I couldn't tell her. But she guessed.

"Will you go down again?" I said. I said this, because I had a feeling that I had a better chance of finding what should be done without her. But the moment she went, I felt a lowering of temperature, the so to speak thermometric shadow of a presence. And immediately I knew that we should look for Rosa's drawings not where Rosa might have been likely to hide them, but where Charles Scarlet would have done. I went through to the lumber room, that had once been Charles' bedroom and now was Kit's, and opened the cupboard where we had found the straps and spurs.

It was dark inside. I had no torch. But I heard a most curious sound—not animal, not loud. It was a sort of gentle dragging, pushing noise. I felt for my cigarette lighter. It must have taken me fifteen seconds to find it and all this time the pushing noise went on. It continued during the snap of the flint and for the briefest moment I saw the cardboard folder moving—not more than quarter of an inch maybe, but moving. And I held the lighter up to see whether it would start again.

It didn't. But a cold dank draft passed my head and hands and—though perhaps this was imagination—I sensed a sort of musty mausoleum odor. It made me shudder with cold and then it passed. The lighter was growing hot in my hands, but I held it close to the cardboard folder. A plasterboard flooring had been laid on the joists and on this flooring was a layer of dust which had driven up from under the eaves. In this dust I could trace a track about eight inches long made by the folder being moved away from the door of the cupboard toward the corner where it was most likely to lie unnoticed.

The folder had been shifted, from a human point of view an absurdly small distance. But what superhuman strength must be needed to move an object in another time!

I grabbed the folder and took it into the bedroom. There was no time to lose. Whoever they were, They knew what we were up to. And one of them was away and ahead of me. I opened the folder. And the first thing I saw was a pencil sketch of the tulip tree, looking from the ground up into the branches. I snapped my fingers. I knew I had it. This wasn't the tree as it was now. It was the tree as it had been when I was a boy and Helen had stopped beneath it with her young Australian lover and they had called up to Charles and me. There was The Crow's-Nest, there was the shadowy ladder dangling downward and there even was a little boy, as imperative as Charles, looking down and beckoning. He and the house and the ladder were surrounded with the same brilliant aural light which had surrounded my mother in the watercolor of the rose garden.

The door opened and I looked round. It was Magda. "I've got it. Quick. Look. She's in the tree house."

"But there *isn't* a tree house!" Magda said.

"I know. That's the danger. You'd better show these to Kit and Nieves while I go and get her."

Magda put the drawing in the folder. "No, George. No! If anyone shows them that, it's Rosa. Must be. Afterward."

She was right. I kissed her, holding her very close and thinking, "If there is an afterward." It depended how far down the tunnel she had traveled, whether I could catch her up and bring her back.

Magda suddenly realized some of the implications of what was happening. "Why can't *they* go? Kit and Nieves."

"She's running away from them," I said. "Besides Kit's tight."

"But the danger . . ."

"More for her than me." I gave her a last kiss. "I didn't marry you to make you a widow in a month. Have you got a torch?"

She had, of course, with all the other useful impedimenta in her bag. "But it isn't strong."

"It mustn't be strong." Calling someone back from another time, I thought, remembering the overshadowing of Michael Lessing, was a hazardous business, even on *terra firma*. Up a tree on a dark night with forces which might gain more power the more one's grasp on the present was relaxed, was a very delicate operation. The powerful beam of a torch shining upward might do the devils' job for them.

As I opened the door of the studio, I had a glimpse of them, Nieves bent over her drawing table, Kit in a deep armchair, studying a brief through his heavy horn-rimmed spectacles, both trying to find their anodyne in work. But it was pretense. Nieves stood up, brush in hand. Kit stripped off his spectacles. "Well," he said, "what do we do? Call the police?"

I could feel their antagonism. They were Rosa's parents; it was they who should know where she was. "I may be dotty, but I think I know what's happened," I said. "But it may take some *time* to bring her back."

"We come too?" asked Nieves.

I shook my head. "It's only in the garden."

"What the hell do you mean then?" Kit had laid his papers aside and was standing up. "About the time, I mean."

"It's time she's gone away in," I said. "I want to fetch her back alone. Magda knows. I don't think I'll fall down—on the job. Give me ten minutes . . . but don't all of you come charging out after then. Not unless I say so. It might be dangerous."

"Is this really necessary?" Kit was challenging me. He had bossed me all my life. Now he wasn't certain.

"It is." Though I wasn't certain now. "Rosa isn't far from *here,* but she's a long way from *now.*" I've had so many instances of personal prejudice masquerading as divine guidance.

As I opened the French windows and went into the garden, I knew that Nieves and Kit must think I was insane. So did I, in one part of myself. Yet it was the only possible explanation of what had happened, so far as I could see.

I closed the windows behind me. Magda pulled the curtain close, as I had told her. I stood a moment readjusting my eyes to the summer darkness. The sweet scent of the nightstock beneath the studio windows beat up overpoweringly in my nostrils, recalling the evenings in the falling light when Helen and I had walked together in this garden, taking an almost ecstatic pleasure in the mindlessness of our adoration of the assault upon our mutual senses, the passion of the dying sun, the incense of the flowers and the pure notes of the nightingale, as scruffy as a chorister, pouring his soul out in the still twilight.

Now it was too late for nightingales. But somewhere a barn owl was hooting, among the trees and roofs and television aerials stenciled against the electric-blue sky.

My eyes became accustomed to the darkness. Just behind me was the studio. What were they doing now? Magda trying to draw Kit and Nieves together to explain—explain what? Something which none of us understood. Now myself least of all.

This garden, heavy with nightstock, was not the beautiful place I had fancied it. Evil hung over it like a leaden dome. The last sun died in the sky and the massed trees confronted me like a solid wall. I suppose it must have been that I had stood there long enough for the restless animal night life to be reassured and begin to move again in the relentless traffic of the dark. The bats turned and wheeled and there was a tiny squeal. A creature, very small, was dead. I felt an impact on my cheek and something began to walk up my face. I clutched it and felt the lovely wings of a moth and the sadness of its death in the mess on my palm.

I blundered up the garden. They were mustering the total forces, natural and supernatural—and the fifth column in the heart, the cohorts of childish fears. I flashed on the light of Magda's torch. It was dim, but as I felt my way forward, I could hear the rats plunging through the deep weeds. They did not seem to be running away as rats should. They were more like ferrets in their lack of fear. I tripped on something and almost fell. It was a bar of old gas pipe and I picked it up as a weapon. I loathe rats; they stand in my unconscious for all that is foul and bestial. I tried to kill one, crouched at the head of the steps before me, teeth bared. But it side-jumped into the weeds.

Nieves and Ramratan had cleared a sort of rough path round the garden—very rough. (There was a whacking great bramble still trailing across like a trip wire.) But after clearing the path, they had concentrated on the lower terraces—folly of course, because the docks, nettles, dandelions and loosestrife were seeding faster than they cleared.

I saw there was a path trodden down—not cut—to the base of the tulip tree and there was a glint in the torchlight. Lying almost hidden in the high weeds was the aluminum ladder which Nieves had bought so that Ramratan could pick the fruit in the overgrown trees. I saw what had happened—at least in a material sense. Rosa had taken the ladder, which was ridiculously light. She'd extended it and climbed up to the first fork of branches—as I had climbed to the tree house forty years before up the rope ladder—and when she reached there, the aluminum ladder had slipped and fallen in the weeds.

I looked up. I took my bifocals off, because with them I can't see precisely more than eight feet. But I realized that my longer sight was worse than I thought. I could not see silhouetted against the dark blue sky anything which was certainly a child. The trunk, the branches and the foliage were too dense.

"Ros-a," I called softly. "Ros-a."

Then I listened. I could hear the traffic of motorcars, some damn-fool motorcyclist without a silencer, the hoot of an owl close by.

Perhaps she did not hear me. I called again louder. Twice. Then from the direction of Belgium came in a passenger plane, its engines throbbing like a festering thorn prick. As it flew over, I saw the lights, the winking safety lights. (What were they doing up there—the commercial traveler, who had been promoted to sales representative, drinking double whiskies on his expense account, lord of the air till he landed and went back to his suburban house in Jellicoe Drive; the wife, in pursuit of her husband? or her lover? They were safer than Rosa, the truant from bed, fleeing into another age.)

There was no answer to my calling. I could expect none. Though only forty yards from home, she was as many years away. And she had betrayed herself. The secret was out. Things would never be the same again between herself and her parents.

The noise of the plane died away. It was on the outskirts of London by now, the green and amber lights of suburbs displayed below like Woolworth necklaces.

I called sharply, "Rosa!" I propped the ladder against the tulip tree. "*Rosa!*" I had passed the age for climbing heights, especially on anything as flimsy as that ladder. "There's no need to worry, Rosa love," I pleaded. "We all want you back. I'll make it all right with them. It'll all be forgotten."

There wasn't any answer. I thought what a fool I was. Perhaps that ladder had been lying in the weeds for weeks. She wasn't up there at all. But I couldn't go back without making certain. If only Magda had been there to hold the ladder for me. I was a coward. It was twenty feet up to that branch and the ladder so light.

There was no sound from above, except the hooting of the owl. But the rats were coming closer. They were not like rats as I have known them. Rats are thieves, fearful thieves. But these seemed to me more like hunters. It was they who drove me up that ladder.

Suddenly the siren sounded. It was the all-clear, which is used by the Wilchester Fire Brigade to signal a fire alert. But it brought back the war—as I suppose it must for all my generation—the glorious horror of the Battle of Britain, with the blue skies scribbled with the white exhaust messages of conflict, punctuated with death plunging out of the sky. And that was how I feared Rosa might end, as I climbed rung by rung toward her, even though I kept up an incantation of reassurance. Or if not Rosa, me. I didn't know to what degree she was possessed. But I knew that she had only to give that slender ladder the merest tip and I'd be down.

I kept muttering to myself, "Oh, God, why did you make it so good for Magda and me?" It wouldn't have mattered otherwise. Then looking up, I saw Rosa. She was looking down at me. I might have been the Devil coming to fetch her. I said, "Rosa, my little girl, my honey. Don't be frightened. It's Uncle George."

I shone the torch in my own face and then I turned it toward hers. I was by then only about eight feet from her. I don't know whether you've ever had the experience of seeing someone you know and then at the moment of greeting, it isn't! The appalling shock!

It wasn't Rosa my torch flashed on. It was her dumpy torso, her large legs, her heavy loose-lipped face, her shaggy hair, in fact it was her body. But she wasn't in control. It was somebody else there. It was like going to a house and finding there was a new tenant.

And as she saw me, or rather as the creature within her or overshadowing her saw me, the body which was Rosa's with an agility of which I swear Rosa wasn't capable scrambled up and away from me another ten feet and looked down at me with an expression of diabolical hatred.

As you must have realized, I am rather slow in my reactions. I was still thinking it was Rosa and how she must be feeling about

Kit and Nieves and wanting me to reassure her. I kept on this silly reassuring talk as I climbed up the ladder and onto the fork where she had been.

And then suddenly as I reached the safety of the fork, I realized that the spirit looking through the windows of Rosa's eyes was as old as Lucifer's. Her lips began to twitch. She, or It, was poising, about to jump from that height on me and carry us both to destruction on the ground below.

Suddenly I saw the whole thing in reverse. I thought I had gone up that ladder to save Rosa from Them, but They were using Rosa to destroy me. There was a rustling sound and then a clang as the ladder slipped away and bounced in the weeds below. I clung to the tulip tree for grim death and at that very moment the thing in Rosa was about to leap on me.

"Oh, God!" I called. "In the name of Jesus Christ, let It be gone."

18

THE FORT BESIEGED

From the upper branches of the tulip tree there came a noise like struggling and then it ceased and through a gap in leaves I saw the black shape of an owl with beating wings stenciled against the sky.

Then there came another sound, half-cry, half-whimper. I turned the torch beam toward it and I could see Rosa, the true unshadowed child, looking down in terror. I don't think she had any knowledge of how she had climbed as high as that. She was like a sleepwalker suddenly waking to find herself poised on the parapet of a roof.

"It's all right," I whispered. "Don't worry. It's all right."

At first she did not recognize me. (She had either forgotten or never really taken in the fact that Magda and I had returned from Italy.) "Oh, Uncle George, you're back!"

She was only five feet above me. "I've brought you a puppy," I said. "Don't you want to come down and see it?" It was a fatuous remark perhaps, considering that even if she climbed down to my level, we could descend no further until help came from the house. But *you* try reassuring a little girl thirty feet up a tree on a dark night, when she is coming round from being overshadowed. It is not easy.

She felt safe where she was and I felt safe where I was. But between us there was a gap where foot- and handholds were tricky. There was no point in my going up to her and she was too scared to try to come down to me.

"Listen, Rosa," I said. "The ladder's fallen. We can't get down until someone comes to put it up again. I know Magda is coming in a few minutes and we can wait for her. Or I can call out and hope that they'll hear in the house."

"Don't call," Rosa said. "They'll never forgive me. Never. Never." She began to cry again and I let her, because it took her mind off worse fears. No little girl ever fell out of a tree while crying at the thought of how angry her parents would be when they found her. But I did say quietly, "They won't be angry, my dear. They'll be so glad to see you safe and sound."

I repeated this over and over again, before it had any effect. Then Rosa changed the direction of her sobbing.

"They don't care," she said. "They never have cared."

"If you could see them in the house now, you wouldn't say that." I was thinking how, short of calling out the fire brigade, we could get her down safely. "They're worried stiff." If there was a short ladder, we could haul it up and lash it so that it would reach the branch where Rosa was. Even a length of rope for her to steady herself would suffice, if the four of them stood beneath with a blanket to break her fall, in case she lost grasp.

"Only when I'm not there," Rosa sobbed. "That's when they care." There was a certain justice in that. They were both so engrossed in their careers that they had failed to give the time needed to reassure her of their love.

Luckily at that moment I heard their voices, Kit protesting against Magda obeying my instructions and coming alone. "Hello," I shouted. "It's all right. All of you, come. We're in the tulip tree."

It took nearly half an hour to get Rosa down. It would have been quicker if Kit had not tried, as Rosa's father, to take charge of the operation. He weighed over two hundred pounds and I managed to persuade him that the light, lithe (and sober) Ramratan was physically better equipped for this part of the rescue, while he and the women held the blanket underneath.

We could see the nervous strain under which the child had been laboring from the fact that the moment that Ramratan reached her, she lost consciousness. Ram brought her down to the fork where I was; but we did not dare to take her down the aluminum ladder until she had regained consciousness with aid of sips of brandy and Nieves's endearments.

She was revived enough to climb down by herself, with Ramratan preceding her and forming with his arms and body a sort of descending pocket which would catch her, if she slipped or fainted. But the moment she reached *terra firma,* her strength gave way. Ram and I carried her in on a chairhold and laid her on a sofa in the studio. She immediately turned her head away from the light and went off to sleep.

Magda knelt down and took her wrist to feel her pulse. Kit poured himself a tumbler of water and drank it straight down. He handed the jug to Mrs. Ramratan. "Fill it up, Kumari, will you? And make some strong black coffee."

Nieves bent over the sofa. "She must go to bed at once."

"Not here," I said. "You and Rosa had better sleep at The Chantry. What about you, Kit?"

"I'll stay with the Rams. We can't all abandon fort."

Magda stood up. "No need to call a doctor."

"You'd better get some night things packed," Kit said. He took the water jug from Mrs. Ramratan, filled his tumbler again and drank it at a gulp.

The women went out to pack and Kit said, "I suppose it's too late to exorcise this place tonight."

I saw by my watch it was already five minutes to eleven. Kit had been married by special license to Nieves, having lived with her for over a year. He might be slow to decide, but he was swift to implement. "You can't have a runaway exorcism," I said. "It's Saturday night; and Father Martin has his first Communion at 7 A.M."

"But we could talk about it. Make the arrangements. He could put me in the picture. The whole thing seems completely medieval, but I suppose there's something underneath the trappings."

I was adamant. Kit could impose on me; but it was unfair to impose on a priest at that hour of a Saturday night. Beside I wanted Kit to sleep on the question. Though he was swilling black coffee and sobering up quickly, any decision made under the stress of worry and the persuasion of alcohol might be repented of in the sober revulsion of the morrow.

"I'll take you round to The Chantry if you like and after Rosa's in bed, we can talk about it. I know a little. And if you and Nieves decide to go ahead, we'll fix a meeting with Father Martin. But it's far more complicated than . . . than calling the plumber in, when the drains begin to smell."

Nieves came in with a traveling rug. She laid it over Rosa and Kit slipped his arms under her and raised her as if she were a baby.

Rosa woke up, blinked in the light. Then she saw me. "The puppy. I want the puppy."

"All right," I said. "I'll get the puppy. Don't worry." I turned to Kit. "You take her out to the car. I'll get the puppy from Mrs. Ram."

Mrs. Ramratan had arranged a cardboard box lined with an old blanket in a corner of the kitchen. But the puppy was out in the yard. She wanted no messes to clear up in the morning.

I went out and looked around the small flagged yard. There was no sign of the puppy, who had probably retired to the coal shed. "Come on," I called, "come on." I flashed the torch into the darkness. For a moment I saw what looked like glowworms, but they were red, cut rubies.

Then a pair of these shot at me, at my face or neck. Instinctively I struck with the back of my arm. The thing squealed, as it fell. For a moment, the shed seemed alive. They were about my feet, streaming past me. I stamped with my heel. Something squished, wriggled convulsively and then was still.

I flashed the light into the yard and there through the hole in the bottom of the gate I saw the last scrawny rump and tapering gray-wire tail vanish. At my feet was a lean dead rat, nearly eighteen inches from the tip of its tail to the end of the blood-smeared snout.

I climbed over the coal and on the far side near the corner I found Rosa's puppy, or rather a bloody mess of hair and flesh and bone. That was all they had left of the gift which was to turn Rosa's affections to this world.

I picked it up. I could not leave it lying there. The rats would be back. I didn't understand what was happening. I'm not sure even now. This may seem absurd. But I wonder if I had prayed for that puppy before I brought it to Anglesey House, if I had dedicated it to God, whether it would be alive today.

And those rats . . . how did they fit in? Are rats and snakes intrinsically evil or made evil by our hatred and fear of them? I suspect, looking back, that the death of the puppy was my fault, the failure of love and dedication, the overweening pride of feeling that *I* had saved Rosa, not God through me. I was in a state of sin, of trying to direct a drama in which I was only one of the players.

I held the tender, savaged body in my hands, wondering what I should do. The Ramratans mustn't see it. They would panic. Say that they couldn't be left alone. I saw a dust bin in the yard. I lifted the lid and popped the puppy in. My hands were covered in blood. The rain-water butt which had stood in the yard had been removed, because it was rotten. I looked around to see how I could cleanse them, without alarming either the Ramratans or the others in the car.

The kitchen door opened. "You found it, Mr. Grantley?" Mrs. Ramratan said.

"Thank you." I summoned up the reserves of childhood in which one could outface servants and I walked past her to the downstairs cloakroom. I washed the blood off my hands, very carefully, leaving no trace on the towel.

Mrs. Ramratan said outside the door, "Mrs. Grantley is asking why you're so long, Mr. Grantley."

"I'm just coming. Tell her I'm just coming."

"And the puppy, Mr. Grantley. What about the puppy?"

"Tell her not to worry." Even then I felt ashamed of this subterfuge. It was a retreat behind the class barriers of fifty years before.

When I came out of the cloakroom, Ramratan was waiting for me. I couldn't forget his courage up in the tree. "Is Sir Kit coming back tonight?" he asked. "You're not going to leave us here alone?"

"He's coming back," I said.

As I look back, I shudder at my appalling sectarian unimaginativeness. I knew the Ramratans were Marxists and I believed that by their disbelief in God they had obtained some sort of immunity from evil spirits. "We're just going to talk. I'll drive him back. Why don't you and your wife go to bed?"

And so I left him, having committed the worst sin which a Christian can commit, that of assuming that those who do not believe in Christ have no need of him.

Kit was sitting next to the driving seat and he saw me come out empty-handed; but the child was half-asleep on Nieves's lap. I opened the boot of the car and then slammed it.

As soon as I got in, Rosa woke up. "Where is it, Uncle George? I want the puppy."

"I've put it in the back," I said. "You'll have it when we get to The Chantry."

I started up the car. But Rosa began to whine. "I want it now. Why can't I have it now?"

"Why can't she?" pleaded Magda.

"*Elle fut tuée par ratons*," I said.

"I want my puppy," Rosa said. "I want my puppy."

"If you don't shut up, you won't get it at all," Kit said, in a voice which shocked Rosa into silence. Then in a whisper, he said, "That rat-catcher chap did a pretty poor job. And yet he showed Rushmore over eighty tails."

"It could be a fresh invasion," I suggested. "Better have him in again to clear this new lot." I was more concerned with getting Rosa off to bed and smuggling one of the other pups to her so that she wouldn't know what had happened.

When we reached The Chantry, Rosa wanted to wait to see the boot opened. But Kit lifted her, kicking and screaming and beating with her fists against his face, and carried her to the little room which Magda had occupied on her first stay.

I went through the motions of unlocking and opening the boot, while the child was being carried up the steps into the house, vowing to myself as I did so that if Magda and I had children, they should be spoilt less and loved more, as Adrian had been when he was mine.

Then I went in and picked the only other bitch in the litter and took her up. I gave her to Nieves and went down to Kit. He had lit a cigar, a huge thing. But he wasn't drinking anything except iced water, a great jug of it, which I had to get before helping myself, rather timorously, to the whisky I felt I deserved. "Help yourself, my dear fellow," he said, "you need it," usurping as usual the place of the host.

He walked the room, like one of the large cats at the zoo before feeding time. "Something's got to be done about this, George," he said. "But I want the facts. What is going on? This is a world I've had nothing to do with. Politics, law—within limits I know where I am. But this is not my line."

"It wasn't when you were at St. John's," I said. "You seem to forget it was you who converted me to Christianity."

He stopped pacing. "Did I? Really?"

"You don't remember the dinner hour, leaning against the radiators, saying that it was all or nothing; not a Sunday religion, but every minute of every hour day and night?"

"My God! You're right. And it's true, George. I still believe that. That's why it was nothing. But this thing now . . . that tape . . . Rosa . . . this talk of exorcism . . . I'm worried. I don't . . ."

Nieves and Magda came in. "She had to have the puppy in the room," Nieves said. "There will be puddles everywhere tomorrow. But Magda says no matter."

"I was saying," Kit broke rather impatiently in, "that I want George to explain this exorcism. It seems such a mumbo jumbo with all that nonsense about bell, book and candle."

I found it hard to explain, because I had never been at an exorcism or really thought about it as a sacrament. "I don't know how it works. I don't pretend to know. But I imagine that it'll only succeed if we have enough faith."

"Faith!" he said. "In what? I believe that there's something . . . something evil . . . devilishly evil about this. But that doesn't mean I believe in Jesus as the Son of God."

It was like Pinky Brown in *Brighton Rock*. "*Credo in unum Satanum.*" At least faith in the devilishly evil was an advance from

Rationalist Truth. "Perhaps you'd better sell the house," I said. "It won't be easy; but it'd be harder still after an unsuccessful exorcism."

"Don't be facetious!"

"I'm very serious," I answered. "Faith can't be given like a Christmas present. It has to be found, like buried treasure. There's no point in your trying exorcism if you don't believe in it."

He put his hands up and grasped the hair either side of his head. He was enraged with a feeling of helplessness. I knew that if only I had tried to convince him of the existence of God, he would have been happy in proving how wrong I was. But I would not give him the satisfaction of that escape. He turned to Nieves, the anticlericalist child of an anticlericalist father. "Do you believe in it, Nieves?"

"I believe in Jorge," she said. "About the evil, he was right. We were wrong, I and you. About the exorcism, perhaps he is right too."

Kit flung up his hands. "Then what do we do?" he asked. "What on earth do we do?"

I heard the front doorbell ring. I looked at the clock. It was past midnight. "I'll go, Magda."

"I'll come too," Kit said. "It's time for me to go."

We went down the stairs together. "I haven't been very helpful, I'm afraid, Kit."

"At least you haven't said, 'God helps those who help themselves.' But I suppose you've been thinking it."

"I was thinking that God sometimes forces people to help themselves." I opened the front door.

The Ramratans were standing together outside.

"What on earth?" Kit said. "I was just coming back."

"You can, sir," said Ramratan. "But us, we'd go back to South Africa, rather."

19

A DANGEROUS CALL

Kit did not go back to Anglesey House to sleep alone. I had the impression that he was relieved that the Ramratans had deserted the fort. It simplified the position that they too recognized the presence of a spiritual evil beyond the category of the "materially wrong."

"But it's no good, George," Kit said to me, as he went upstairs to bed. "I can't make myself believe what I don't believe. And you can't expect me to. Intellectual honesty is what I've always clung to, and I shan't abandon it."

"You can't," I said. "Intellectual suicide isn't the price of faith." I had never felt so close to him. I was aware of a tension within him, rather like a head of steam mounting in an engine. The affectations, the escapes into irony, rhetoric and alcohol had gone. Something, I was sure, was going either to move or to explode.

Next morning we found that the Ramratans had already been back to Anglesey House and brought plentiful supplies of food, including a large capon.

Rosa and Nieves were still asleep, when Magda and I came down. We were going to Sung Eucharist, so we just had coffee. Kit came down as we were finishing. "I think it would be a good idea if I came along too," he said. "Then we might have a word with Father Turner afterward." He poured himself a cup of coffee.

"You've decided?"

"If God exists," Kit said, "He won't make Rosa the victim of my inability to believe. By definition, He is all-loving, all-merciful." Kit was right. I had tried quite unfairly to pose him with a dilemma. It was the unwitting stratagem of a sectarian.

On the way to the church, Kit asked me what a Sung Eucharist was. The church he had attended with his mother in Notting Hill Gate had been gauntly evangelical with the celebration of the Lord's Supper less an act of communion than a demonstration of Protestant principles. "It's just the Communion Service, sung to Marbek."

"Well, I like singing," he conceded. "But I expect I've forgotten it all."

I remembered from St. John's School days that Kit had a fine baritone voice. He had sung in the school choir and solos at school concerts. In the intervening years he had used his voice exclusively for advocacy. But he hadn't forgotten the service. I noticed that he soon abandoned the prayer book. After all these years the words were still familiar. And Marbek seemed to give him little difficulty. Magda was between us, but I could perceive the pleasure which he derived from singing.

Kit was sitting furthest from the aisle. When the time came to go to the altar rail, I went out and stood aside for Magda to go first so that she could re-enter the pew first. Kit remained where he was kneeling on his hassock, self-excommunicated by integrity. He seemed tragically cut off, a solitary outpost of unbelief in the house of God.

We made our communion and went back to our seats, passing as usual through the side chapel. I was so drawn into myself that I did not realize until we came to the pew that it was empty. I looked up toward the chancel and there in a shaft of sunlight towering above the figure of Raikes, the verger, stood Kit.

Magda had seen it too. She stood aside to let me pass first into the pew to where Kit had sat. Then as we knelt together, she whispered, "It's happened!"

I prayed that she was right. It did not seem to me possible. But it was equally impossible that Kit would have gone to the altar rail if it hadn't happened.

I looked at Kit as he came back and bowed his knee. Magda was right. It *had* happened.

At the end of the Sung Eucharist Father Martin always comes to the porch in order to greet those going out. Kit remained praying. He sealed us into our pew. Magda nudged him. "We've got to go, if you want to talk to Father Martin."

He looked at us. He was in another world. "Father Martin? But of course."

Father Martin had shaken hands with the last of the communicants and was coming back into the church ready to prepare himself for Matins.

I introduced Kit. "We have a problem," I said. "Could you come to lunch to discuss it, Father?"

Father Martin hesitated. He had another engagement.

"We can wait," Kit said.

"No, I think Mrs. Corbett will have to wait," Father Martin said. "I would be pleased to come." He went back toward the vestry and the three of us stood at the entrance of the church.

"Magda, George," Kit said. "D'you mind? I want to go back. You understand?"

When we went into The Chantry, we found Nieves waiting for us. "Where's Keet?" she asked. "Not *al iglesia*, no!" She did not seem as outraged as I'd expected.

"I think he believes again," I said.

"It's impossible," she said.

"Go and see," said Magda. "He's in the church. Go and see."

"Me?" Nieves looked alarmed. "I can't go in no church."

I took her by the hand. "Kit wants you," I said. "I'll take you in the car."

When we came to the church the five-minute bell was slowly tolling.

Nieves got out of the car and I took her up the steps and between the pews into the church. Raikes wanted to give us two prayer books and two hymnals, but I took one of each. I gave them to Nieves and led her to the pew where Kit was kneeling. "Bless you!" I whispered.

Nieves looked at me, lost and wild. As the voluntary started, I saw the mustering of the choir and made good my escape.

When I got back to The Chantry, I found that Magda had given Rosa breakfast and dressed her. Rosa was out in the garden playing with the puppy which we had told her was hers. She hadn't asked where her parents were.

"She must have her lunch before us," I said. "We can't talk freely with Father Martin, if Rosa's there."

Magda nodded. "But has it happened? Really?"

I've always been suspicious about emotional Salvation Army conversions. But the vision on the road to Damascus, the blinding reversal of belief, is historic fact. Something like this could have happened with Kit. What it was I could not know. But he would not have gone to the altar rail unless his integrity had directed him. Unlike me, he was an all-or-nothing man. "It must have happened," I said. "I'm going to see Rosa."

She was lying on the hard-baked lawn, playing with the puppy. I went across and stood over her. Her untidy hair had been tied back in a pony tail. As she looked up, seeing my shadow, her features were softened. There was nothing of the middle-aged child about her now. She was a little girl, rather odd but also rather beautiful. I sat down beside her and tickled the puppy's belly, feeling the immature teats beneath the soft hair. "What are you going to call her?"

"Spreckles," she said.

"Why?"

"Because I want to ride," she said, looking at me with her curiously gemlike eyes. "I told you I want to ride."

I laughed. "D'you think Miss Spreckles will enjoy hearing you shout 'Down, Spreckles, down!' or 'Look what you've done, you *naughty* Spreckles!'"

Rosa burst out laughing too. "I'll have to find another name. It can't be Sukey, though."

"Why not?"

"That's the name I gave the other one."

"What other one?"

"The one the rats got."

"How did you know that?"

"Well, they did, didn't they?"

"But nobody told you; you never saw it."

She bent down and kissed the little puppy, her head bowing downward to provide a screen between the animal and me.

"Peter couldn't play with Sukey, if she stayed this side," Rosa said.

"Why not? If Charles could, why not Peter?"

"I don't know, but that's what Charles says. I asked him once. But he just said, 'Because, silly!' Charles can play with Peter and with me. But *I* can't play with Peter, because he's 'too far back.' Not unless *I* go across. And I don't want to, not for always. I want to get back for meals and being warm in bed."

"It sounds very queer to me," I said, as if this were the most natural conversation in the world. "Being too far back, I mean. They're *both* the other side."

"Did Charles tell lies, when *you* knew him?" Rosa asked.

I tried to think back. I supposed he did, but not much more than I did myself. "It wasn't that so much," I said. "But I did feel . . . well, he was like two different people."

She looked at me in surprise. "Oh, he is. I'm sure he is. And one of them is nice. But the other one . . . that's the one that makes him tell the lies."

"You mean, there *is* no Peter?"

"Of *course,* there's Peter," she said impatiently. "Charles went across to play with Peter, so there must be. No, I think They're hiding Peter."

"You mean, because They want you to come across?"

Rosa put her hand in the puppy's mouth and let its tiny jaws worry her flesh. "I don't know," she said. "I'm sure Charles does too, I mean want me to, the nice one. I think Charles is lonely on the other side with just Peter. He'd like to come back for good, but he can't except to me. He says there were lots of children during the war and after his Mother died—but I'm the only one who's played with him. Do you think that's why he likes me, Uncle George, and not because I'm me? He says the others left him cold."

I felt a *frisson* at this literal use of the slang phrase. But I could not explore further because at that moment Mrs. Ramratan called Rosa to come in for luncheon.

As I watched her go to the house, carrying Spreckles in her arms, I wondered how long might be this chain composed of Them and the child suicides. Was there behind Peter, perhaps at the time of the Wars of the Roses, the Black Death or the

Norman Conquest another earthbound boy or girl looking for a psychic playmate and used by Them to bring Peter across from the life which seemed to hold so little for him in the body? How far back did the chain of lonely, desperate children recede? To the Roman encampment on the hill behind us? Or even to the neolithic village buried beneath the Roman site? The patient ancestry of evil appalled me and the hold it still possessed over the human soul, despite all the technical achievements of scientific man.

The Evernesses came back in the Vicar's car, a Ford Anglia of uncertain age. I could see from Nieves's expression that she had been given a faith only in her husband, but that was a faith which had been lacking previously. Kit, however, was extraordinarily changed. The sense I had had before of a person who was dark within himself when he was alone, but artificially illuminated for others, preferably with a reinforcement of alcohol, gave way to a sense of a man who was bright within.

Over sherry Father Martin said, "Sir Christopher has been telling me about the problem, George. The question is the sort of exorcism we need. I've never had to do one, thank God. But if we're to exorcise Rosa, we shall have to have the Bishop's permission; and I'd like a priest with experience. It's dangerous."

"I don't think you should exorcise Rosa," Kit said. "She isn't possessed."

Father Martin looked at me. "Would you agree?"

It was hard to say. The night before, when she was so overshadowed that she was prepared to jump on me and throw us both to the ground, I would have said that she was possessed at that moment. But it was only temporary. The command in Christ's name to be gone had been enough to banish the evil power. I said, "I think Rosa needs to be blessed. You ought to confirm her as soon as possible. She has a psychic gift which is wonderful. It must be consecrated, or it'll do her harm. But exorcism would be wrong: like trying to cut out someone's imagination as if it were a malignant cancer."

Luncheon was announced. "That's good," Father Martin said. "No personal exorcism. Then it's just the house. I could cope with that myself."

We went into the dining room. I wondered whether I should ask the father to say grace. I decided not. Everybody remained standing apart from Nieves. Then she suddenly noticed and stood up.

"Benedictus benedicat, in nomine Patris, Filii et Spiritus Sancti."

When we were all served, Father Martin said, "I suppose we shall have to use the service in the 1549 King Edward VI Prayer Book." He turned to Kit. "There is no exorcism in the later Book."

"Isn't that for the casting out of demons?" I asked. "I think this is more complex." I told them of my conversation with Rosa in the garden. "I think this is on two levels. 'They' are forces of evil, demons if you like. But Charles and Peter—perhaps even others before them—are victims; as they've been trying to make Rosa a victim. I think the victims need to be blessed."

Father Martin said, "You realize that's heresy. There's no Christian foundation for the notion that human spirits can wander bodiless. If a place is infested with an evil, the evil isn't defined but is presumed as demonic. Your whole concept is a pagan view of body and spirit."

"I'm not a theologian, Father," I said. "I'm merely telling you what's happened. The nice Charles Scarlet is very much the same boy as I knew in 1916. But at times he's overshadowed by one of Them; just as Rosa was, in the tulip tree last night. Can't the soul of a dead child be overshadowed by an evil spirit, in the same way as the soul of a living one?"

"Orthodoxically, no," said Father Martin. "Which means we may have to concoct a heretical sacrament."

"But when?" asked Kit. "Can you do it tonight? I've a heavy day tomorrow."

Father Martin shook his head. "Sunday is *my* heavy day. I've got to prepare for this; not just liturgically, but spiritually."

I knew what he was thinking of. This sudden conversion of Kit's might be permanent, but could just be the product of fear for Rosa and if the exorcism didn't work, Kit might relapse. Of one thing Father Martin never thought, I am sure. That was the danger to himself. He wanted to get the exorcism right, just as a doctor wants time to think and take a second opinion before prescribing treatment in a dangerous and unusual case.

"I'm sure, Magda, we can put them up here at The Chantry as long as the Ramratans will help." Magda nodded. "So long as you don't object, Nieves."

"I can go down and work during the day," she said.

Father Martin looked at his watch. "If I'm to take Rosa to Sunday school . . ."

As Nieves went away to get Rosa ready, we talked generally about exorcism. "You mustn't think, Sir Christopher, that this is a sort of mechanical process; like mending a car which has got something wrong with it."

"It's more like magic," Kit suggested.

Father Martin looked at him sharply. "I think," he said, "this is a spiritual, not a magical, thing. But I don't pretend to understand how it works, any more than I understand how prayer works."

"'God moves in a mysterious way,'" Kit said. "I used to think the theology of that was as poor as Cowper's verse."

"I don't know," Father Martin said. "'God is His own inter-preter' is a good line."

Nieves opened the door. "She's gone, Keet," she said. "Rosa, she's gone!"

"What do you mean, 'gone'?" Kit stood up and addressed the question as much to the Ramratans, who were standing behind Nieves in the doorway, as to his wife.

"Not in her room!" Nieves said.

"Not in the garden!" Ram said.

"She is nowhere," said Mrs. Ram.

We were all standing now. I thought of my last sight of her with Spreckles in her arms. "The puppy? Where's the puppy?"

"Gone too!"

There were only two possibilities I could see. Rosa had gone to Sunday school on her own; or she had for some reason, probably diabolical, been drawn back to Anglesey House. "Quick," I said. "Father, you go to Sunday school. Perhaps you'll see Rosa on the way. Kit and I will go to Anglesey House. The rest of you really search this place, the attics, the cellars, all the places in the garden. It's probably a false alarm."

I prayed it was, but in my heart I feared that somehow these spirits, whom I had imagined tied to a single place, had a mobility

I hadn't suspected. Kit and I bundled into my car and were off before the Father, streaking by short cuts at speeds which I, a normally careful driver, thought were justifiably hazardous.

"She couldn't get in the house," Kit said. "It's locked."

"But is the garden? Did the Rams lock the door from the cut? That tulip tree's the danger."

As I stopped in the cut, Miss Spreckles, brown beret on head and face tanned like an old shoe, walked her Equitationists down on their ponies. Kit eased himself out of the car, muttering "This riding fetish," and went into the garden. I caught him up on the first terrace. I saw a rat scuttle into the delphiniums, the plants wave as it made for safety.

Kit ran forward, looking up to the tulip tree and calling "Rosa! Rosa!"

It seemed to me, coming behind him, that he was suddenly tripped or tackled. He cried out as he fell forward, spreading his outstretched palms to break the fall. But his speed and his weight were too much. As he crashed, there was a horrible expulsion from his lungs; and a crack, at least it seemed to me, an audible crack. And there he was lying, wounded, in my way.

I saw what had tripped him, the bramble I had noticed the night before. Materially it was as simple as that. I bent over him. I could see he was in agony. His face screwed up in pain as he said, "Rosa. The tulip tree. Quick, George." And then I think he fainted.

But I'm not sure, because I had to go to the tree and look up and make sure that Rosa wasn't there, even though I knew before I reached it that she wouldn't be there.

They were far more cunning than we, as one might expect, these things that St. Paul called "principalities and powers" of evil. Little Rosa did not matter now so much in the battle that had been joined. Last night, it had been me that they had tried to destroy, because at that time I was the person who understood most of what they were doing and so was the principal enemy. But their failure had won over Kit with infinitely greater spiritual powers than I can ever have and they had turned against him, using Rosa as bait once again.

I say this in retrospect. But all I thought at the time was "Thank

God, the child isn't up the tree," and went to Kit. He was in a bad way. His face was very white, with unhealthy sort of gray shades to it. He had turned round and was sitting on the steps, holding his heart or his ribs.

"She isn't there," I said. "I'm going to take you to the hospital, Kit."

He looked up at me. "I've cracked ribs before," he said. "And it's just the same sober or drunk. We'll find Rosa first."

"Don't be a fool, Kit. You can't stand."

He was in great pain. "You might help a pal up."

I wanted to force him to admit that I could take him to the hospital first. "Don't worry, old boy. I'll find Rosa. I've done it before now."

I didn't mean this as a goad. But it acted as one. He stood up by himself. "Come on. Let's find her." He held out his arm and I took it and helped him to the car.

I said, "Aren't you being rather foolish?"

"I've been extremely foolish for a very long while," he answered. "This new folly doesn't matter much. So long as you find Rosa."

I drove slowly round to the Church Hall, keeping a lookout for the child. But there was no sign of her. Kit needed no persuasion to stay in the car, while I went into the packed Sunday school.

I stood in the back. Father Martin said, " 'Thy will be done' means that any prayer we make for ourselves may turn out quite different from the way we expect. . . ." I caught sight of Rosa. She was sitting with Spreckles in her arms.

I went back to the car. "She's perfectly all right. The whole thing's a false alarm. But I'm going to take you to the Cottage Hospital to have those ribs strapped. You can't be X-rayed on a Sunday."

"I can see how dangerous belief can be," Kit said, holding his ribs.

"What d'you mean?"

"I mean . . . it would be possible to think that it wasn't just a bramble and my carelessness. I mean, that might be Their way of getting at me."

"I shouldn't think that," I answered instinctively. It seemed too fantastic even to contemplate. But on reflection, I think it possible that Kit was right. We were so concerned with the danger to Rosa as the victim that we didn't realize that They were using her as a lure as well. They had nearly killed me in the tulip tree the night before and they had wounded Kit, whose new-found faith, as Father Martin pointed out, made him the most potent instrument of the Divine power.

By the time I had Kit strapped and back at The Chantry, it was time to fetch Rosa back from Sunday school. We were taking no chances of letting her walk back alone.

"Tell me, Rosa," I asked. "Why did you go off like that?"

She did not answer; just gave me an evasive smile. For the first time, I felt that her conscious innocence had been violated. The sooner we had that exorcism, the easier I would be at heart.

Magda was standing waiting on the steps of The Chantry. "Who is your doctor?" she asked. "Kit is very ill."

20

THE HERETICAL SACRAMENT

Kit had pleural fluid in the left lung. The doctor said there was danger of bronchial pneumonia, unless he stayed in bed and took complete rest. He prescribed some antibiotic to be taken every four hours for the next five days. "This is one of the occasions when you'll have to bless our 'blunderbuss' medicine, Grantley," he said to me. "In the old days, I wouldn't have given much for your friend's chances."

On Monday afternoon I went round to see Father Martin at his request. "Are you still convinced that child is not possessed?" he asked.

"No, I'm not sure," I answered, "not as sure, that is, as I was yesterday lunchtime. I mean, what led Rosa to set out for Sunday school with the puppy without telling any of us?"

"Was she going to the Sunday school?" he asked. "I caught her up. She was . . . I won't say embarrassed—confused is more the word. But she made no fuss about coming, in fact, seemed rather glad. But she could have been going to Anglesey House."

" 'Influenced' is the word I'd use rather than 'possessed.' "

"Why don't you want her exorcised?"

"Because I'm afraid it would harm her," I said. "She hasn't reached the age of making adult distinctions. If she had, we could explain that there was nothing intrinsically either good or evil about her psychic gift, though it made her more vulnerable than most of us to evil spirits. If we exorcise her, she'll think that the gift itself is evil."

"I'm not altogether convinced it isn't."

"There was nothing evil in her seeing my mother in the rose garden. And whatever your exorcism does, it won't drive away her gift. When she sees other spirits, she will think that she is evil; and we won't be able to help her. Then there really would be a danger of her going over to the other side."

Father Martin nodded. "I spoke to Mills on the telephone last night. He takes the same view; even says that as a Christian psychic she might do very valuable work for us, when she grows up. He's writing me a letter with suggestions of what we might do. I'll receive that tomorrow morning. I told him I wanted to do the exorcism at 3 P.M. tomorrow afternoon. That was before I knew about Sir Christopher."

"Does he have to be present?"

"It would be better if he were," Father Martin said. "A sudden gift of the Holy Spirit like his brings with it an enormous access of power. We need everything we've got. Mills wants to organize prayers among his circle, at the same time."

I hadn't realized the degree to which the success or failure of the exorcism might depend upon us, or rather the spiritual power which we might generate between us; but of course Father Martin was right. I suggested that we should work toward Tuesday afternoon at three o'clock but review it according to the doctor's advice next morning.

On my way home an impulse carried me into Scarlet's. I bought some bast and as John was looking up the price, I said to him, "We're going to exorcise Anglesey House tomorrow afternoon."

He gave no sign that he had heard, except that his hands ceased to flutter the pages of the catalogue for a moment and I was aware of acute tension.

"It's planned for three o'clock," I said, leaning forward and speaking quietly, though we were alone in the front shop, Mrs. Worplesdon having lured the only other customer into the depths of the back. "I wondered if you would like to go." I don't know what prompted me to make the suggestion, whether it sprang from a cruel desire to penetrate the armor of his reclusion or from an intuition that his presence might help him or us.

"It does not belong to us any more," he said quietly, accepting the idea of an exorcism as normal.

"But Charles was a cousin of yours," I pointed out. "And you were in his room that night."

He stopped fumbling through the catalogue. "It'll be half a crown, Mr. Grantley."

I felt in my pocket. "It's for Peter Ingleside, too."

His face, always pale, took on a ghastly shade of white. His hands clenched on the bast. He knew who Peter Ingleside was, I swear. Like Charles and Rosa, he could *see* what I and others merely *felt* as frigid shades. That was the secret of his terror both in childhood and now, a psychic gift of which he went in dread.

"At least," I said, handing him half a crown, "pray that we lay them."

On Tuesday morning, Kit was so much better that we called the doctor to say there was no need to examine him. Kit rang Dawkins to tell him not to cancel his brief next day and getting up at eleven, he spent the late morning with Rosa. He was trying to prepare her for "the service to get rid of Them." What he said, I do not know; except that he promised her that she could take lessons with Miss Spreckles and if she learned to ride could have a pony of her own. That rather than the exorcism seemed to be what made most impression on her.

We drove to Anglesey House at 2:45 and five minutes later Martin Turner arrived in the Anglia with old Raikes, the verger. As he did so, two people whom I had noticed loitering at the entrance to the cut came over. The elder was one of the many Angleseys, Michael, who was in his second year at Oxford on a

County Scholarship, the son of Thomas Anglesey, who owned the Wilchester Arms Garage, a dark-eyed server with a deep, warm voice, whose handsome features were scarred with the passionate eruptions of acne. The other was Mrs. Ambrose's nephew, Tom, the senior choirboy, a tough freckled youth, bursting with health. With Raikes, whose face was drawn with the almost incessant pain of an injured hip, they made a fairly representative cross section of Father Martin's male congregation.

Father Martin introduced them and then they retired to Kit's office while we waited in the studio, where I had arranged seven chairs and seven cushions on the floor before them. (I had been hesitant about asking the Ramratans, but Kit had brushed me aside. "They may be Marxists," he'd said, "but that doesn't mean they don't need protection," a view in which the Ramratans concurred.)

Rosa, at Father Martin's suggestion, waited in the office until they were ready and then came into the studio to warn us.

We stood up as they entered. Raikes came limping first, wearing a cassock and carrying the cross. Tommy Ambrose and Michael Anglesey followed, acolytes in cassocks and cottas, equipped, the former with thurible, the latter with holy water stoup and sprinkler. Father Martin with surplice, stole and violet cope, appeared to me invested with the priestly authority which was not just his human *persona* in superlative degree.

Their presence in this artist's workroom, with its throne, its easels, canvases and objects collected for their beauty, oddity or exoticism, made a curious harmony.

After a short prayer, Father Martin asked us to sit down. He said, "I want to explain what we shall do in this service. We are not here just to drive evil away from this house, we are here to bless the house and make it good, to bless the people living in it and make them good.

"This is not something which is done magically by prayers and incense and holy water and the bearing of the cross. These are just the outward and visible signs of a making pure of this house and of our hearts and souls and minds in the truth that God will dwell in this place and in us. You must all of you understand this because what we are going to do depends not just on God but on all of us here in this house and on those elsewhere who are praying for us. We cannot work without Him and He cannot work without us. That is the first thing.

"Now for the second thing. We know that there were two boys who killed themselves in this house. There was Charles Scarlet who killed himself in 1916 and Peter Ingleside who killed himself—" he had forgotten the date I had given him, the very same day in August 210 years before—"a long while before that. We are taught that it is a sin to kill ourselves, but it is not for us to judge either Charles Scarlet or Peter Ingleside. We do not know what agonies they have already undergone and anyway we are told not to judge and we will not be judged. In this service, we will pray to God of his mercy to free these two boys from being tied to this place and pardon them, if it is His will. We are told to pray for the dead. And those who have died by their own hands perhaps need our prayers most of all. So I want you all to remember Charles Scarlet and Peter Ingleside not merely during this service, but in your prayers in the future. And I mean that especially for you, Rosa, because you have seen more of them than anyone has. Perhaps you have been given this gift of sight so that you could tell us of their need and we could pray for them."

Rosa nodded, flattered at being singled out from us all.

"But there is a third thing," Father Martin said. "It is possible— in fact, I think it is probable—that Charles and Peter did not start this. I think that they were the victims of some spirits of evil— what in the Middle Ages our forefathers described as demons, or *daimons* as the ancient Greeks called them. In this service, as well as asking God to bless Charles and Peter, we shall ask God to curse Them, these evil spirits, these demons or *daimons*."

At this point he nodded to Rosa, who handed round a typewritten service sheet. As she did so, Father Martin continued.

"This service falls into three parts. In the first we shall pray for the banishment of evil from ourselves and from this place. Then we shall go in procession through every room in the house and through the grounds, cleansing by the sprinkling of holy water and censing it with our prayers. As we process from one place to another, we shall say verses from Psalm 118, beginning each time from where we left off."

Having finished his explanation, he asked us to kneel in prayer. And when he opened his mouth next, it was to speak not as our friend, but as our priest before God.

"If Thou turnest away Thy face, we shall be troubled; Thou shalt take away our breath, and we shall fail and shall return to our dust. Enter not into judgment with Thy Servants; for in Thy sight shall no man living be justified." The wonderful sentences rang through the studio, stirring even those of us who did not fully understand their meaning. "He hath made us to dwell in darkness, as those that have been dead of old. Therefore are our spirits in anguish within us; and our hearts within us are troubled.

"Turn not away Thy face from us, lest we be like them that go down into the pit."

There was a silence in which the true meaning of that sentence came upon me. This was the moment of danger; this was the moment of challenge to evil spirits which for centuries had possessed this place unchallenged, claiming every so often the lives of those they could tempt across, working their evil in the hearts of others, Albert lusting after Helen as Miriam took her time in dying, Helen betraying herself for security and betraying Albert for desire of Andrew.

Then Father Martin made the sign of the cross in the name of the Father and of the Son and of the Holy Ghost. "I command you, unclean spirits, that ye come out and depart from this house and garden." His voice thundered down the long low studio among the easels and the screens, the interesting tree roots dangling from beams like birds, the Moorish pots and Mexican masks and experiments in wire. "Ye cursed spirits, remember your sentences, remember your judgments, remember the day to be at hand, wherein ye shall be committed to destruction prepared for you and your angels; and presume not hereafter to exercise any tyranny toward God's people whom Christ hath bought with His precious Blood, and by His Holy Baptism called to be members of His flock. Amen."

I glanced at Rosa, wondering whether she would be alarmed. But she appeared fascinated.

Suddenly his voice turned to tenderness. "O Jesus, who wilt 'wash away the crimes of Sion by the spirit of judgment, and by the spirit of burning,' mercifully listen to our earnest supplications of those departed in this house, especially of Miriam Anglesey Scarlet, of Albert Scarlet, of Helen Kent Scarlet and their son Charles Scarlet, also of Peter Ingleside and his family. Visit them not in anger for the frailties of their mortality, neither call them rigorously to account for every idle word, for they have not renounced their faith in Thee; and if unhappily, they were led astray by the concupiscence of the eyes, the concupiscence of the flesh, by the pride of life or its despite, by the overshadowing of the powers of darkness, enter not heavily into judgment with them, for in Thy sight shall no man living be justified. . . ."

After, when I told Father Martin how surprised I was to hear him couple the names of Miriam, Helen and Albert Scarlet with that of Charles, he answered, "I was just as surprised. I had not intended it; but suddenly it struck me that the guilt of the child's suicide must lie in part with the parents and the sense of guilt even more heavily, the grief of seeing the visitation of their sins upon the child."

This addition invested the service for me with a significance I had not expected. In the last few months my admiration for Helen had given way to disillusion and even contempt; and then in the happiness of marriage I had forgotten all about her. But immediately Father Martin included her name among those for whose rest we were praying, the blessing of the house became vividly real. That room in which we were kneeling, which to the Evernesses was just a studio, held so many memories which I needed to lay, from that first exciting moment when after her own boy's death she offered me the love she had never given to him to the darkening years of her decline when, mind and memory and body failing, she had called me "Charles," her "own boy," the "pride of her heart" or began to weep and begged me over and over again to forgive her.

I had thought as the service began that we were laying the past for Rosa, sanctifying her gift and separating it from the evil resident in the old house and using for that purpose the faith which Kit might never have regained if he had not seen his daughter threatened by powers of evil he could not explain by his narrow secular philosophy of right and wrong. But as we proceeded from room to room and about the garden, blessing each place, it became for me, and I think for all of us, not an exorcism but a dedication; a sacrament which later, when we knew that Magda had conceived, Magda and I asked Father Martin to perform for us in The Chantry, not a break with the past but its sublimation.

I had begun in fear as to how Father Martin would conduct a service which he had never performed before, had in fact improvised for the occasion. I had listened too much to tales of failure and danger. But this was so much the real thing that I did not even think, "This is the real thing." We seemed to pass in a luminous fire of purification no chill shade could withstand. We stood beneath the beam from which the Scarlet boy had swung and God was with us. He was with us when we sprinkled and censed the tulip tree.

And then we came to the yard where the rats had savaged the puppy and the Father said his benediction. "Pour down we beseech Thee, the gifts of Thy loving-kindness upon this place, that those who shall dwell therein may be defended from all the dangers that may happen to the body, and from all evil thoughts which may assault and hurt the soul; through the might of Jesus Christ our Lord.

"Peace be to this house and to all who shall dwell therein from this time forth and forevermore. Amen."

And then they went in and disrobed and drove off in the Ford Anglia.

21

IN THE END IS MY BEGINNING

It is as hard to say when something ends as when something starts. I began my narrative with Kit's letter asking me to look for a house. But the story as it unfolded went back to Peter Ingleside born in the seventeenth century and perhaps to an age before the birth of Christ.

In the same way my writing this down as faithfully as I can may have repercussions in distant times and places of which none of us in this narrative has knowledge.

Things did not end abruptly with Father Martin's benediction and departure. The drama moved immediately into a new phase, rather as the tragic Greek trilogies were followed by a comedy. As we waved good-bye, the telephone rang in Kit's office. It was a personal call to Kit from the *Daily Sentinel*. A reporter asked if there had been an exorcism. Was it successful? It was followed by the *Clarion*, the *Recorder*, the *Argus*; all in the space of half an hour.

Kit told the exchange to block all calls and for forty minutes there was peace. Then the reporters started to arrive in person.

When refused interviews, they peered through the windows, took photographs of the house from the street, even climbed on the roof of Miss Spreckles' stables to see what, if anything, was happening. One of them scrambled over the wall and was ejected by Ramratan, while a colleague took photographs of his ejection.

A telegram arrived from the Rationalist Truth Society: "CANNOT CONTACT YOU PHONEWISE SHATTERED BY NEWS IF TRUE PIGSON."

"Who's Pigson?" I asked.

"It's really Pogson," Kit said. "I suppose I'll have to ring him. Mortality's the only thing he's got to live for."

While Kit was speaking to Pogson, another couple of telegrams arrived, one from a national daily offering £500, the other from a Sunday paper offering £1,000, for exclusive story rights. Half an hour later the TV vans arrived and did not leave until the police were called in. Movie-right offers did not begin until the next day.

But as far as we were concerned the invasion of privacy by the meddlesome forces of this world was a cheap price to pay for the repulse of the invasion of the evil forces of the next. Kit prepared a brief, dignified and tentative statement for the press, beyond which he refused to go. After all, at that time we had no certainty, except our spiritual conviction, that the exorcism had been successful.

The only external pointer came a few days later, after Rosa had her first riding lesson. She produced from the cupboard under the eaves the bundle of paintings. She showed them first to Nieves and Kit and then at their suggestion to Magda and me. They were the fascinating and frightening records of a suicidal temptation; but the fact that she could exhibit them argued that the temptation had passed.

When I looked them through, I said, "And that's the end, Rosa?" thinking, "Thank God that's all over."

"Oh, no," she answered. "I did another one this morning."

My heart sank as she went to fetch it.

"D'you like it, Uncle George?"

It was almost like a copy of the picture which had given me the clue to her disappearance, from the bottom of the tulip tree looking up into the branches. There was The Crow's-Nest and there the Scarlet boy standing on the platform looking down. But it was all dimmer and he wasn't beckoning. He seemed to be waving good-bye.

"When *was* this?"

"It was when he was leaving," Rosa answered.

"I think it's marvelous," I said, "the best thing you've done."

Rosa smiled with pleasure. "I liked it."

That was over a year ago. Rosa has learned to ride and is the proud possessor of a pony, which she spends hours grooming and exercising. When Nieves was privately baptized and confirmed, there was some discussion as to whether Rosa should be confirmed at the same time. Rosa decided that she would prefer a public confirmation with her schoolfellows. Though not the "most popular girl in her class," Rosa has made a number of horsy friends and also a couple who paint.

For some time Kit was frightened that what appeared as a sudden gift of faith for the specific purpose of the exorcism might be as suddenly withdrawn. But finding it was not so, he consulted the others and then suggested to me that I should try to unravel what had really happened during that strange summer of 1959. I have learned a great deal in the process, but I am conscious that there was more in it than I have perceived and perhaps it is not over. There is always some twist which makes the expected strange, the dreaded welcome, our cherished ambition empty and the recognition of defeat a victory.

Ingram Content Group UK Ltd.
Milton Keynes UK
UKHW042246030523
421159UK00004B/191